ONLY EVER YOU

A LOVE STORY

CD REISS

This is a work of fiction. Names, characters, organizations, places, events, and incidents are either products of the author's imagination or are used fictitiously.

Published by Montlake Romance, Seattle

www.apub.com

ISBN-13: 9781503905290
ISBN-10: 1503905292

Cover design by Caroline Teagle Johnson

Printed in the United States of America

ONLY EVER YOU

CHAPTER 1

RACHEL

"Rachel, we know you," Mrs. Wellcome said with her hands steepled on her desk so she could click her nails together. Our school principal had a helmet of wheat-colored hair that seemed separate from the satiny fringe of bangs over her eyes. "We know you don't have a filter on your mouth. But encouraging another student to engage in fisticuffs is unacceptable."

"I don't know if she *encouraged* him." Sitting next to me, my mother defended me as best she could, but she was missing the larger point.

"It's not right," I said. "They pick on him every day no matter what we say. If they don't understand English, then we had to speak their language."

My hands were balled into fists. Maybe not the best way to show contrition, but I was still mad. I was missing my AP English class over something that seemed obvious. Every day Sebastian and I walked to school together. Every day Scott Turner and Brock Kendall called Sebastian "Artyboy" and "Dweebastian." They would try to grab his sketchbook, and we would try to get past them without a fight.

That morning, they'd gotten his sketchbook away and made fun of his work. A crowd had gathered to hear taunts about all the sexy comic strip heroines he drew. They asked if he jerked off to them. Everyone laughed, and I went crazy. Just crazy. I was so blind with rage I barely remembered swinging at Brock. When he swung back, Sebastian jumped on him, and it all went downhill from there, with the bullies turning into victims as soon as an adult had shown up.

"You could have come to us," Mrs. Wellcome said without a trace of irony.

"We did! Like a hundred times."

"It's true," Mom said. "And you have to admit nothing improves."

"We don't fight hurtful words with violence," the principal said. "Neither Scott nor Brock has ever touched either of you, and now Scott has a bruise under his eye."

"Good!" I cried.

"Rachel," Mom murmured tersely.

Rachel, nothing. This whole conversation was garbage.

"Have you ever been so fed up with everything that's wrong that you'll die if you don't do something about it? Like, just die if it goes on one more minute?"

"I think—" Mom started.

"Like, it's really clear to you," I continued. "Right is right, and wrong is wrong. And it's wrong to hurt someone every day. It's wrong to make them feel ashamed and scared. But it keeps happening because no one who can make it stop thinks it's as wrong as you do. So you have to make it right yourself. You *have to*."

I pounded my fist on the desk, which, in the silence that followed, I realized maybe hadn't been the best idea.

"I think there's a lot of blame to go around," my mother said. "And the school bears part of it. If these boys have been harassing my daughter and her friend, it should have been dealt with." Mom had been called to school early and wasn't her usual self. Blonde hair in a long ponytail. Sneakers instead of pumps. She hadn't even put lipstick on, but she was composed enough to defend me.

Mrs. Wellcome stopped clicking her nails and folded her hands together.

"You're an excellent student, Rachel," she said. "You've made it through eleventh grade with a spotless record. So it hurts me to do this, but I have to suspend you."

"What?" I shifted forward in my chair as if I was about to lunge.

"How long?" Mom asked.

"Three days."

"I have a chemistry test on Thursday!"

"And," Mrs. Wellcome added with the slightest hint of sympathy, "you'll be removed from the cast of *Our Town*."

"But you can't." My anger transformed from fire to the pressure of oncoming tears. "I'm Emily."

"I know, but if we let it go, we're setting a bad precedent."

My face went hot. Oh no. I wasn't going to cry. Not here. Not in front of her.

"What about the boys who harassed her and Sebastian?" Mom asked.

In what could only be explained as an attempt to soothe my mother, Mrs. Wellcome smiled. "We'll talk to them about it."

Mom was not soothed. She stood and leaned over with her knuckles on the desk.

"You're suspending my daughter for defending a friend against daily bullying, and you're doing nothing to the bullies? Is that what you're telling me?" She held up a hand to stop the answer she'd just asked for. "Don't tell me. Don't speak another word, Mrs. Debra Wellcome. I know who you are and what you are. I also know who my daughter is, and she's already a better human being than you'll ever be." She put her hand on my shoulder. "Come on, Rachel. Let's go home."

Without waiting for a reply, my mother led me out.

CHAPTER 2

SEBASTIAN

Sitting outside the principal's office waiting for Mom, I felt great. So good. I'd landed Scott Turner square in the face. Bam. I didn't have much weight to put behind the punch, but I'd felt the impact through my shoulder.

And the way he'd looked at me after I'd done it? Fear and wide-eyed surprise. My brain had taken in every detail. The slack lower lip. The leftover fighter's tension in his shoulders. The inverted V of his eyebrows. As I drew it in my science notebook, I exaggerated the shading in the eyeballs so they looked as if they'd pop right out. Little drops of sweat at his temples. I'd make his lips the color of raw liver when I had my pencils.

I couldn't wait to show Rachel. She was going to crack up.

Principal Wellcome's door opened, and Rachel and her mom came out. Mrs. Rendell didn't look like herself without makeup and nice shoes.

Rachel didn't look like herself either. Her lips were pressed tight together as if she was holding her breath, and she looked straight ahead, intent on something, even though there was nothing there. Her eyes were red with an effort to block tears.

I stopped feeling great.

Wellcome must have punished her. Detention, I figured. Maybe an essay on nonviolence.

"Rachel," I whispered. She came to me as her mother signed them out at the front desk. "What happened?"

My mother, Carol, came in just then. She looked harried and rushed, hair falling out of her single braid and her crystal necklace hanging off center. She and Mrs. Rendell conferred by the front desk.

"Three-day suspension," Rachel said thickly. "And no school play."

Seeing her chin quiver made my eyes sting. Rachel didn't cry. She was every female superhero I ever drew.

"I'm sorry," I said. "I'll tell them it's my fault."

"It's not your fault," she hissed. "It's their fault. They're the awful ones. Brock and Scott. I wish I got suspended for giving each of them a bloody lip."

Rachel was awe-inspiring fury. Was it wrong to think of how beautiful she was when she was in so much trouble that she was near tears? She was breathtaking on most days, but that morning my best friend was cloaked in righteous splendor.

"I'm going to tell them it was me," I said. "I'm going to make it right, Rachel. And you're never going to have to get into a fight for me again. I swear it."

For once, instead of seeing her as someone who did and said things I couldn't, I was inspired.

Rachel and I lived across from each other on a quiet cul-de-sac. The Rendells had moved in when I was eleven, three weeks before my father had a sudden heart attack. They treated my mother; my little sister, Tiffany; and me as if they'd lived across the street forever. I had every trouble in the world after Dad died, but loneliness wasn't one of them.

I'd tried to bargain with Wellcome to get Rachel immunity, but nothing had worked. I'd gotten three days as well, but my mother was a liberal parent who wanted us to call her by her first name. If the school wanted to discipline me, that was fine, but she thought the entire episode should be a learning experience.

On day two of the suspension, Rachel came over to work on the Western civ homework that was due whether we were in school or not.

"Are you all right?" I asked her as we worked at my kitchen table. Carol was at her job, and Tiffany was having a normal fourth-grade life.

"I'm fine." Her head was bent so low her dark hair draped a few inches onto her paper.

"You've been really quiet."

"Good." She erased a line from her essay. "I'm not going to fly off the handle again. I'm going to think before I speak, especially if I'm mad." With the side of her hand, she brushed away eraser dust. "I'm thinking about my future. I have plans, and I don't want to screw it up."

The fight with Scott and Brock made me feel empowered and strong. It seemed to have the opposite effect on her.

"You won't screw it up."

"I will if I have a bunch of black marks on my permanent record. Only nine percent of applicants get into NYU." She put her elbows on the table so she could count each step on her fingers. "NYU is the first thing. Two birds with one stone. I live in New York and go to college at the same time. Next. Spend two years on film and TV sets, learning the ropes. Three. Grad school. USC or UCLA. Those are the two best for film. That makes me twenty-six when I graduate. Focus one hundred percent on work for two years. Married by twenty-eight."

Married? I stopped breathing. Married to whom? Who was this guy?

She continued. "First child by thirty, then—"

"How are you going to find someone to marry if you're one hundred percent focused on work?"

She glared at me. "I just will."

"But what if you don't? Your whole plan's messed up. Step four precludes you from getting to step five."

She put her pencil down and folded her hands together.

"Would you say that if I was a man?"

"No, but—"

"You'd expect a man to focus on his work, then get married whenever he wanted."

I never could guide a conversation with her.

"Look," I said. "All I'm saying is you might need a plan B. A stopgap."

"A stopgap?"

"In case of emergency, break glass. You're thirty. Rich as sin, of course. Successful beyond your wildest dreams. Men are at your feet, but they're all jerks, and you don't want to marry them. You have a choice." I swallowed a nervous laugh. I had to sell this by making it seem sensible. Not funny. "Give up on your life plan, or marry your best friend."

Her face didn't change when I said it. She had an antireaction, going from a movie to a still-frame photo in a split second.

"What if you're already married?"

"Well, duh," I said, pushing papers around so I didn't have to address the fact that I'd divorce Milla Jovovich in a hot minute to be with Rachel Rendell. "We can't get married if I'm married to someone else."

She screwed her mouth to one side of her face and tilted her head.

"Yeah," she said. "A stopgap. I like it."

She *what*?

"You do?"

She ripped a sheet of blue-lined paper out of her spiral notebook. "Let's set the terms."

Together, we wrote a silly contract laying out the terms of a ridiculous deal that would never come to fruition. The fact that she was willing to even consider an event horizon for marriage made the suspension the best thing that had ever happened to me.

CHAPTER 3

RACHEL

Fourteen Years Later
(Give or Take)

Nothing in life had gone as planned. Not the career. Not the husband. Nothing.

But Mandarin Lane, the cul-de-sac in San Diego, was always there for me. The sun always shone in the blue sky. The clouds were always puffy and white. Every autumn, the Santa Ana winds blew over the deck chairs.

I lived in Hollywood, which tripped off the lips when I met people from out of town, especially if I was thinking impressive, two-story, single-family Craftsman thoughts. But Hollywood was home to plenty of dumpy apartment buildings, and I lived in one of them. The washing machines in the basement ate quarters like Skittles, and the dryers were about as effective as shaking my blow-dryer at my clothes. My roommate, Ruth, sent hers out to the laundromat in a pink bag. They came back in a cube.

Every two weeks, I went to my parents' house. Mom fed me and helped me fold. Dad asked questions about my job. The week after Thanksgiving, I helped put up the holiday lights. Mandarin Lane engaged in full-contact Christmas decorating.

"Is Bruce coming for Christmas?" Mom asked, stringing untangled lights up to Dad, who was at the top of the ladder. She wore red yoga pants and a half-zipped sweatshirt that stretched across her reconstructed breasts.

When Mom had breast cancer, Carol Barton and her Guy-with-a-Pickup-Truck, Roy, had decorated our house while we were at a doctor's appointment. I'd thought it was a waste, but Mom had been so grateful she cried.

"Bruce and I broke up," I spit out after having avoided the subject for an hour.

She dropped the string of lights to put her hands on my shoulders.

"Oh, sweetheart! Are you all right?"

"I'm fine. I will be. Whatever. I thought he was different," I said. I always said that. I didn't even believe it anymore, but acting like I did was better than giving up. "He was a cheater." I looked at my shoes, humiliated.

"Have you tried that new phone-swiping thing? What's it called?"

"Grindr," Dad called from the top of the ladder.

"Tinder," I corrected. "And yes."

"You can go on it again," she said. "You're a beautiful, smart . . ."

Here we go. I had to fight an eye roll.

"Accomplished, wonderful—"

Changing the subject, I called up to Dad. "There's usually four bulbs between each clip. You have five there."

"How about you listen to your mother, and I'll do the counting?" he shot back, fixing the string anyway.

"Men love success," Mom said. "You said you were getting an episode this season."

I was a writer's assistant on *Romancelandia*, a terrible show about a thing that didn't exist. *Law and Order* did "ripped from the headlines" crime. We did "ripped from the tabloids" romance. I was too old to deliver coffee and take notes, but a writer's assistant job was hard to get, and no one else was banging down my door.

"They haven't decided what to give me yet."

"Who knows who that'll attract?" Mom said. "Maybe a better caliber of man."

I caught sight of Carol walking across the street. When she'd left her job years before to become a professional astrologer and tarot card reader, she'd abandoned waistbands altogether in favor of colorful muumuus.

"Rachel," she said, kissing my cheek, "Sebbie didn't have your address. He wanted me to hand deliver your card."

She handed me a red envelope. Just my name. No return address.

I hadn't seen Sebastian in ten years. After high school graduation, I'd gone off to NYU. He'd gone to design school at Stanford. We came home for different holidays.

More accurately, during college, I'd spent holidays with my boyfriend, Shane's, family in Maine. Then he went to Harvard Business and decided he needed a woman with better prospects. I'd seen Sebastian on Mandarin Lane the Christmas after we graduated. I didn't remember much from that week. I'd been so crushed over Shane I doubt I was able to have a decent conversation.

The card was hand embossed and strung with thin gold ribbon, and the writing was in Sharpie. For a guy who could draw like Picasso,

Sebastian had the handwriting of a left-handed doctor with a broken pencil.

> *Merry Christmas, Rachel!*
>
> *We're thirty this year. Big 3-0!*
>
> *Remember we had a deal? I moved back from Silicon Valley. I'll be on Mandarin Lane for Christmas. Hope to see you then.*
>
> *—Sebastian*

"You're coming for the holiday?" Carol asked after I read it.

"Oh, she'll be here," Dad said, coming down the creaky ladder.

"I guess I'll show up." I put the envelope in my back pocket and forgot about it until Christmas.

CHAPTER 4

RACHEL

Christmas Eve

Sandra, the showrunner on *Romancelandia*, was so busy she could only hear my story pitch on Christmas Eve. This was normal. No one ever stopped working. Not for love, money, or national holidays. When we were out, we talked about work. When we were home, we wrote. When we went to bed, we slept so we could work harder the next day.

It was the perfect life for me except that I was still at the bottom of the ladder looking up.

The guild set aside two shows per season to be written by someone who wasn't a staff writer. Those slots were usually given to assistants because we worked like dogs and didn't make staff-writer money. The payout for those scripts was—for us—substantial and sometimes the only thing that made the job worthwhile.

Now was my chance.

"He's a hacker," I said. It was hard to sound excited when my palms were sweating and my heart beat so hard it hurt, but I gave it everything.

Sandra sat behind her desk with traffic on Wilshire Boulevard chugging away behind her. She was nearly six feet tall with long brown hair, black-kohl-lined eyes that were cupped with gray late in the day, and a dour face she'd Botoxed into rigidity. It made reading her reactions near impossible, and pitching a story was already hard enough.

"A hacker." Sandra planted her elbows on the desk. She had a one-inch-long swatch of Scotch tape across her pointer and thumb.

"She's an FBI agent tracking him across the dark web. He's dropping clues in all these exotic places."

"And he's the sexy nerd sitting right under her nose?" She snapped another piece of tape off the dispenser. She exhibited the tape tic whenever she sat still.

"No!" I exclaimed. "A sexy Romanian coder!"

She plucked the tape off her fingers and rolled it into a ball. Shit on the half shell. Not good.

"Our show is about hope. It's about growth. It's about two people overcoming their differences and finding lasting love. It's not about exotic locations and criminal activity," Sandra said, tossing the sticky ball into the trash with a few dozen others. "I'm going to do you a favor."

I didn't want a favor. I wanted the residual checks and the affirmation that came with a writing credit on a show, but I didn't express it. I'd honed the skill of shutting up before I said something stupid to a fine point.

"The execs want something, and when they want an episode, we give it to them."

"Okay." When the guys upstairs had asked for a Brangelina story, we'd given it to them. When they'd asked for an HEA for Lorena Bobbitt, we'd made it work. This favor was guaranteed to be produced, but it could be anything in between.

"You've heard of the 'Delete It' viral video?"

Of course I'd heard of it. Everyone had. I'd even watched it out of morbid curiosity. It started as a run-of-the-mill sex video until the woman saw her boyfriend's phone propped up on the dresser.

She leaped for it, screaming.

He dove for it, laughing.

The screen went black, but you could hear her shouting, "Delete it, delete it, delete it!"

Obviously, he hadn't, and millions knew it.

"You're joking," I said, then clamped my jaw tight and looked at my hands twisting in my lap.

"Her life afterward. She finds true love. Hero beats up the ex. It writes itself. You won't even have to pitch it."

Any normal writer's assistant would have jumped at it. I couldn't get excited any more than I could open my mouth to object.

"Rachel," she said, folding her hands in front of her, "we love having you here. You're the best room assistant I've ever had. You type like the keys are on fire, and you miss nothing."

"But?"

"You're not fulfilling your potential. I need to move you up, or I'm going to move you out."

"That's not fair."

I wished I could have grabbed those three words midair and stuffed them back in my mouth, but Sandra seemed unfazed by the fact that I was acting like a toddler.

"Break your story with CJ. I know you'll come up with something great."

Breaking a story meant fixing it or brainstorming it into existence. But I hated the idea of the "Delete It" video so much that I wished it were literal.

The 5 freeway was a parking lot. Waze said Mandarin Lane was going to be three hours of white-knuckling, brake-tapping traffic. I spent the first half of the drive thinking of ways to turn humiliation into happiness. Needing to talk it out, I put on my headset and called Ruth, who worked for Enoch Hobbs at WDE Talent & Literary. She was on the other side of the country, meeting her boyfriend's family.

"I'm sure you can come up with something," she said. "It's just standard messy backstory."

Ruth had been in the Stark (a.k.a. Shark) program at USC while I'd been in for screenwriting. She had a sharp story sense and never hesitated to tell me when I was off base.

"I just keep thinking of her face when she saw that phone." I picked up my cold coffee but put it down without drinking. There was an hour and a half of driving in front of me, and I already had to pee.

"Use it. Make it an emotional connection."

"But she's a real person."

An exit was coming up. I got in the right lane. I was going to have to stop at a gas station for the bathroom.

"You're not going to use her name, silly," Ruth said. In the background I heard the click, click of her reloading her mascara wand. She spent a ton of time in front of the mirror.

"I just wish I could ask her first. Or, like, warn her not to watch it. Make sure she's okay, at least."

"She's fine."

"She's . . . ?" I missed the exit. "How do you know?"

"No one stays invisible."

Should I just take her word for it? What did *fine* mean to Ruth? What did it mean to me?

"If I could talk to her," I said, "maybe I wouldn't feel bad about writing this."

Ruth's pause was overlaid with *hurms* and *mmms* to let me know she was considering it as she put on lipstick that would miraculously last all night.

She hated saying no.

"Never mind," I said. "Probably better if I don't meet her."

"You got this, girl," Ruth said. "This is your shot. It's gonna be so huge."

I turned into my parents' driveway at 6:04 p.m. and parked behind Dad's SUV. I was starving, and I really had to pee.

The side door was open. As soon as I walked in, I could smell turkey and mulled wine.

"Is that you, Rachel?" Mom's voice was one of many coming from the dining room.

"I'll be right in!"

I rushed toward the half bath in the back hall, and because I was hungry and dehydrated, I didn't look where I was going.

Which was why I reacted with a wide-eyed gasp when I almost crashed into him. And maybe that was why I didn't recognize him right away, besides the fact that he wasn't human. I mean, he had all the traits. Six feet. Black hair cut just below the ears and set in careless yet precise disarray. Expressive eyebrows over sapphire eyes. Human, except he looked like he'd stepped out of a magazine cover.

This couldn't be . . .

"Hey," he said.

Jesus, the smile. Shoot me now.

"Sebastian. I . . ."

Were those *biceps* stretching the sleeves of his cardigan?

"It's nice to see you."

His voice. Not squeaky but deep, confident, adult. Was that my bladder pressing against all my female parts?

Get your shit together.

This was Sebastian Barton. So skinny he'd once escaped a particularly bad taunting by slipping through the vertical bars surrounding the schoolyard. So weak I'd had to help him carry his books home. This was a kid who ducked his head and flailed roundhouse-style at Scott Turner, shocking him enough to get a clean shot. A kid I got suspended for because Scott was a bully as well as a crybaby who fell like a house of cards.

He snorted when he laughed, was allergic to air and water, was socially stunted and intellectually advanced, walked like a grandma, and dressed like a grandpa.

"Nice cardigan," I said, crossing my legs and bouncing a little.

"It was my grandfather's."

Thank God some things hadn't changed.

CHAPTER 5

SEBASTIAN

She hadn't changed at all. She had an easy beauty, and I wasn't just talking about her looks, which were still stunning. She cracked a joke about my sweater without actually cracking the joke. She got it. She got me. She'd always understood me.

"Your grandfather still has amazing taste." Her legs were crossed, and she bounced up and down.

"*Had* amazing taste. Are you all right?"

At that moment, four-year-old Lala Garcia pulled her father down the hall, crying, "Poo potty, poo potty." He rolled his eyes as he passed.

"Stay single, man." They went into the bathroom.

Rachel looked down the hall, bouncing. I assumed it was the Christmas music. Or maybe she always did that, and I'd forgotten?

No way. I didn't forget anything about her.

"I heard you sold your company," she said. "Congratulations. I don't know if that's what you say when someone sells for millions?"

"It is, but I sunk a bunch of it into a finance modeling . . . never mind. It's boring."

"I'm sure it's not."

"Tiny company not even worth talking about." I lowered my voice. "Carol's disappointed. She thinks if I'm in finance, I'm going to die young like my father."

"Is that you, Rachel?" Her dad, Rob Rendell, casserole in quilted-mitten-covered hands, had taken a detour between the kitchen and dining room.

"It's me," she said, bouncing. "Merry Christmas."

"They're in here!" he called into the dining room.

"Are they talking about the wedding?" her mother said from behind the wall.

Rachel's eyes met mine, wide with surprise. She even stopped bouncing for a second.

"They saw the card?" I asked. She nodded as voices started talking over each other.

"Rachel turned thirty in April," Carol said.

"And Seb three weeks ago, right?" Mrs. Rendell was trying to sound casual.

Tiffany cried, "What's going on?"

"You didn't hear?" Mr. Rendell said as he disappeared into the dining room with his casserole. "Rachel and—"

"—had this deal—"

"—and Sebbie are getting—"

I held my hand up to Rachel, who looked overwhelmed.

"I have this." I stepped into the dining room and clapped my hands once. All eyes were on me. Good.

Rachel's mother had on a loud Christmas sweater and a flashing clip that held her long salt-and-pepper hair in a twist. My mother, Carol, wore her standard muumuu with ten pounds of beads and crystals around her neck. My sister, Tiffany, was in a hoodie, staring at a phone in a Tiffany Blue case. The two oldest Garcia kids, in an untucked holiday shirt and askew dress, couldn't sit still while their parents chatted with ours about our marriage pact.

"Listen up," I said. "Rachel and I—"

"It's about time," her father said.

"I always knew," Carol added.

"Dad!" Rachel had come into the dining room behind me.

"Lasagna!" Two-year-old Oliver leaned over the hot casserole dish, banging his silverware on his plastic plate.

"A deal's a deal," her dad said, cutting the lasagna with a spatula.

"Is it true?" Mrs. Rendell asked, hands over her heart.

"No." Rachel's fists were balled up, and her legs were tightly crossed.

Mr. Rendell pointed an odd-shaped wooden spoon at me. "He said—"

I cut in. "Rachel and I had an agreement to get married if—"

"I ran the dates." My mother's big soft brown eyes fell on me. "That's what I've been telling you."

"Are you serious?" Mrs. Rendell was bent over the table to look at my mother.

"I showed you their charts."

My mother, the online psychic, astrologer, and tarot card reader, was a fantasy maker. Her biggest fantasy had always been that one day I'd marry Rachel.

"They were always such good friends," someone said. "I remember—"

"You showed me when she was eleven," Mrs. Rendell said to Carol. "She's not a child bride!"

"I'm thirty!" Rachel cried.

"Wait!" I barked. Everyone shut up. The kids stopped banging their spoons.

Rachel was looking at me with her eyes a little wider, mouth a little slack with surprise. She bounced once.

"Go to the bathroom," I said, suddenly realizing what she was dancing around about. "I'll take care of this."

"I can wait."

"We made a dumb deal when we were kids. If we were single at thirty, we'd get married. It wasn't a serious thing. Okay? It was never a serious thing."

Silence. Then Oliver banged his spoon on his plate. Throats cleared. Dad stuck the serving spoon in the lasagna. Evan and Lala returned from the "poo potty."

"Gross," Tiffany said, looking up from her Tiffany-encased phone long enough to meet Rachel's glance. "Marry a dweeb." Nose wrinkled, she put her eyes back where they always were.

"He's not a dweeb." Rachel defended me. I smiled, remembering all the times she'd objected on my behalf.

"You could date." Mrs. Rendell shrugged, picking up her glass. "Rachel's single."

"Weird!" Tiffany said.

"So's Sebbie," my mother offered.

"Sebastian," I corrected.

"It's not . . ." Rachel's face twisted into a grimace, and she bent over slightly.

"You really should go," I said, and this time she took off like a shot.

Rachel and I pointedly ignored each other the entire dinner. I'd been looking forward to seeing her, but a few extra words on a Christmas card had screwed it up.

Tiffany texted me from across the table.

—stop looking at her before I puke—

I turned away from Rachel, turned off the phone, and gave my sister a dirty look.

Over the years, Rachel had turned into a hazy memory of a girl who made me laugh when I cried and who stood up for me when no one else would.

"You win the block this year, Ms. Barton," Rachel said to my mother. Her parents had never allowed first names.

"Roy was hell bent!" Carol answered. Roy had started out trading odd chores for tarot readings. Now, according to Tiffany, his pickup truck was in the driveway all the time. "I cleared out Home Depot on the twenty-sixth last year. Everything on sale, and he put it all up."

"He threw it all on the front yard without a thought to composition," I said.

Did I sound like an ass? Probably. But I was annoyed that Rachel was sitting at the other end of the table.

"Come home and help me next time, Mr. Artist."

I jumped at a sharp pain in my thigh. Oliver was at my feet, jabbing me with his fork.

"You have lasagna?" he whispered from under the table. The turkey had done me in, so I did have half a plate left over.

"You want it?"

"Did you know . . . ?" Carol started as Oliver climbed up to my lap. "Sebbie—"

"Sebastian." Correcting her was pointless, but I had no choice. Rachel was there. I wanted her to see me as an adult, not a nerdy kid with an *ie* at the end of his name.

"Sebastian's animation program was used in that new show? The one about the birds?"

Everyone raised their glasses for a toast. Oliver sat on my lap and gobbled up my leftovers.

Rachel gathered the plates.

Right. Here it was. I gently got the boy off my lap and into my chair so I could grab some dishes.

She was already at the sink, scraping food into the garbage and loading the dishwasher.

"Hey, Rachel." I put the plates on the counter just as her phone rang. She looked at it, held her finger up, and went to the back patio for privacy.

Crap.

I could hear the whispers in the dining room as I walked back.

"She hasn't said anything."

"He's been single long enough."

"I'm so glad he got rid of that one."

When I was in the doorway, Mr. Rendell saw me and said loudly, "Isn't there a game on?"

They all spun to me.

"Sure is!"

Everyone got up. That was how I got stuck doing the dishes and taking out the garbage.

CHAPTER 6

RACHEL

My parents had plenty of patio furniture, but I sat in the dark corner with my back against the railing, as far away from the house as possible. Then, and only then, did I answer the phone.

"What do you want?" I asked Bruce.

"I just wanted to wish you a merry Christmas."

He'd been my world for two years, and he'd cheated on me for three-quarters of that. Yet his voice was a dagger in my chest. I didn't want him back, but I missed him at the same time.

"Why?"

"I was thinking about you. Thinking you'd be at your parents' place. Can you wish them a merry one for me?"

Fuck him. He'd kissed my mother's ass as if she were the one who needed to fall in love with him. And the way he watched ball games with my father, pretending he gave a damn. It was all an act, and he was still courting them. The cool air made my fingertips numb, or maybe it was suppressed anger pulling circulation away from my extremities and toward my heart.

"Sure."

"Yeah," he said after a pause. "It's nice to hear your voice. You sound good."

"So do you."

Actually, he didn't sound good or bad, but I played along. I was an expert at not letting my temper get the best of me.

"I gotta be honest," he said as if this were a new thing for him. "I miss you."

If I had to be honest, I missed him too. I loathed him, but I missed him.

"I mi—"

A hollow clap and crash came from the side of the house.

"I have to go," I said, hanging up before I said something true and stupid.

I jumped off the deck and ran to the side of the house to find the plastic bin tipped and Sebastian standing in a pile of garbage, holding a broken bag.

"Sorry," he said, righting the can. "I wasn't trying to interrupt."

"You did me a favor." I reached behind the water heater for the broom that had been there since the dawn of time. "I was about to say something stupid."

"It really is nice to see you," he said, picking up fallen garbage with his fingertips. "Even though our parents are trying to marry us off to each other."

"It's nice to see you too. You look good." I was being unspecific on purpose. I didn't want to talk about his body, the way he inhabited a whole slew of new musculature; the high forehead, which had been such a liability when we were kids but now made him look smarter; or how the dark hair that fell over it made smart look so sexy. His skin had cleared up. I was tempted to compliment him on that but managed to shut my mouth.

"What was that thing Bobby Spencer used to do?" I shut one eye and stopped sweeping long enough to point to Sebastian with a crooked thumb while ticking the back of my tongue against my teeth. "Looking good, baby."

"You totally fell for it."

"I did not." I swept my pile together.

"You did."

"Grab the shovel so I can get the glass in."

He got the shovel from behind the water heater and angled it so I could sweep in the garbage.

"I was a sucker for the good-looking ones," I said. "I wonder what happened to that guy."

"Sound mixer, I think." He dumped the contents of the shovel.

"A grown-up job," I grumbled. "Must be nice."

That was stupid. Being jealous of a guy who sat in a dark room wearing headphones and staring at sound waves was bad enough. Saying it out loud made me look like a desperate whiner.

"I spilled it, I sweep it." He gently took the broom from me. "I thought you worked on a TV show?"

"Romancelandia." I slammed the side of the shovel on the edge of the pail a little harder than I should have. I always told Sebastian more than I should have, and that obviously hadn't changed. Without the stars and rainbows or cynical blitheness, there was only honesty left. "The show everyone makes fun of. The one all my USC friends complain about. 'Why does that shit get made, and we can't get something decent on?' 'Bullshit pandering to women,' blah blah. And I'm not even a writer. I'm a writer's-room assistant."

"You can move up, though?" He poked the broom between two cans to get out the last of the debris.

"Sure." If I didn't say something, he was going to ask another question, and I was going to blurt out the fact that I was going to move up because of the "Delete It" video.

"I heard you had a girlfriend," I said, leaning on the shovel.

He dug for something stuck in the space between cans.

"We broke up." He finally dislodged a small white box.

"Sorry to hear that." I picked up the box. I recognized the compounding pharmacy logo from my time helping my parents with Mom's cancer.

"Her parents put up with me, but they were evangelical. When they couldn't change my mother, they tried to get me to stop speaking to her. After five-plus years I'd had enough."

"Fuck them." I turned the box over. "I'm sorry, but fuck them. Your mom's awesome."

"Yeah." He looked at the prescription name with me. "What is it?"

"Probably nothing."

It wasn't nothing. Zofran. Nausea meds. Maybe. It had been a long time since I knew every medication better than the pharmacist. But I knew they gave out Zofran for chemo-induced nausea, and I was sure we'd tossed the meds she didn't need when she'd gone into remission.

"Anyway," he said when I was staring into the garbage pail as if I wanted to root around for more medicine boxes, which I did. "I think you're doing great."

I tossed the box away.

"The writers I work for make all the money, and they're younger than me. My mentor's two years younger than I am. My *mentor*. She dropped out of undergrad, and I have a master's degree." I ran my mouth as if this guy I hadn't seen in ten years were my therapist. "I work all day and write my own stuff all night. No one wants to read it. I can't even get an agent. Can't get a meeting. And even if I got a meeting? Practically vomit when I have to pitch something." I closed the pail. "I'm sorry I'm dumping all of this on you. It's just that some of the people I went to school with are having projects made. I'm just this loser who gets excited about stories no one will ever see. And there I go, dumping on you again like a bitter old crone."

"Bitter old crone suits you."

I slapped his arm, but he was undeterred.

"You just need a mole right here." He touched my nose.

"Shut up."

"Is that a hair?" He touched his chin while looking at mine, and my hand flew up to cover the imaginary growth. He laughed, and I laughed with him.

"Jerk." I gave him a push to the shoulder. No bone. Just solid muscle and unpushable, deep-throated man. "Is this even real?"

I reached for the scruff under his chin and wound up actually grabbing some, which pulled him closer to me. He allowed it easily, as if he was headed in that direction already.

And then, like that, I could feel the presence of his body near mine like a mass with its own gravitational pull. His cologne or soap or his natural scent was part lemon, part leather.

This was not Sebbie. I was trading insults and advice with some gorgeous stranger as if he was a friend.

And he was, but also . . . he wasn't.

I let go. He didn't back away. His eyes flicked from my mouth to my cheeks and back to my eyes. I felt his breath on my lips as I shifted closer to his gravity. Because this wasn't Sebbie, but Sebastian, and I knew him well enough but not too much.

"I—"

He never finished. The side door banged open, and my mother leaned out. We separated like kids caught kissing behind the gym.

"You guys had a *contract*?"

"Mom, really?" I cried.

"Did you keep it?"

"Of course not."

"I have it," Sebastian said. "Actually. It's in my old room somewhere."

"Oh, can we see it?" Carol called from behind Mom.

"No!" I shouted.

Everyone looked at me.

Why didn't I want them to read it? What was the problem? Sebastian and I had been sixteen, good friends, having fun with a promise we'd never keep.

The contract was nothing more than nostalgia and nothing less than evidence that what I'd wanted out of my life wasn't going to be delivered. It was proof that I wasn't where I thought I'd be by this time. It was an admission of failure. It wasn't about a man or marriage. It was about my career. About being all grown up. I thought I'd be settled by thirty, but instead, I was going to have to settle.

That contract was my voice-over.

In a world where you sign contracts you can't keep . . .

Sebastian was looking at me, but more than looking . . . he was *seeing* me.

"You know," he said, turning back to our mothers, "I'm not sure I have it anymore."

"Yes, you d—" his mother started.

"Carol!" Sebastian snapped his voice with an authority I never thought I'd hear from him. "I said no."

"I think . . ." I took a deep breath before continuing. "I think you should check. It'd be fun to see it."

"Really?" The question wasn't rhetorical. He was giving me an out.

"Yeah. I'll go with you. Come on."

CHAPTER 7

SEBASTIAN

Rachel walked next to me across the street without saying a word.

I'd loved my ex, Tammy, as much as a guy could love a girl who spent five years trying to change him. I'd figured Rachel was just an adolescent infatuation. I'd never feel anything like that again. I was an adult now, with manageable adult feelings. But when Rachel asked about her, I was ashamed at what I'd sacrificed for someone who would never love the real me.

Rachel followed me to my old room and sat on the edge of the bed.

"Where's the telescope?" she asked, pointing to a spot by the window.

"Traded it in." I opened a desk drawer where I kept all the drawings that were too good to throw away and got out a manila folder. "Here it is."

I sat next to Rachel and handed it over. She opened it to the handwritten sheet of blue-lined three-hole-punched paper pressed between a kitten version of Red Sonja and the folder's cardboard.

"To whom it may concern," she said. "God, how dumb. We wrote a deal memo, not a contract." She started reading again. "We, the undersigned, do hereby agree that when Sebastian Barton reaches his thirtieth birthday—" She looked up at me. Our arms were touching so we could both see the contract, and her face was close enough to kiss. "It was two weeks ago. Happy belated birthday."

"Thank you." I read where she'd left off. "If both parties are unmarried and without a boy-slash-girlfriend, they will get married before Rachel's thirty-first birthday."

"March," she said. "Wow. Short engagement."

"Who's rushing? This contract," I continued, "is set forth between the parties as almost adults of sound mind and body who promise to enter into a marriage contract for the purpose of having children and other companionship with no other promises made about conception methods."

Her cheeks broke out in a dusting of pink. She was thinking about sex. With me.

She continued. "This contract shall be entered into effect if both parties are single—where *single* is defined as absence of marriage—or serious relationship, where, quote, *serious relationship*, unquote, is defined as regular dinner dates on Saturdays."

"We set a really low bar," I said.

She turned the page over. On the bottom, I'd John Hancocked the thing as if I were signing for my lottery winnings. A passage had been crossed out.

"You redlined this part about us dating first," I said. "Before we actually got married."

"Why would I do that?"

"You didn't want anyone to think you actually liked me."

"That would be stupid. I mean, if we were getting married, I obviously like you."

"That's different than not wanting to be alone."

She shrugged, giving me the point.

"It was a self-fulfilling prophecy," she said, looking closely at the signatures, then smoothed the paper on her lap. "They say if you want to be successful, you have to act successful. But failure is a snowball rolling down a hill. It attracts more of itself."

"Wow, that's terrible. Marriage isn't a success or failure thing."

"I know. Technically. But it would be nice to achieve one single thing I set out to do." She passed the paper to me. "Anyway, we didn't sign in blood."

"We spit in our hands and shook on it."

"I don't know how I forgot that."

"An exchange of DNA makes it official."

"My mother always did want us to get married." She smiled as if lost in thought. "When she had breast cancer, she mentioned it. Not the contract, but like, 'Whatever happened with you and Sebastian?' That kind of thing."

"What did you tell her?"

"I didn't tell her anything. But I did ask her how you were doing."

"What did she say?"

"She said you were in Silicon Valley and doing really well. But I was really worried about her, not me or you. So if she said something more specific, it didn't stick."

"That must've been a hard time."

"You never really find out what a pain in the ass your mother can be until she's really sick and won't admit it."

"Sebbie!" A voice came from the street. It was Carol in the middle of the front walk.

"Yeah?" I called out the window.

"Can you grab the containers with the blue tops?"

"Coming!"

CHAPTER 8

RACHEL

As we went back out into the street, I fell a little behind. I took stock of the way his shoulders narrowed down into a tight V at his waist. This wasn't the skinny, pimply little Sebastian who could barely carry his own books home.

"Hey," I said, catching up, "I didn't ask if you were single either. Presently. Not that it matters for the contract." I waved the papers.

"Of course not."

"Because this"—I slapped the paper with the back of my hand—"this is silly."

"It sure is."

"So? Anyone after Tammy?"

He stopped at the front door and answered before he pushed it open. "No one for almost a year. You?"

"Couple of months." I cleared my throat. "I'm a little . . . well . . . I'm a little raw."

"He's an asshole to let you go." His words were a statement on Bruce, but the way he looked at me was a statement about the sheer blindness of any man who would cheat on me.

My face got hot. I turned away so he wouldn't see me blush.

"So cute," my mother said after reading the contract aloud for the twentieth time. Over cake and pie, everyone was a little sloshed and very relaxed. The kids were watching cartoons with Sebastian, who peered into the dining room whenever he heard his name. Outside, the flashing Christmas lights went on at sundown.

"Saturday-night dinners." My dad shook his head. "You kids."

"What did you want us to say? A thrice-weekly—" I stopped myself for the sake of the kids. "You know."

"Is that what you're calling it these days?" Dad asked.

"Thrice?" Mom said.

"That's about right," Carol added.

Sebastian had appeared in the doorway, and when he laughed, my cheeks got hot. I threw a napkin at him.

"I'm holding back vomit," Tiffany said in a singsong voice.

"You two really should think about it," Carol said, digging into her pocket and coming out with a gold drawstring bag. "I could throw some cards."

Sebastian stood behind me and put his hands on my shoulders. Even through clothes, the touch sucked my attention.

Carol pulled out a well-worn Crowley deck and slid it over to me. "Cut the deck into three with your left hand."

"Oh, really," Mom said, sober enough to roll her eyes and soused enough to lean forward in curiosity.

"Fine," I said, separating the deck into three piles. Sebastian's hands were still on my shoulders, resting on my shirt, except for his left thumb. As I cut, it drifted across the surface of my skin, and I shuddered as the touch tingled. I didn't shrug him off. I could smell him so close. Lemon and leather. Maybe I was a little soused myself.

Carol flipped the top three cards.

"Two of cups. Five of wands. The Sun. Well, well."

"What's it mean?" I asked.

"Two of cups is love," Sebastian said from behind me, his thumb taking another stroke. "Five of wands is speed."

"And the Sun is a culmination," Carol said, flipping another card. "The Tower. Hmm."

"I'm pleased to announce," he said, "we've skipped the dating and engagement part of the process, and we're moving right on to marriage."

The whole idea deserved all the sarcasm in his voice.

"Well," I added, playing along. Putting a hand over his and looking up at him, I said, "The five of wands means we'd better get to it."

"Dinner Saturday?" he asked.

"Naturally." His fingers wove into mine as our eyes stayed steady on each other. Our words mocked the idea of marriage, but his touch represented something more truthful.

"Make him buy," Tiffany said just as her phone camera clicked. Gaze broken, we looked at her. She'd taken a picture of us and was already tapping the glass.

"You're not posting that." Sebastian's hands slid off my shoulders.

"It's in stories." She put her phone down, smiling. "It'll be gone in twenty-four hours."

We got our phones out.

He found it first. "You can't even spell."

In the picture, I was looking up at him with a half smile that exuded comfort and warmth, linking my hand with his. He was tilted to see me, not as visible from that angle, but no one could miss the same warmth in him. The bells, bluebirds, and hearts Tiffany had put all over didn't obscure the fact that we looked like the happiest couple in the world. Not even her caption.

WEDDING BELLZ FROM HELLZ!

Carol collected her cards. "You remember Joy Tabona?"

"She's doing wedding planning," Mom added. "She did Matt and Brian's wedding at Cotillion Arms."

"It was wonderful." Carol slid the cards into the drawstring bag. "Even Roy was impressed."

"You took Roy to a wedding?" Sebastian asked.

"You have no idea," Tiffany muttered.

"She's got a long waiting list." Carol turned the conversation back to safety.

"I'll have her over." Mom stood as if it was decided.

"Mom!"

"Just to see!"

"I don't even have a ring!"

My comment was meant to prove that there was no wedding. How could we be engaged without a ring?

"You can have mine," Carol said.

"No, no." Sebastian removed his hands and sat next to me. "I'll get my fiancée a ring on my own dime." He smiled at me.

It was all a joke. A big, funny fantasy for our families' benefit. One that let them believe I was sticking to the goals I'd set for myself.

I stood up and gathered cake plates. "I'm sorry. I have to get some work done."

"It's Christmas Eve," Dad objected.

"You don't make it far taking days off, Dad."

I swept into the kitchen. Before anyone could join me and continue making a joke of my life, I went upstairs to outline a romance about a humiliated woman finding love.

CHAPTER 9

RACHEL

When I'd fallen asleep at midnight, there were still voices downstairs.

The next morning, Santa brought me a notebook, doughnut-print pajamas, Swarovski crystal earrings, an iTunes gift card, and a pair of fuzzy rainbow socks that I put on immediately.

My mother had a wiped-out look I remembered from chemo, but I attributed it to the late night.

"How late were you guys up?" I asked.

"Two in the damn morning," my father grumbled. "They were following that Instagram post of you and Sebastian. Do you know Tiffany has half a million people following her? All strangers."

"She's very active online," Mom said as she helped me stuff crumpled wrapping paper into a plastic bag.

"She could stop looking at her phone for five minutes." I pointed to the space under my father's footrest. "There's a bunch of green paper under Dad's chair. Can you get it?"

She collected it but didn't pass it over right away.

"You two did look cute together."

"Mona," Dad said. "Don't push."

"I didn't realize how well known he is." Mom shrugged, handing over the green paper. "He's a catch."

"Good for him." I stuffed the paper in the garbage bag. "I'm not."

"The bride doesn't have to be."

"Mona!" Dad snapped.

Outside, a car door slammed. I craned my neck to see out the window. Sebastian was putting his stuff in the back seat. He hugged his mother.

I had to put this whole thing to bed immediately.

Before I could ask myself what was so urgent, I ran out, crossing the cul-de-sac in my fuzzy-rainbow-sock feet.

"Hey," he said when he saw me, crossing until we met in the middle of the street.

I was out of breath, and I didn't know what to say. He'd gotten so damned tall and handsome, but he was still that kid from the block who helped me with my homework.

"You all right?"

"I, uh . . . just wanted to say goodbye."

"Yeah." He transferred the keys to his Audi from one hand to the other. "It was great to see you."

"Me too. I mean . . ."

He put his hand on my shoulder and kissed my cheek. I dropped my arms and turned my head a little—not because I thought about it but because I didn't. My lips ran over his jaw as he pulled away.

"I live in Santa Monica now," he said, backing away. "Maybe I'll see you sometime in LA."

"I'm not playing this game," I said, sounding more annoyed than I felt. My arms were cold, and I was stupid and embarrassed.

"What game?"

"The getting-married game." It was my turn to back away. "So anyway. Have a good drive back."

I got two steps toward my parents' house before he called out to me.

"We should go out."

That got me back to the middle of the street.

"I like dinner." He shrugged at the obviousness of it all. "You like dinner."

"I don't think it works that way."

"I think you're wrong." He was so confident in his assertion that I believed him. He had that. As much of a nerd as he'd been, when he stated a fact, you could bet it was a fact.

"And we did spit sign getting married," he continued, "so we might as well get on with it."

Even though I knew he didn't mean to make it sound like an obligation, his joke jabbed me where I was softest. That was my cue to let it go. Let my better nature suppress my impulses.

"I'm not desperate," I said. "I'm just behind schedule."

"I know. I was—"

"See you next Christmas."

I didn't wait for him to answer. I walked back to the house without looking back.

CHAPTER 10

SEBASTIAN

Christmas was a holiday, but things still had to run. Funds traded overseas. The algorithms had to be constantly tweaked, and no one else was around to do it.

The lights were dimmed, and the hundreds of screens at hundreds of desks were black. In the biggest office at the other side of the space, Seema was lit by a flat screen. She had honey skin and long black hair, a full figure, a husband, and two kids. She'd been a rising Bollywood child star who took a break to go to Stanford, where we met. She returned to acting for a few years, saved her money, met her husband, and invested in turning a mathematical model into a business.

"Merry Christmas," I said, slapping my bag on the desk that faced hers.

"You're late."

"Traffic." I turned on my machine.

She pressed her fingers together and tapped her thumb against them, meaning *waa-waa-waa*. "I have half an hour here before Teddy files for divorce."

"You'll be out of here in twenty." I fished an orange box from my bag and tossed it to her side. "Here. This will make it up to you."

When she saw it, her mouth dropped open. "Sebastian!" After pulling the brown ribbon, she opened it, revealing a scarf with a complex print of equestrian doodads. Belts and buckles and shit. "This totally makes up for it." She opened the silk square to look at the print, blocking her face. I sat down. "It's gorgeous." She folded it with the honor of a Girl Scout on flag duty. "How did you know?"

"You said you rode horses when you were a kid, and you wear scarves. Not rocket science."

"I didn't get you anything."

"Our friendship is over."

"It is. How are you engaged and didn't tell me?"

I was about to ask her what she was talking about when I remembered she followed my sister on Instagram.

"I'm not. It was a joke."

"She seems nice."

"She is." I clicked to our dashboard. "How's Singapore doing?"

"Why do you have that face on?"

Her accent got heavier when she got personal.

"Nothing."

"Mm-hmm." She wagged her finger like a metronome. "Nope. Nope-nope-nope."

"We're at work." I refreshed my screen, but nothing changed.

"There's no one here and not much to do, so why the face? Just tell me. I won't Kappa Sig you."

Once she'd found out I'd spent a year in the nerd frat at San Jose, she'd never let it go.

"It's boring. Personal stuff. Blah, blah."

"Did you call Tammy for Christmas? Did she string you along again?"

Seema, needless to say, did not like Tammy. As a Hindu married to a Methodist, she saw no reason religious beliefs couldn't comingle. Tammy and her family had seen it differently.

"I didn't call, and I won't." I picked up a pen just to express my irritation by tossing it back on the desk. "It's the Instagram wedding girl. I knew her when we were kids."

"Is this the one who beat up that bully?"

"Yes."

"The one you made carry your books?"

"I didn't make her do anything."

"Mm-hmm."

"She just hated seeing me struggle."

"That's a nice person."

"I know!" I shouted at myself, not her. "She put her career on hold to take care of her mother when she had cancer."

"Very impressive nice-person credentials."

"I couldn't stop mentioning this marriage pact we made. I acted like it was enforceable." I put my face in my hands. I couldn't look up when I said it.

When I got my hands off my face, Seema was leaning forward as if she wanted to jump over the desk.

Seema shook her head slowly. "Seb, Seb, Seb."

"Here's the thing. I'm sure that for like half a minute, she was attracted to me. One hundred percent sure. I can't have fucked this up forever. I should call her. Right?"

I had her parents' number, and I was as sure she was there as I was sure she'd liked me for a second in the hall.

"Don't."

"What?"

"Not today. It's Christmas. If she's mad, let her be mad. You're sure she saw you differently than when you were kids?"

"Utterly confident of that."

"Utterly?"

"With utterness."

"Then don't risk ruining it completely, and don't stalk her."

"It's not stalking."

"Trust me. Let her forget what you said and remember how you looked. How she felt."

"Okay. Damn. I saw her, and it was all like *bang*. I was so in love with her."

"If it's karma, it will happen."

"Who were you in love with?" Wade poked his head in, pressed shirtsleeves rolled up over a thirty-thousand-dollar watch. He was our head of sales and, if I was being honest with myself, my only guy friend.

"What are you doing here?" Seema asked. "Don't you have a family?"

"Money doesn't take Christmas off." He threw himself in the chair across from us and rubbed his hands together. "So who's the girl?"

"An old friend of his," Seema said, sliding her coat off the back of her chair.

"It's nothing," I agreed, wishing I had an email to answer.

"Don't bullshit me, bro." He pointed two fingers at his eyes, then mine, then his again. "I see you. She hot?"

"She's hot."

"That's my cue to leave," Seema said. We wished her a merry Christmas. When the door closed behind her, Wade leaned forward.

"Tell me about this girl."

"Old high school crush."

"You gonna ask her out?"

"Maybe. She just got dumped. I don't want to push."

"Ask her out to lunch. Dinner is pushing. Lunch is food."

"Dinner is food too."

"You need a woman, my dude. I got skills, and I got good tips. Splitting hairs with me isn't going to get you laid. And if you ask me . . ."

"I didn't ask you."

"You want to be this way forever?"

"Forever's a long time."

"You bet it is."

Getting laid was the third thing on my mind, but the first two were closely related to the third.

"You're right." I took out my phone and opened up a message to Rachel.

"Whoa, whoa." He snapped the phone away. "Slow down there, cowboy. Not *today*. Jesus. Let her think you don't want her for a few days."

I took the phone back. "Fine."

"Give it until after the holidays."

"That your final word of advice?"

He stood up. "For now, bro. Merry Ex-mas."

I got back to work after he left. He was right. I shouldn't crowd her. It would be a long few days, but after the holiday seemed just right.

CHAPTER 11

RACHEL

Something bothered me about Christmas Eve.

A lot of things bothered me. Bruce's stupid call. My mother's eagerness to marry me off to Sebastian. The fact that he was some kind of catch, and I was nobody. The way he'd changed from a late-blooming boy into a man.

That last one didn't bother me as much as my reaction to him did. I couldn't stop thinking about him. When I worked on my viral video script, the hero looked and sounded like him.

VINNY

You can turn this around. I know it's been hard for you. But you have something special.

VIOLET

It was my dream to be an actress, but I never thought my big break would come in the form of a sex video.

Lame.

I often typed a few scenes to get the tone before working on an outline. It helped me find the overarching themes and capture the voices of the characters.

Not with this. Every word I typed was lame and forced. I didn't believe any of it. The idea that Violet would just pick herself up, dust herself off, and continue with her life after the humiliation of the "Delete It" video was as ridiculous as the idea that Vinny would be able to overlook it.

Maybe I needed to have more faith in Vinny.

The night before I had to go back to work, the last thing that bothered me about Christmas Eve bubbled up, and I couldn't spend another second holding it in.

I had Sebastian's number from years ago. I scrolled through a few old texts from college and sent a new one.

—Hey. It's Rachel—

Even starting the conversation was relief enough to get back to work.

VINNY

You take your breaks where you can get them.

It wasn't enough to make the work good.

—Hey. It's Sebastian. How are you?—

—Pretty good. I wanted to ask you something. Do you have a minute?—

—For you, always—

He was more enthusiastic than I expected. I shut my laptop and sat back in my chair.

—Did my mother look OK to you?—

—Yes. Why?—

—The Zofran in the trash. We threw out all her old meds when she went into remission—

—What's that medication for?—

A rational question from someone who didn't know the ins and outs of cancer caretaking.

—Nausea from chemo. Or nausea generally but she hated it because it wiped her out. So if she's taking it? It's for chemo—

He was going to forget to answer my question, and I needed to know.

—So, she didn't look tired?—

Dots appeared and disappeared on the bottom of my screen, and then the phone buzzed. It was him. The background noise was ambient music and clinking plates.

"Rachel?"

"Are you at dinner?"

"Yes, but—"

"I'm bothering you. I'm sorry."

"No, you're not."

"I am."

"I wouldn't have called you if I couldn't talk."

Beaten by logic, I tucked my feet under me. "So she looked all right?"

"I haven't seen her in ten years. She looked older, but I didn't notice anything else."

"Okay. That's good. Thank you."

"Now you have to tell me what's on your mind."

The background noise changed from the interior of a restaurant to the sound of cars whooshing by.

"I really don't want to interrupt."

"Don't make me come over there."

He didn't know where I lived, but that didn't matter. His threat was delivered with humor and concern. The years between us folded together. He was my friend, and he cared.

"I'm afraid the cancer is back, and she's not telling me."

"That's kind of a big thing to fail to mention."

"I know, but she's Saint Mona. She always said that if it came back, she wouldn't tell me because it would interrupt my career again. And when she was all hot to get us married . . . seeing me settled before she dies is like a real thing for her."

A muffled woman's voice said something in the background.

"I'm coming," Sebastian said away from the phone.

Was I interrupting a date?

I was ridiculous, calling him about this now, and the shot of jealousy was even more ludicrous.

"I have to go," I said, untucking my feet and standing as if I were late for something important.

"We should talk again."

"Yeah. Sure. Later."

We said our goodbyes and hung up.

Feeling cut off and dissatisfied, I opened my laptop. My "Viral Love" outline needed to get done. I typed about Violet and Vinny, but I didn't feel like I was writing. I was going through the motions.

Bored with even the thoughts in my head, I opened a script I'd loved that Sandra had rejected.

AMY

There's something about me that doesn't feel right with the world, and I don't know how to fix it.

I hadn't looked at "Broken Promises" in a long time, but like a friend you'd lost touch with, once I saw it again, I could finally see why I'd loved it and why I'd dropped it. It had good bones, but the dialogue was nauseating. Clunky. Seventy shades of purple.

I saved it as a new document and changed a few things just for fun. Then changed more just for the love of it.

CHAPTER 12

SEBASTIAN

Wade walked the hedge fund guys out to the valet. Seema and I were alone with half-empty coffee cups and the check.

"Who was that on the phone?" Seema asked as she took the check from the waiter, even though he'd handed it to me.

"It's personal, nosyboots."

"When you walk away from a dinner meeting with Dominant Funds, I get to be nosy." She slid her company card out of her wallet and snapped it down. The waiter took it. "Is everything all right?"

"Fine. It was the girl I told you about."

"The one Wade told you to wait on a few days? She contacted you?"

"Yeah."

"Why do you look confused?"

I scanned the room to distract myself, but my eyes landed on a couple in the corner. The woman was talking, shaking her finger as she made a point, and her date was nodding. "She's changed. When I knew her, she was a fighter. Fearless. Outspoken. She always wanted to do what was right. Now—just her voice—she sounds like the world's crushed her."

"Not your type."

It seemed wrong to say Rachel wasn't my type after all the candles I'd burned for her, but what Seema said was completely true. I liked opinionated, fearless women.

"What?" Seema asked.

"What, what?"

"You've been sitting there for I don't know how long analyzing a pack of sugar."

"You're right."

"About what this time?"

"She's not my type."

Seema took the receipt back from the waiter.

"You don't do wounded birds." She clicked her pen.

"I don't." I leaned over to see what the dinner cost us. My partner quickly calculated a 25 percent tip and wrote it down.

"You like strong women." She closed the folder. "You're not out to fight for the damsel in distress."

"She's the one who taught me how to fight, Seema. Before her, I was a passive dweeb."

"I don't know anything about this woman," she said, pushing the check away and picking up the last remnants of her wine. "But I can look at you and see you have unfinished business with her."

"It's all business with you."

"You know that's not true." She drained her glass. "I have a scheduling conflict on New Year's Eve. Two tickets to the mayor's Christmas auction at the Ebell. You take her."

"That's a big first date."

"Who says it's a date? Bring her as a friend. Get to know her again." She looked over my shoulder. "Wade's coming back, so unless you want to get a lecture on why you shouldn't bring her—"

"Adjourned."

I was glad to end the conversation.

—

Home from the dinner with Dominant, I uncovered my telescope. It was dusty and pointing to a star I'd bought for Tammy. She had the certificate. It would collect dust until she threw it away, but the star would always have her name on it.

The time and emotion I'd put into her weren't a great investment. I'd only known what it was like to want. The feeling of being wanted had been too good to let go, even when it was hurting me.

Through college, I couldn't get laid to save my life, so I put all my energy into school by taking computer science alongside art. Some boys had their growth spurt at fourteen. Mine came at twenty-one. I went from five-seven to over six feet in ten months.

Through the telescope, the star was far away, dim, sending old light to a new person. I recalibrated to Venus. It was either a hunk of poisonous rock in the sky or the planet of love. Take your pick.

I'd met Tammy when I was the twenty-four-year-old president of a three-man startup. I was overworked, obsessed with venture capital, and steeped in the toxic male culture of Silicon Valley. I wanted to be Elon Musk. She wanted to know if I wanted salad or fries with my burger. When I said both, and hold the mayo, she said there were no substitutions. I could tell she was used to being uncompromising.

As much as the culture around me devalued that in a woman, the deepest part of me found it attractive. Tammy had a true sense of wrong and right that she got straight from scripture. Though I loved her moral compass, I could never share her true north.

So while I built AnimaThing to rigid perfection, I let her compromise me. My mother was practicing witchcraft. I disagreed until I stopped bothering and just didn't talk to my mother as much as I should have. I let her isolate me, but I never committed to her religion.

When I sold AnimaThing to Pixar, Tammy put an end to my vacillations.

I could join her church and get married in it, or I could leave.

Leaving had been easy. Finding someone else hadn't been.

All that time, I was looking for a Rachel Rendell. A strong, loyal, fierce tiger of a woman with a warm heart didn't appear. Falia had been ambitious but cold. Nancy had been smart but distracted. None had gone past a couple of dates. I hadn't gone to bed with any of them.

I didn't realize I was looking for Rachel until I turned thirty.

And now, even Rachel wasn't Rachel.

I covered the telescope while it was still pointed at Venus and went to bed.

CHAPTER 13

RACHEL

The first workday after Christmas, I was in the bathroom with Ruth getting ready. She spent most of her nights at her boyfriend's place, making her the perfect roommate, even if she was a slob. The bathroom vanity was an explosion of hair implements, makeup bags, and lotions. Somehow, we managed to know where everything was.

Ruth handed me her phone. Instagram. Of course she followed Tiffany Barton. Everyone did. She had a screenshot of *BELLZ FROM HELLZ!* Sebastian and I looked just as happy together on the Tuesday after Christmas as we had on Christmas Eve.

"This was a joke."

Ruth leaned toward the mirror to get her mascara on. "Is this the same Sebbie you told me about? The ninety-pound weakling?"

"Yeah."

"He's rocking that grandpa cardigan."

"I liked it," I said, stroking on lipstick.

"Yeah, I mean it. You find a guy who looks that hot in a grandpa sweater, you found a guy for life."

"We're not even dating." I pressed my lips together and released.

"So I don't need to find another roommate?"

"No. God, no." I picked my mascara out of the pile and changed the subject. "How's Mario?"

"He set up a private dinner at the Expo Park Rose Garden on New Year's."

"Sounds romantic."

"It is," she said, giving her hair a fluff. "What are you doing for the New Year?"

I wasn't a total loser.

I had friends. Plenty of friends. People from school, from work, from other friends. There were plenty of places to go, but none were appealing.

"There's a party in Venice, but the drive? Bleh."

Ruth undid the third button on her blouse and turned to see how much cleavage was exposed.

"How's the sex-video script coming?" She fastened the third button.

"It's terrible. Worst thing I've ever written."

"You hate everything when you're working on it."

"This one is especially bad because I'm making money from someone else's humiliation. I feel gross even thinking about it."

"What if you could meet her? The girl?" she asked without missing a beat in her regimen.

"The 'Delete It' girl?"

"Yeah. You could ask her if she's all right."

"You know her?"

"Personally? No. But can I get her on the phone? Yes."

Would that unload the sense of wrongness? Could I profit from someone's pain and feel good about it?

"Let me think about it."

We worked through lunch. I typed one-liners and story ideas for a "second chance" romance. I grumbled to myself about how completely unrealistic it was for the hero to just disappear and not ask anyone in their small town how she was doing. How he came back to their small town a rich hero and knew nothing about her. How he loved her so much when they were younger but left anyway.

No one gave up that much for love.

At least, no one had given up that much to love *me*.

My phone dinged with a text. Sebastian.

Were we friends now, again, after all this time? I liked that idea. Sure, I had friends, but he was old and new at the same time. Comforting and exciting.

—What are you doing for New Years?—

—Dancing on tables. I just got a custom lampshade to put on my head—

—The possibilities are endless. So, I guess you have a location for the table already—

—I have options—

Not a lie, but not the truth since all the options stank of cosmopolitans and puke.

—Would you like one more?—

Was the pope Catholic? Did McDonald's have golden arches? Was I more excited than I should have been? Probably.

—Yes. I didn't say they were good options—

—I have a thing at the Ebell Theater on Wilshire. Super stodgy and boring. I can't get out of it, but if you come I won't want to—

—Do I have to dress up?—

—Probably?—

Could I borrow something from Ruth? She was skinnier than me, but maybe we could cobble something together. We were the same shoe size, and she had a closet full of dressy heels. Shoes made the outfit.

—OK. We're on!—

—Really?—

I smiled. His text seemed like he'd blurted it out without thinking.

I was about to answer when the texts disappeared, and the phone rang.

Bruce. Third time in as many days. I did what I'd done with the last three in as many days. I declined.

—Really. I wouldn't let a friend down—

I shut the phone. They weren't allowed in the writer's room, and I had to get back to work.

I'd gotten the job in the *Romancelandia*'s writer's room based on a pilot script Bruce had gotten into the right hands. It was called "The Barista Diaries," but the subtitle had made me the hottest commodity in Hollywood for all of four minutes. It was, "How to Not Spit in His Half-Caf-Double-Shot-Two-Caramel-Pump-Latte Even When He Deserves It."

Spoiler. She spit in his latte when she had mono, and nobody lived happily ever after. Neither did I. I took a lot of meetings, but nothing stuck until Bruce followed up with a few calls on my behalf. I was offered the job at *Romancelandia* because of him—or because I didn't cap the title's *i* in *in*.

An assistant gig was less than I thought I'd get when "Barista Diaries" started making the rounds, but I had no choice. My mother was well enough for me to take a seventy-hour-a-week job, and I was grateful to my boyfriend, so I did.

And here I was, rejecting his call, on the periphery in a room of twelve writers, typing everything they said as if forgetting a word would melt the network.

What's the grand gesture? . . . he's outside her window in the rain . . . he strings her name over the Hollywood sign . . . done . . . are there any more doughnuts? . . . I have this idea about a baker . . . small town . . . he's a vet . . . there was a Diane Keaton movie like that . . . not Annie Hall . . . do you remember Woody Allen, the way he tugged the hair coming out of his collar? . . . I do that . . . not a romance hero twitch, dude . . . what if he stops when she's around?

I could do the job with my eyes closed and my mind shut off, which was good in a way but also terrible, because I kept coming back to the bottle of pills in the garbage.

The box was in the garbage. Not the bottle. As if she'd gotten the prescription, taken the bottle out, and put it away for the treatment.

No. No *no no.*

She couldn't be sick again. That wasn't allowed. She wasn't allowed to cut her hair so it wouldn't make a mess when it fell out. There were no more breasts to take away. No more damage that could be done.

Dad. Dad couldn't take it again. He'd been emasculated by a few million cells he couldn't see. He'd gone to the basement and wept when I cut her long hair. There was nothing left to take from him either.

My sinuses tingled, and my eyes got wet.

Cancer had taken everything from them. There was nothing left.

"Rachel." Sandra's voice cut through the tears.

"Yeah!" I tried to sound alert but wiped my eyes before I turned.

"Did you get the line about their souls clicking together like puzzle pieces?"

Had I? Why the hell would I even need to? We'd only put that line or a version of it in a dozen actors' mouths. Why would anyone need to write it down? I was suddenly angry at every word of mawkish sentimentality I was expected to be excited about when love was cancer and short hair. It was loss and grief. Love wasn't in the stars or anywhere else.

"He doesn't even know her anymore!" I exclaimed. "He can't just waltz right in and expect her to be the same person." I met the eyes of the staff writers. Henry was midchew on a doughnut. Randy swirled a carrot stick in hummus. CJ nodded to encourage my stupid outburst.

I turned red. I was allowed to speak, but I was supposed to know my place.

"Go on," Sharon said.

It was her script, but if she was telling me to go on, I was going to go on.

"She can't melt for the same old lines. She's got to say, 'That worked when I was eighteen, buddy,' and he has to meet her halfway. Change his tactics for who she *is*, not who she *was*. Less *The Notebook*, more *Sweet Home Alabama*, with genders reversed."

"She's right," Ellie said, pushing her script away and pressing her forehead to the table.

"Good call." Henry closed his script.

Chairs squeaked as the room packed up. I was left with my mouth hanging open. When Sandra stopped by my desk, I thought she was going to demand I meet her in her office for a ream out.

"Can you make seven production copies of 'Heartbreaker Hero' for after lunch?"

"Sure." She turned away. "I'm sorry," I said, and she stopped. "I wasn't trying to insult the story."

"Never apologize for trying to make it right."

The super stodgy and boring thing at the Ebell Theater was actually the mayor's fund-raiser for a children's charity. One of those X-thousands-of-dollars-a-plate things people complained about when they complained about fund-raising.

Ruth's closet came through with a floor-length silver halter dress with tiny pleats that made room for my body where it was bigger than hers. She did my hair in rhinestone pins and loaned me a pair of silver shoes Courtney Cox had given her in the limo after an awards show.

"I don't think I look stodgy enough," I said in front of the tall mirror we kept in the front room.

"I have a black suit," she said, wiggling her foot into a strappy heel. "But they'll mistake you for a waitress."

"I'm so silver."

Ruth peeked past the blinds. "We're not used to parties without TMZ cameras and at least three washed-up actors with women all over them. This is the kind of party where someone like you shines."

"Someone like me?"

"A serious person." Peeking out again, she said, "I think he's here. I want to meet him."

"Ruth, he's just a friend."

"I know."

"Please don't make a big deal."

She rolled her eyes and opened the door, stepping onto the walk. I grabbed the gray faux fur bolero we'd chosen and followed her. Sebastian was coming up the stairs.

"Whoa," he said.

"I overdressed," I said when I saw him. He looked wonderful in a charcoal suit with a white shirt that he'd kept open at the neck. But I was dressed for a man in a black bow tie.

"No," he said.

Ruth cleared her throat.

"Oh, hey. Sebastian, this is Ruth. My roommate. Ruth. My dear friend, Sebastian."

They shook hands and exchanged pleasantries.

"I need to go change," I said.

"Later!" Ruth slipped back into the apartment and closed the door. The lock clicked.

"You look beautiful," he said. "Don't change."

"I won't fit in."

"I'm the one who doesn't have a tux." He crooked his elbow. "Come on. There's an open bar before the auction."

I slid my hand into his arm.

"My favorite."

He led me to a red zone where a black Mercedes sedan was running. Before I could ask why he'd left the lights on, a woman got out of the driver's side and opened the back door.

"A driver?" I said.

"No one wants to drive on New Year's."

I got into the back seat, and he slid in next to me.

I didn't say anything until the car was moving.

"Thank you. This is already more fun than any other party I was invited to."

"Thank you for choosing me over all the other plans. Not that it's the first time."

I scoured my memory.

"You mean your twelfth birthday party?"

"Yep."

His party had been the same day as Georgia Drake's annual cake and game extravaganza, which he wasn't invited to. Anyone who bothered to RSVP to Sebastian's declined, and the rest were just not going. Carol bravely asked if they could combine parties and was turned down. When Sebastian's mother moved the date to the following week, no one changed their RSVP.

I didn't go to Georgia's. My mother gave me money, and I'd treated Seb to a movie.

Seriously, it wasn't as if I'd had a choice. I hadn't even liked Georgia that much.

"All that's old stuff, Sebastian."

"I forget nothing."

"What did we see, then?"

"Cast Away."

On cue, we both shouted, "Wilson!" and laughed all the way to the Ebell.

CHAPTER 14

SEBASTIAN

Rachel hadn't overdressed. Not even a little. She fit right into the art deco space with its bronze and marble ornamentation. I was the one who looked like a kid who didn't know the meaning of *black tie*.

"Drink?" I asked.

"Sure. White wine."

With Rachel on my arm, we crossed the ballroom under a net with gold balloons sagging from the ceiling.

I got her a chardonnay. When I got my drink, she wrinkled her nose.

"Bourbon?"

"Forces me to sip. Keeps me honest."

She held up her glass. "To staying honest."

We clinked.

"Happy New Year," I said, letting the sour burn of the drink keep me to small sips. Her gaze darted around the room.

"I've never been in here," she said. "Do you come every year?"

"No. My partner's the charitable one."

"Partner?"

A simple word said as a question. So many expressions flashed across her face I couldn't have caught them all. Inquisitive. Worried. Embarrassed.

Maybe jealous? Maybe.

"Business partner. One of her kids is sick."

"Oh, that's—"

Wade's voice interrupted.

"Who let the nerds in?" He wore a custom tux with rhinestone studs. The lipstick on his date's pouty lips matched the smear on his collar. "Jesus, you look like a scumbag."

When the car in front of you stopped suddenly, and you hit the brakes, sometimes you held back the passenger, as if any human arm had the strength to stop two tons of inertia. That was how I felt when Wade joked with me next to Rachel. I put my hand in front of her as if I was going to have to hold her back.

But she was frozen, staring at the middle space in front of Wade's rhinestone buttons.

"And you look like a douchebag," I said.

Wade held up his cosmopolitan. "God bless America."

I couldn't help but feel Rachel's relief. We all touched our glasses and made introductions.

"Natasha needed to show face," Wade said, drawing her closer. "We're off to the *Hollywood Reporter* party in Bel Air."

"You'll fit right in," Rachel said before sipping her wine as if she wanted to hide her face. Her cheeks turned pink. I laughed when I realized she'd meant to jab at Wade.

Rachel seemed half an inch off center about it.

In the courtyard, someone tapped a microphone.

"You guys better go before you get sucked in to the auction," I said before turning to Rachel. "Wade hates losing."

We shook hands, air kissed, professed how nice it was to meet. Wade put his hand right above Natasha's ass when they walked away.

"I'm sorry," Rachel said as I picked up my auction paddle.

"About what?"

"He insulted you, and I realized you're friends, but by then I had residual anger."

I put my arm over her shoulders and walked her out to the courtyard. The night was perfect. Cool, clear, with the rush of the fountain to accompany the hum of voices and the string quartet. Folding chairs had been set in front of a podium.

"You're the same as you always were," I said as we took seats.

"I'm not. I didn't defend you. Not until it was too late, anyway."

"You haven't seen me in a while."

"Why did you stay away so long?"

"Did you miss me?"

"Kinda."

I expected a denial or brush-off, so my delight at her answer was coupled with shock, and she laughed at my reaction.

"Of course!" she said. "What do you think? You're forgettable?"

"No . . . well . . ."

"Give me a break. You were my friend. Of course I wanted to see you." Her hand dropped over mine. "Christmas, at least."

She kept her hand on mine. I tried not to read too much into it. She'd always been affectionate. This was nothing.

My thumb wasn't convinced. It objected strongly and insisted on proving a point by moving against the curve of her wrist ever so gently to let her know that even if its owner was too cautious to let her know he had feelings for her, the thumb was brave.

Silently, she kept her hand over mine for a second while my thumb finished the rotation; then she put her hands in her lap.

The silence was too awkward. It could be broken with a joke, but my sense of humor was taking a powder. All I had was distracting honesty.

"I didn't come because, for part of it, I was with someone who took all my time."

"You could have brought her."

"My mother made her uncomfortable."

The auctioneer stepped up to the podium. He wore a tux with a bolero tie and a top hat, and he had a curly moustache.

"Ladies and gentlemen! Take your seats!"

"Your mother?" Rachel asked. "Carol Barton? Seriously? She's one of the nicest people I've ever met."

I cleared my throat. There was no explaining Tammy in the middle of a party. Not if I wanted to enjoy myself.

"I know. And I knew. But I was in a habit of not coming back anyway. I dropped in to see Mom here and there. Odd days. But on holidays, I worked, or I traveled, but mostly . . ." I paused while I tried to find words. The chairs were filling up. We stood to let a group by. "I was trying to tell myself I was different. I'd grown out of it or whatever. And every year it got harder to go back because I was wrong to stay away, and making sure I was busy was a way to justify all the years before. So here we are. Tiffany's a grown woman, and my mother . . . she's dating Roy, or what?"

"There's definitely a thing with them. I don't know if it's 'dating' per se."

I rubbed my eyes. I didn't need to think of my mother hooking up or having a friend with benefits. Maybe if I'd shown up once in a while, it wouldn't have been such a shock. Maybe if I'd come around when Rachel was home, I wouldn't be sitting next to her on New Year's Eve wondering if she was still as beautiful inside as she'd always been, because without a doubt, she was more beautiful outside.

"Next up!" the auctioneer called. "This 1942 gold Academy of Motion Picture Arts and Sciences Award statuette, frequently described as an 'Oscar,' for achievement in cinematography."

"She seems happy," Rachel whispered. Her hand twitched, then fell back down, as if she wanted to touch me again but thought better of it.

"Between Roy and my father, I'm starting to think she likes men who are nothing like her."

"There's no one else like your mother, Sebastian."

The auction was going strong, but neither of us wanted an Oscar.

"So," Rachel said when we were sitting again, "what brought you back this year?"

My drink was empty. It must have gone right to my head.

"I remembered your birthday being so close to Christmas and then the fact that we were thirty."

"The contract?"

I hadn't come back for her. That wasn't what I'd told myself when I told myself to go home for Christmas. But if I hadn't thought she was going to be around, I would have talked myself into a full workday and dinner at Seema's house.

I wasn't ready to tell Rachel that.

"Just made me think of how much time had gone by," I said.

"Well, don't be such a stranger."

She put her hand over mine again.

"Sold!" The gavel came down.

CHAPTER 15

RACHEL

The first time I put my hand on his, he stroked my skin just the tiniest bit, and my body went into red alert. Four alarm. Code three. DEFCON one.

So naturally, once I wasn't paying attention to *not* doing it again, I did it again.

I wasn't usually this forward. Especially with someone I wasn't officially considering forward motion with. So I sat there and stared at our hands, waiting for him to move his thumb again or not, wishing he would and hoping he wouldn't, or hoping he would and fearing he wouldn't. Maybe I was just taking a retest to see if the last incident was a real thing or a twitch before I decided if it mattered.

The test went on way too long. Awkwardly long. I couldn't move, and he didn't.

"Next up!" the auctioneer said from a million miles away. "A framed poster signed by the cast and crew of *Cast Away*."

That was enough to move my eyes to his.

"Wilson!" we both shouted. The room burst out in laughter with us.

"Starting bid of one hundred dollars to the couple shouting the name of a volleyball."

"Two hundred," a man called from the front.

"Five hundred!" Sebastian raised his paddle.

"Seb!"

"What? That's our movie!"

"Posters like that are a dime a dozen."

The auctioneer didn't have a second to call the next offer.

"Seven hundred!" The man stood. Tom Hanks. We were literally bidding against Tom Hanks.

"Seb, you'll never beat him."

"It's for kids in need." He raised his arm. "Twelve hundred!"

"Two thousand!" Tom pointed at us with a smile and called, "Twenty-five hundred if they agree to take it home."

Everyone applauded. Seb stood and bowed out.

The gavel clacked.

"Sold!"

Seb looked down at me with a smile that wasn't that much different than the one he had when we were kids. But more perfect. More real. More confident.

Or maybe he hadn't changed. Maybe I had.

"And the look on your face!" I could barely get the words out I was laughing so hard. When Sebastian put his drink on the bar and made the same face he made when he'd opened his SAT score, I laughed even harder, feeling the effects of my third glass of wine and the company.

The band cut the music, and a man in a top hat and tails took the microphone.

"Ladies and gentlemen! The New Year is a countdown away!"

"Come on." Sebastian took my arm. "It's bad luck if we don't kiss at midnight."

He pulled me to the center of the ballroom.

"Is that the rule?" I asked, putting my arms around his neck. I was unreasonably happy and relaxed. I didn't feel like myself at all.

"It is."

"I heard it was something else."

"What?"

"Ten!" the room chanted.

"I was with this guy in college." My fingers drifted through the hair at the back of his neck. "He said if you're not fucking at midnight, you'll have a bad year."

"Nine! Eight!"

"Did that work?"

"Seven! Six!"

"Didn't give me good luck, but he did get lucky before he ghosted me."

"Five! Four!"

"Luckier than he deserved."

I smiled. Sebastian was still the only guy who believed the lie of my great worth.

"Three! Two!"

"You were always a good friend."

"One!"

The bell rang, and the band played the old cliché "Auld Lang Syne." I was loopy enough to sing along, throwing myself off balance. Sebastian caught me at the waist and bent over me.

His face took up most of my line of sight. Behind him, the net opened, and the balloons fell. I could kiss those lips. Just for tonight. I put my hand on his cheek. He was clean shaven, smooth, warm, firm where I let my thumb drift over his skin the way his had over mine.

He got closer. The balloons were crowded out by him. I closed my eyes with anticipation, waiting for his lips . . .

. . . which landed on my cheek, kissing it tenderly before he pulled me back to a standing position.

"Does that count?" I asked.

"Of course it does," he replied, but I was so tipsy and happy that I believed it.

—

Sebastian took me to my apartment door with the *Cast Away* poster under his arm. It was easy to lean on him, even after the wine wore off.

"Do you have a place for it?" he asked as he leaned the frame against the wall.

"It's a really big Tom Hanks face looking at me."

"Maybe not the bathroom, then."

I pulled my keys out of my bag, laughing. "You sure you don't want it?"

"Nah," he said. "Doesn't go with the furniture."

"Well, good." I put the key in the lock and stopped. "Because I love it. Thank you."

"Thanks for coming," he said. "I had a great time."

"Me too."

"Don't be a stranger."

"Don't disappear again."

I opened the door and slid the poster toward it.

"Here." He took the frame from me and put it inside the door, then stepped back out. For the first time since we'd met again, he was fidgeting and nervous. Like he'd been in school. I'd forgotten how he used to be and had taken the more confident man for granted.

"Thanks," I said.

"Hey," he said. "Are we . . . uh . . ."

"Friends?"

"Yeah. Are we friends now?"

"Now?" I couldn't let him forget what we'd been to each other. He wasn't new to me. He was the best part of my past. Even eight inches taller and built like an athlete, he was Sebastian, and he was my friend. "Now and always."

"Right. Of course."

"Good night."

"Good night." He stepped away but didn't leave my door until I locked it behind me.

CHAPTER 16

RACHEL

The copier was churning out collated stacks with a rhythm of whooshes and clicks when my mother called.

"Hey, honey."

"Hey, Ma."

"Your father and I are having an argument you can solve."

They weren't arguing. They never argued.

"Okay," I said. "The Great Santini will save your marriage by answering one question."

"Your father thinks you and Sebastian aren't going to go through with that contract."

"Mom, really?"

"He says you're not even dating, and it's crazy. I told him that you always keep your promises, and Carol was over and said Seb always had a crush on you."

"You're discussing this with *Carol*?"

"Rachel." CJ poked her head into the copy room. "You free?" She could have modeled if she weren't five four. Instead, she'd written an incredible spec about being a black woman in the dating scene and had been immediately hired as a staff writer.

"After this?" I asked CJ.

"Rachel, honey?" Mom said. "I don't want to keep you but . . ."

"You're both right," I said into the phone. "I have to go." I hung up. "Sorry," I said to CJ.

"I'm going on a research trip for 'Hedging His Bets.' Wanna join?"

"Let me finish up here."

She tapped the doorjamb. "Meet me at my car."

The copier burped out the last script.

We were in CJ's Fiat doing a healthy fifty-four miles per hour on the westernmost end of the 10 when I finished pitching the take on the video that the network wanted.

"Wait, wait." CJ held her hand up, changed lanes, and continued. "She becomes a lawyer for revenge porn victims, and she's single until she's how old?"

"We need more older heroines."

"She's chasing him around to sue him for half the show."

"But he's innocent!"

"We need kissing. Where's the kissing?"

"The tension is—"

"Has anyone ever told you what romance was about?"

"Happily ever after. Optimism. I get it."

She got off an exit deep in Santa Monica and turned toward the ocean.

"I'm rooting for her to catch him and put him in jail, the way you have it," she said. "Sure, they're worthy adversaries, but I want to root for love, girl—how are you going to make me root for love?"

"She's lonely. Her job is everything. We want her to be happy."

"She can be happy with anyone." She pulled into a garage, and a ticket popped out of the machine like a tongue. "We have to want her to be happy with *him*." She plucked the ticket out, and the arm went up. "We have to be afraid she'll lose him. Now, what if they knew each other in college or something?"

It always came back to some little trick that smoothed the way.

"Because I want it to be like real life. It's always . . . they knew each other already. Or it was a one-night stand on Saturday, and he's her boss on Monday. Or he comes back to town ready to win her. I want it to be like real life. I want it to be *hard*."

CJ pulled into a space and clicked the car into park. "I think people have enough of that."

That was the mantra. *Romancelandia* was an escape. I didn't know if I could write an escapist fantasy if my mother was sick again.

"Can I tell you another one?" I asked.

"We have a few minutes."

"You remember the 'Broken Promises' pitch?"

"The one with the lawyer and the activist? Sure."

"I'm thinking of making it into a romance."

"Now you're talking."

CHAPTER 17

SEBASTIAN

Back at the office, I couldn't answer emails at my desk for another minute. My phone was burning a hole in my pocket. I wanted to call Rachel. The disconnect between the object of my teenage infatuation; the dissatisfied, frustrated neighbor I'd seen on Christmas; and the beautiful friend I'd almost kissed on New Year's Eve was uncomfortable. I had to tie them all together.

When would a friend call? Two days? Three? When there was something specific to say? Could I come up with something reasonable? A question. *Hey, do you remember . . . ?* Or *What was the name of that place . . . ?*

Wade caught up to me in the hallway.

"You were supposed to wait until *after* the holidays," Wade said, pointing his coffee cup at me. "New Year's is a holiday."

"She called me. I had an extra ticket."

"She called you? I like that. Okay. So any action?"

"Not the kind you're asking about."

"Dude, you gotta shake this thing."

"This thing?"

He took my arm and stopped me, checking the ends of the hall to make sure we were alone.

He was at least four inches shorter than me, so when he made an important point, he picked his heels off the floor. He thought I didn't notice.

"The thing your ex-girlfriend forced on you."

"Give me a break."

"No, no, you're a red-blooded thirty-year-old man, and she forced you into an unnatural state of inexperience."

I started walking again. "I should never have told you."

"It's unnatural."

Seema was at the end of the hall with her jacket and bag. "What's unnatural?"

"Bye." Wade blew past, avoiding the question.

"Nothing," I said. "Don't you have a walkaround now?"

Walkarounds were when one of us had to show journalists the company.

"Can you take it?" she asked me. "I had Evana set out the table, but I have a meeting with Tijaan's head of school."

"Is he in trouble again?"

She rolled her eyes. Her son was a great kid, and he was always in trouble. "I know it's not your thing . . ."

I wasn't the face of the company. I didn't do media outreach or PR. That was the deal. But Seema needed me to suffer through it. How hard could it be? Show a couple of writers around. Teach them the lingo. Broad overview. No problem.

I don't know why I didn't put two and two together.

Mostly because it wasn't two and two but an indivisible exponent with no solution, but still. Writers were coming. Rachel was a writer in a city full of writers.

When we'd designed the place, I'd kiboshed glass doors at reception because I didn't want people in the waiting room to see in, but the whole mess could have been avoided if I'd been able to see out. Instead, I strolled into reception as if I owned the joint, which I did, and she saw me while I was still scanning the room for my guests.

And boom, my heart jumped into my throat as if it were trying to make a run for it.

She saw me, and her eyebrows arched with recognition.

And but, damn. The unexpectedness of her right there, in my office, was the problem. Seeing her cut through all my reservations.

On Mandarin Lane, I'd thought she wasn't my type anymore. And two nights ago I'd convinced myself we could be friends.

Wrong on both counts.

My type was built on her. Even with her hair looped in a rubber band. Even in jeans and a button-down shirt with the cuffs rolled up. Even the way she hugged her laptop was so real, so down to earth, so unaware of the beauty she was covering up that she sucked my resistance away.

"Mr. Barton!" The woman next to her had rich, dark skin and a halo of kinky hair. "Thank you so much for meeting us. I'm CJ Davis. This is—"

"Rachel," I finished for her.

"You guys know each other?"

"We went to high school together," Rachel said.

That smile. A little nervous. Was she overwhelmed? She should only know what was going on in my own head.

"She told me about her mentor," I said.

CJ crossed her arms and nodded, speaking as if she knew something we didn't. "Really?"

"Spoke very highly. But she didn't mention you were coming. Funny, after all these years . . . three times in quick succession."

I wanted to say something about kismet and fate, but they weren't here for the guy whose mother had eaten spicy food to induce labor so she wouldn't have a Capricorn. They were here for Hedge Fund Algorithm Guy.

"It's like the stars aligning." Rachel said what I'd been thinking.

I cleared my throat. My emotions were going to have to be managed, one way or the other.

"Why don't you guys come on inside?" I said, leading them past the doors.

Seema's assistant had set up the conference room with notepads, bottled water, nuts, and fresh crudités, because that was what she did. The little blue dishes looked fussy all of a sudden.

"It's a little dead this week," I said, sitting across from Rachel and CJ.

"That's fine," CJ said. "We're on a deadline, so I can make it work."

"Tell me about your project, and I'll see what I can do to help."

CJ did the talking. She had a crisp, matter-of-fact manner about it. Hedge fund guy falls in love with the interior decorator for his new office. They were looking for insight into the business, the lingo, enough information to give the script the right color and feel. Rachel's eyes flicked over her laptop screen, fingers flying as she typed, smirking as my phone buzzed on the table's surface.

I glanced at it. Rachel had texted from her laptop.

—I'm sorry—

I couldn't answer her. Not while CJ and I were talking. But she relieved my need to ask a question by reading my mind and answering.

—For showing up here like this. I didn't want you to see me like this—

I flipped the phone so the screen was hidden. Rachel made a show of looking at her screen. Lips tight against making any kind of expression.

God, I wanted to unlock those lips with my—

"Our products work as modeling tools for hedge fund quants," I said.

"Quants are people, right?" CJ asked. Rachel typed, but her eyes looked over the screen. Not at me but through me. I straightened my tie.

"Yes. I think for your purposes, you don't want to talk to them. You might want to talk to our developers."

"That sounds perfect!" CJ said with a big smile.

"Why?" Rachel asked, closing her laptop. "We too stupid to understand the complicated stuff?"

"No." I tried to wipe all the defensiveness out of my voice. The way she challenged me was Old Rachel, and I liked it. "I can show you whatever you want, but you just needed a little color, and it's just a—"

"Romance?" Rachel said. Our eyes locked over the table. She was testing me, and it wasn't uncomfortable. It felt right and good and real.

For me. Not for CJ, apparently. I could spar with Rachel all day, but I didn't want to get her in trouble. Lucinda, one of our developers, came in, and the four of us walked down the hall. CJ was abreast with Lucinda in front; Rachel and I were behind them.

"See you like what?" I whispered.

"Nothing. Never mind."

"Are we friends?"

"So?"

"So how shouldn't I see you?"

"This is huge," she said as we passed the Pit, where three dozen coders sat in front of computer screens. The floor-to-ceiling windows overlooked the Pacific Ocean.

"It's not that big a deal."

"I thought you were going to be a starving artist."

She held her laptop in her arms in the same position she'd carried my books all those years ago.

"And you signed a marriage contract anyway?"

"I thought my husband was going to marry very well."

The elevator doors opened just as we got to them.

"He is," I said, but she just kept walking right into the elevator with Lucinda and CJ, and as she turned to face me, I held up my left hand and extended my fourth finger. The doors closed on her and CJ's shock.

—

After I left her and CJ with Lucinda, I spent the weekly staff meeting wondering if she was the same warrior I'd loved or if she was more the woman who'd held her laptop to her chest as if she needed protection.

I was obsessed.

I had to know.

Her text came in as I was leaving the meeting.

—I need to check that we're kidding—

Before I could finish typing a response, I caught her coming out of the bathroom with her laptop under her arm.

Alone. Me and her. Nothing between us but the question of who we were and how we fit.

"Seb, I—"

She didn't have a chance to finish. I crowded her back into the bathroom and locked the door behind us.

"Kidding about what?" I said.

"About getting married."

"Why would that even be a question?"

"Our parents have been in negotiations about it."

My mother couldn't keep herself from talking if she tried, and Tiffany and I were her favorite subjects.

"It might be a little soon for marriage, but—"

"Soon? I don't like you seeing what I do for a living while you're in a glass-walled office overlooking the ocean. I mean, I'm not marriage material, and the odds are that's never going to change."

"I don't see why a date's off the table."

"Do you know what's going to happen if we date?"

The list of possibilities was as long as my arm. I could have counted them off, from "We decide we hate each other" to "We end up in bed." But I didn't, because I was still trying to figure her out.

What did she want to hear?

With her wide eyes and parted lips, what did she want? Did she have a fondest wish where I was concerned? Was she leaning forward? Was her expression soft and yielding?

My mind spent too long deciding what to say, so my body spoke for me.

I kissed her hard and was met with teeth and stiff resistance. It was a kiss I'd wanted since I'd had hairless armpits and a voice somewhere in the low soprano range. I'd dreamed about it. Fantasized about it. Thought about it so hard in the middle of the night I could practically feel it.

But never, ever in my fantasies did she push me away so hard I fell back against a towel dispenser, watching her face twist into surprised rage as the machine spit out a ragged rectangle of brown paper.

"That was—"

"Fucked up. I know."

"Then why? What is wrong with you?"

She was livid, just like she would have been. Just like she *should* have been.

The tiger within Rachel was in there, and my attempt to tease her out had probably alienated her. She'd be right to never speak to me again.

"I'm sorry," I said with my hand on the door lock. "I misread you. It won't happen again."

I started to open the door, but she held it closed.

"If we date, my mother's going to get her hopes up that I'm going to settle down. And I'm sorry, Seb, but if we break up while she's in chemo, it's going to crush her."

"You don't even know if she's sick again."

"You're right." She pointed a rigid finger at me as if I were her mother. "I'm going to make her tell me. This martyrdom bullshit is over."

"You're really beautiful when you're telling it like it is."

She slid her hand off the door. Having been called out, the warrior was sent into hiding.

No. I wouldn't accept that. I wouldn't allow it.

"Let's just go out and catch up," I said. "Saturday."

"Can't. Saturday's the soonest I can talk to Mom."

I unlocked the door. "I'm sorry about . . . the thing."

"Kissing me?"

"No, wasting paper towels. Of course kissing you."

"Next time, give a girl a little warning."

Next time? Her eyes darted to the door. Was she calculating the distance to her getaway? Or making sure it was closed?

"How about now?" I asked.

"Now what?"

"Fair warning. Now."

I stepped a little closer and put my hands on her arms. Not right away. I let them hover an inch away before touching her to give her the chance to move away. A chance I was sure she'd take.

"Seb, really?"

But she didn't move away.

Not this time. When I laid my hands on her biceps, she leaned in to me just a little. I smelled the floral lotion on her skin and a hint of cool water on her breath.

"Really." I slid the laptop from her arms and placed it on the counter. "This is your warning."

You're doing this. I cannot believe you're doing this.

"It doesn't feel like a warning," she said, and again—I noted—she didn't move away.

"Flashing red lights." My lips brushed her cheek, heading for her mouth. She felt better than I ever imagined. Reality had fantasy by the balls. "A buzzer, maybe."

"Just a kiss?" she asked, her lips moving against mine.

Before I could consummate what she was agreeing to, I was smacked by a swinging door.

"Oh!" CJ said. "I'm sorry! I was looking for you."

Rachel snatched up her laptop and walked out. CJ raised an eyebrow with good reason, since I was in the ladies' room. I left, and we all gathered in the hall.

Awkward.

"Well," Rachel said. "Thanks for showing us your tedious financial-sector company."

"Thank you for coming," I said and let them walk away. I could have done or said much more, but not without getting her into trouble. She glanced back at me when they turned the corner, as if she wanted to make sure I was still there.

CHAPTER 18

RACHEL

"What the hell was that?" CJ exclaimed once we were in the car. It was after five, and I was hungry.

"What was what?" I was stalling. She had plenty to ask "what the hell" about.

"The bathroom? And he gave you the finger? When we were getting in the elevator?"

"Oh, God, no. Not that finger. It was his ring finger . . . it's complicated. Can we go?"

She threw the tiny car into reverse and backed out.

"We're getting on the ten. You have plenty of time to explain."

I gripped the edge of my laptop. "I wanted to organize my notes."

"Yeah." She changed gears and sped down the ramp. "No. Out with it. Tell me everything. You guys were looking at each other like there was this whole other conversation going on."

We were at a near-dead stop on the freeway when I turned the radio on. She shut it off and made a circle in the air with her finger as if to say, *Get on with it.*

"Sebastian was the biggest nerd in school."

"You know what happens to nerds. They get gorgeous and rich."

"Right, well. Yeah. Maybe. We had this thing that we'd get married if we were single when we turned thirty."

"Oh my God."

"Well, everyone has that kind of thing, right? You forget about it. You move on. You start a career. Your mother gets sick, and you're a failure as a writer and a person, then—"

"What? Wait—"

I didn't wait.

"And he turns up, and yes. Gorgeous and rich. I get it. And he still likes me because he thinks I'm still the queen of the ball, not an assistant to twelve people—some of whom are younger than me—not even able to get a single 'just a romance' of my own green lit. Everything about my life is a joke. Even the idea that I'm getting married. One big joke."

Maybe not *and* everything in between. Everything in between had been his mouth and his broad shoulders. The way he took my laptop away and left me exposed. My cheek had never felt anything as soft as his lips. I'd almost gone weak kneed with anticipation.

I stared at my last message to him. That was my last word on the subject, and he didn't need another reminder that this was done. I was pissed and hurt, and I didn't need to feel like this.

CJ rubbed her face and dropped her hand in her lap.

"Girl. You're a walking, talking romance trope."

"Whatever."

She held up one finger. "Childhood sweetheart."

"Not really."

Two fingers. "Marriage pact." Three fingers sprayed out like shouty lines. "Fake fiancé."

"No. Not yet." I shook my head to clear it. "Not ever."

"Ah!" Four fingers. "The trope for the twenty-first century. This is why you can't write romance. You're living it."

"Well, then I don't know why people watch romance to feel good."

"Wait for the ending."

The freeway opened up, and CJ went a full forty miles per hour.

What if I was living in a romance trope? What if it was early in the first act, and I was too blind to see what was right in front of me?

Living the cliché wasn't any more fun than writing it. At least if I were living in a TV script, I'd be guaranteed a happy ending.

When I got to my parents' house that weekend, my mother was napping. I threw my stuff in the laundry, set my laptop on the washing machine, and got to work on the video outline.

That went marginally well for the length of the soak cycle. Then I opened "Broken Promises."

JAKE

I can't leave you. Look up at the stars. They've written our names in the sky.

Total puke line. He uttered it to her when he was seventeen, before taking off to Harvard (cliché school if I ever heard of one) and disappearing into privilege and money. She was left with a broken heart and a feeling of unworthiness, not wanting to disrupt his future (martyr move, if you ask me). Then he went broke and returned home (like that ever happened) just as she started getting investors for her children's charity (totally facile way to get us to root for her).

I couldn't believe I'd ever typed such garbage any more than I believed I could have ever loved it.

As I was deleting it, the wall phone rang, and since I'd lived in the house for so long, I was in the habit of picking it up.

"Hello?"

"Hello," a woman answered. I recognized the voice but didn't place it immediately. "This is Dr. Gelbart's office."

"Doct—" I didn't finish the sentence when I remembered who it was. "Arianna? This is Rachel."

Gelbart's office knew me. I'd been my mother's caretaker. Arianna was a young tech who, last I remembered, had been supposed to get married last September. I knew their schedule (open Saturday, closed Monday), the doctor's cell phone (Virginia area code), and what kind of candy to send him when *thank you* wasn't enough (Kit Kats).

"Hi, Rachel! How's the new job?"

"Great, great. How was the wedding?"

"Ah-may-zing."

Of course.

"So? What can I do for you?"

"Your mother has a biopsy scheduled on Tuesday?"

I bit back my first mouthful of responses. They included, *What? Why?* and the more subtle and thus harder to suppress, *Tell me everything; then tell me how to fix it.*

The dryer shook hard, then stopped, scraping where the drum was bent.

The calendar was by the side door. All I had to do was look at it.

Tuesday. *Dr. G.*

Right there. I would have assumed it was a checkup, but no. It was a biopsy.

"On the calendar!" I said with a tablespoon of saccharine.

"Great! Nice to talk to you, Rachel."

"Thanks, Arianna."

I hung up.

"Dryer stopped!" my mother chimed in from the doorway.

"You're awake."

She came in wearing slippers and drawstring pants with a T-shirt that had Dad's union logo on it.

"What do you call it?" She tightened a low ponytail. "A power nap?"

I popped the dryer open and kneeled in front of it, mostly so I wouldn't have to look at her.

"You took those a lot when I lived here," I said. "Naps."

"Between the chemo and the Zofran? Who wouldn't."

My clothes waterfalled into a lavender plastic basket. "Good thing you're not on them anymore."

"I'd rather just give up than go through that again."

I froze with my head in the drum, reaching for a cornered sock.

Did she just say she'd rather die than go through treatment again?

"I'm sure Dad wouldn't let you give up."

"He doesn't want to see me like that again. And what it did to you? It ruined your career."

"Just stalled it a little. For the best."

"What are you working on?"

I hadn't heard or felt her move close to me, but she was leaning over to read what was on my laptop.

"Work."

"Oh, this is so sweet!" she said. "'Our names are written together in starlight . . .'"

"Ugh." I closed the computer. "Stars don't write. And that's not what it says."

"But that's what he meant."

I hitched the lavender basket on one hip. Her line was better.

"Mom, are you okay?"

"Of course."

She laid the laptop on my warm laundry.

"Are you sure?"

"I am." She patted my cheek.

We went through the kitchen to the dining room, where I used the big table surface to fold my piles. The whistles and meaningless male banter of a football game came from the living room.

"We called Joy Tabona." Mom shook a towel out of the basket and folded it.

"The bitch from school?"

"The wedding planner." She smoothed the towel.

I kept my eyes on my folding, trying to find a way out of this. From the other room, Dad let out a half cheer, half grunt that meant the Chargers had done something good but not that good.

"Your father and I can't do it ourselves, and what else should we spend our money on?"

She folded a fitted sheet by herself, tucking the elastic curves into each other. She'd taught me how to do it one hundred times, but it had never stuck.

She looked fine.

Had she looked fine when she was sick?

Sometimes.

Sometimes she'd looked okay.

Was she planning a last hurrah?

"For what?" I tried to sound cheerful and flip, but my voice caught on the last word.

"Your wedding!" Dad called from the living room, shouting over a beer commercial.

"My *what*?"

"You said you were marrying Sebastian."

"I did . . . when?"

Dad trundled in, pulling a beer can out of a San Diego Padres Kan Kooler.

"Mom said you told her."

"I asked you the other day. Was it supposed to be a secret?"

The last time Mom had called, she'd been asking me to settle a fake argument.

He says you're not even dating, and it's crazy.

I told him that you always keep your promises.

I'd said they were both right.

"Okay, Mom—"

"You're pushing her, Mona." Dad passed us to go into the kitchen. "I told you about pushing her."

"I just want to see it settled. Just . . . everything arranged. Joy does wonderful bridal showers."

"I hate bridal showers."

"Just the wedding, then. Or not. We don't have to hire her or anyone. I don't want to push." My objections stuck in my throat as Mom plopped the perfectly squared fitted sheet over the top sheet and stuffed them into the matching pillowcase. "Can't hurt to talk to her, though."

She smiled at me and went to the bathroom as if it were normal to arrange your daughter's wedding before she was even engaged. Or even dating.

It was obvious now, between the bottle of pills and this desperation to make sure I was "settled," that Mom's cancer had reappeared. She wanted to hire a wedding planner so she could make sure my life was put to bed before she told me she wasn't getting treatment.

My father came back with a fresh beer.

"Dad," I said. "What's going on?"

"She's doing what she does. She wants you to be happy, so she's making it happen."

"I am happy." My growl exposed my lie. I folded a shirt as if the creases were a military operation.

"I'll talk to her."

"Why is my happiness suddenly an emergency?"

The doorbell rang.

He didn't move. He just looked down, pausing before he answered.

Why? What wasn't he saying? Was he sworn to secrecy?

"Honey?" Mom called from the hall. "Can you get that?"

My father was a crap liar. I'd get it out of him. He'd admit the cancer was back if I pressed.

"It's not suddenly anything," he said. "You've always been first for her."

He put the beer down and went to the front door.

Really a crap liar.

My mother was dying.

"I'll get it." I ran past him.

CHAPTER 19

SEBASTIAN

"Honey," my mother said through my earbuds. I was on the treadmill facing my personal view of the LA Basin. "Joy Tabona's coming today, and we need to be there."

"Okay? Why?"

"She's a wedding planner. I love Mona, but she's going to have you throwing garters and serving beef wellington. I know that's not *you*."

"There's not going to be a wedding, Mom."

"I thought you had feelings for her?"

A word of advice for my kids: never tell your mother anything.

I hopped off the treadmill and slid a towel off the rail.

"That was years ago," I said, way past denying my infatuation with Rachel.

"And you said New Year's was wonderful."

"I never used the word *wonderful*."

"Well. Your charts say it's going to happen this year. And Venus goes direct in Sag on February sixteenth to the twenty-seventh."

"I know," I interrupted. I loved her, but I didn't believe the stars gave a shit about who I married or when. "But it's not a thing."

"Rachel's car is in the driveway, and Joy's on her way."

"I'm not getting married."

"Maybe Rachel's marrying someone else, then?"

"Maybe," I grumbled. "I have to go."

"I love you."

"I love you too."

I hung up and tossed the phone on the marble countertop harder than I should have.

Rachel wasn't marrying someone else. She wasn't even dating anyone as far as I knew. There was no way she was getting married. It was a mix-up. A misunderstanding. My mother's social math tended to come up with weird solutions. Her misread signals and imaginary motivations drove her to find sense in star charts and tarot cards.

So she was just making something up, but there was a truth in it. Rachel would find someone else if I let her.

I had a narrow window of opportunity. Before she'd stormed out of the bathroom, she'd responded to me. I'd felt her react when I'd kissed her cheek. She'd tingled. I didn't imagine that. It had really happened.

I had to get to San Diego before the window closed, and I had to get there fast.

My mother hadn't wanted a Capricorn baby, but I was due on December 23. For years, she told me she hadn't wanted a Christmas baby because of confusion over gifts and attention, but she let it slip that she'd gotten a taste for raspberry-leaf tea when she was pregnant with me, and I looked it up to get her some for Mother's Day.

Her lies were exposed. When I confronted her with the fact that raspberry-leaf tea was known to induce labor, she laughed.

Capricorns were materialistic and oriented toward finances, while Sagittarians were idealistic and free spirited. She was afraid I'd be like my father, who was a banker and, if my mother was to be believed, an unhappy Taurus. From what I remembered of him before he died, he was a pretty decent guy.

Ever the obedient child, I did as my mother asked and was born under Sagittarius.

Needless to say, tea or no tea, I was who I was. The steadiest little Sagittarius in the star system. When I saved my money, Carol told me to spend it freely. When I spent it, she thought I didn't enjoy it enough. I don't think she was ever disappointed in me, but she worried I was going to be miserable.

The only time she was ever happy for me was the only time I was truly miserable . . . when Tammy and I broke up.

"She wasn't for you," she'd said. "That whole family was weird."

Of course, Tammy's evangelical parents and brothers had kept their opinions on Carol to themselves for the first two years before they started asking about her "witchcraft." I defended her. She was my mother, after all, and had turned her hobbies into a real career with hard work and study. Even Tammy defended her, which I found charming until I realized her defense was a hedge against her confidence that both my mother and I could be turned onto the narrow path with enough exposure to it.

I didn't know what I'd been thinking for five years.

No, I knew what I was thinking.

I thought Tammy was the only woman who would have me. I was in constant fear of losing her. I went to the gym to be worthy of her, but in the end, only my body could give her what she wanted. My mind and heart could never follow where she wanted me to go.

Splitting with Tammy had been a sort of relief. The pressure to change was gone, but I lost routines and stability I'd cherished. My mother had come to Silicon Valley right after the breakup and found me liberated and heartbroken at the same time.

"She was repressive," Carol said, then repeated with *emphasis* so I'd know exactly what she was talking about. "She *repressed* you."

"Carol . . ."

"Any woman who keeps a man waiting for sex for five years—"

"It was a mutual decision."

"I know she made it seem like it was. But you admired her fortitude when you should have been admiring your own."

She was trying to make me feel better, so I let her.

"Aries or Taurus are most compatible for you," Carol had continued. "Stick with Aries. Your father was a Taurus, and it killed him."

"A heart attack killed him."

"You know who's Aries?"

"Who?" In those first weeks, I'd just let her voice comfort me even when she babbled.

"Rachel."

"Rachel from across the street?"

"I ran your chart with hers, and—"

"She thinks I'm a dweeb."

"But look at you now, sweetheart." She'd taken my chin in her hands, and I'd let her. "Look at you now."

I'd taken the Porsche out of a sense of urgency and, if I was being honest with myself, a need to show off.

"What is *this*?" My mother came out when I pulled into the driveway next to Roy's dusty brown pickup truck. She looked at my car with a knotted brow, as if it were a checkbook she couldn't get balanced.

"Oh. My. God." Tiffany was right behind in a crop top and shredded jeans. "You have a douchemobile."

"Shut up, Tiff. It's a loaner," I lied. Wade always said using as few words as possible helped sell the biggest, most direct fibs. Rachel's car was in the driveway across the street, behind her father's SUV.

"You need me to take these lights down? It's a week after New Year's," I asked my mother as I decided what I wanted to do.

"Roy will do it."

I looked at the brown pickup, then at Tiffany, who directed me to the front door, where a fiftysomething mustachioed man in jeans and a T-shirt stood with a coffee cup. That would be Roy.

"I got it, son."

Suddenly, it was clear that Roy and my mother were a thing.

I waved to him, then turned to Tiffany, speaking in a low growl. "What the hell is going on?"

"She's a grown woman, *son.*" She expressed her acceptance and annoyance with me in one word. "If you'd been around, you wouldn't have that stupid look on your face."

I had a few easy retorts that would have just denied the obvious. She was right. I'd been absent and blind. I should have known from how she talked about him. At the very least, I should have seen it on Christmas Eve.

A Chevy crossover pulled up to the Rendell house. "That's *her,*" my mother whispered in a voice that could be heard two counties over.

Joy Tabona got out and popped the back hatch. She wore a floral dress and heels. She'd been the prettiest girl in high school, next to Rachel, and hadn't lost her looks.

Tiffany had her head in the Porsche window. "It smells like you in here." She stood straight and put her hands on her hips. "It's so not a loaner."

I gave her the *shut up* look, and she sneered.

Mom pushed me toward the house across the street, where Joy was reaching into the back of her crossover to slide out a black rolling case. "Beef wellington," my mother said as inspiration to me for battle.

I jogged up to the silver crossover.

"Let me get that," I said.

She gasped when she saw me. Still big blue eyes and black hair, now all woman instead of all girl.

"Sebastian?"

"Yeah. Hi, Joy." We cheek kissed.

"You look amazing."

"You too. Here . . ." I got the roller suitcase out and snapped up the handle. She took it. "Thanks."

She looked past me at the house she knew I'd grown up in—and of course at the red Porsche in the driveway. When she looked back at me, I motioned for the front walk, wishing I'd left the car on the end of the street.

"You first."

She walked ahead and rang the bell.

CHAPTER 20

RACHEL

In a plot twist I should have seen coming a mile away, Sebastian was at the door with Joy. He made his black grandpa cardigan with wood toggles look like a *GQ* cover. She looked fine and finished—still the prettiest girl in the neighborhood—and I was wearing sweatpants and a T-shirt with a survivor of a bra underneath.

"Hey!" she said, just as chipper as you please. I stepped out of the way so Dad and Mom could greet her. Sebastian stepped in as my parents set Joy up at the dining room table.

"Did you plan this?" I hissed.

"Hell, no. We have to tell them."

He glanced to the dining room, where my laundry was being pushed to one side of the table. Joy pulled binders out of her rolling bag.

"Rachel!" Carol's voice came from behind him. She was running across the street with her paisley muumuu flowing and Tiffany right behind, staring at her phone.

"Carol!" Sebastian snipped at his mother.

She brushed past him and gave me a hug. "So good to see you! I hear Joy Tabona's here. I wanted to say hello."

Before we could say a word, she was in the house, kissing and greeting. Tiffany joined in, still looking at her phone. Roy the Handyman was right behind, nodding at me as if he were a member of the family.

"Gang's all here," Sebastian said in the foyer as everyone gathered in the dining room.

"Well, at least we only have to say it once." I closed the door.

"Just, first? Before we go in? I'm sorry about the other day."

"I'm sorry too. I knew you didn't mean any harm."

Maybe that wasn't the best expression, because his eyes narrowed for a second. "You owe me a kiss."

"How did you go from apologizing to what I owe you?"

"You were into it. Don't deny it."

Remembering that moment, yeah—I'd totally been into it. And with him standing close enough to whisper a conversation, I could probably be into it again.

"And," he continued, "we have to make up for New Year's. It's bad luck not to kiss your date."

"Oh!" my mother cried. "This is lovely!"

We both turned to the parental gaggle, where binders were splayed out on the table.

"Shit," I grumbled.

"Look at this!" Mom held open a book for me as I approached. She seemed so happy. I hadn't seen her look like that since she went into remission, and if the cancer was back, I didn't know if I'd ever see her like that again.

I took the binder and looked at the picture. It was a place setting with a construction paper heart on the plate. A name was handwritten in Sharpie on the top.

"Each guest writes a wish for the happy couple," Joy said. "I like to do things where the guests become part of the ritual."

"That is nice," Sebastian said over my shoulder.

"Thank you." Joy's words were accompanied by a glance at the fake groom that set my hair on end. She was *looking* at him.

"I like this," Carol said. "With the organic, locally grown dinner menu and the recycled napkins."

Joy had been an inveterate boyfriend stealer, which wasn't usually the case in the second-chance-high-school-sweetheart trope, but life wasn't a romance, and people were complicated.

"It looks like army rations," Roy said, making my father laugh.

"My clients were Los Angeles conservation activists."

Joy looked at his arms the same way I had when I'd seen him for the first time in years. I saw the thoughts right in her head, because I'd had them too.

He filled out nice.

"Yeah, well, here's the thing . . . ," Sebastian started, taking the binder I was holding and closing it. He cleared his throat.

Mom pulled the chair out, and Dad helped her sit. Was she that weak already?

Dad put his hand on her shoulder. Not good. I'd seen that gesture before, and it was very, very not good.

And Joy? She touched Sebastian's hand when she took the binder, biting her lip when their eyes met. Literally. She. Bit. Her. Lip.

"The thing is—" Sebastian started.

"We want to plan our own," I cut in. I felt Sebastian's surprise next to me and grabbed his hand. His fingers laced easily into mine, and when I looked at him, his expression was a little alarmed but also encouraging.

"I'm sorry, Joy," I said to her. "I don't want you to waste your time."

"It's fine," she replied. "I understand."

"We can still do the paper hearts, though!" Mom said. "If it's all right with you?"

"Sure!" Joy said.

"On recycled paper!" Carol jumped in.

"Oh. My. God," Tiffany said. "Does my dweeb brother even know how to kiss? That last girlfriend was such a prude."

"How would you know if it didn't happen on Instagram?" Sebastian said.

"Do you even *like* each other?" She was glued to the robin's-egg-blue device.

"Tiffany!" Carol tried to snap away her phone but missed.

"He's the most wonderful man I ever met."

"Yuck."

Everyone started talking at once. Sebastian pulled me away into the kitchen and out the back door. He slid it closed and sat on the edge of the teak bench.

"What's going on?" he asked.

"I'm sorry. We should go back and undo it. It was an impulse. It's just . . ." I took a big breath. Put my hands on my hips. Let them drop. Shifted my feet.

"Sit down."

I threw myself on the bench next to him, leaning back against the railing while he leaned forward, looking over his shoulder at me. Those arms. Damn. This was a guy who could barely carry his own books. Now he could carry me.

"You know when I said I thought my mom's cancer was back?"

"Yes."

"At this point, I'm sure of it. So sure. And she's not admitting it."

He leaned back. Our shoulders touched. I had plenty of room to move away but didn't, because . . . those arms.

I took a deep breath and continued. "And she'd be so happy if I was settled with a 'nice guy.'"

"Why the air quotes?"

"What air quotes?" My hands had been folded in my lap.

"You don't need fingers to make air quotes. I heard them. You don't think I'm nice?"

"You're nice, okay? But this is weird." I twisted to face him, even though it meant we weren't touching anymore. "You don't just marry a nice guy before you date him."

"Is there a rule against us dating?"

Well. No, there wasn't. Except for the fact that he was my friend. He was the unsexy boy across the street who made me feel needed. The kid whose jaw was square because his body hadn't filled out and whose gait was floppy and awkward because his feet were man size years before the rest of him.

"We kind of already had a date on New Year's," he added.

"It was fun."

An insane thought that had been planted in the dining room sprouted on the back patio.

"I want to go out with you again," he said. "And you still owe me that kiss."

The insane thought grew branches, developed leaves. It was going to root if I didn't spit it out.

"Let's fulfill the contract," I said. His face went blank, and I knew I was going to have to explain. I was committed. No laughing it off. No pretending I was joking. "Let's . . ." My last chance to take it back was in the next sentence, but screw my chance at *not* doing something. "Let's get married."

"What?"

"Let's. Get. Married."

"Why?"

Why was always the big question. Why does the audience care? Why are they not changing the channel? Why do they tune in?

"Okay, bear with me." Mentally, I committed to the pitch. "This could be really something."

"I'm listening." As if sensing my enthusiasm, he made a decision to hear what I had to say, twisting around to face me and draping his arm over the back railing.

"My mother is very possibly sick. She won't tell me because she thinks the last time she was sick, she held back my life. If she sees my life isn't stalled, she'll either tell me the cancer's back, or she'll just feel better emotionally. So this begs the question. What if—thinking I'm doing fine—she tells me, 'Rachel, I'm sick.' Well, look, we want to date each other. We just keep doing it, and the engagement drags on and on until she's better."

"And if she doesn't tell you?"

"I think planning a wedding, even if it's in some vague, undefined future . . . I think she'll *feel* better if she thinks I have my life figured out."

He rubbed the divot where his chin met his lips. Watching the way the short beard there folded and sprang back was hypnotic. No matter how you sliced my stupid idea, I wanted to date him long enough to kiss that divot.

"What's in it for me?"

"Your sister will stop thinking you're a dweeb."

"Nothing I do will change that."

"Women dig a guy who's engaged. Look at Joy."

"Not interested." He glanced over my shoulder. I followed. Carol and my mother were pretending not to look out the glass door.

If I couldn't get him to take a carrot, maybe I could use my stick.

"I'll tell your mother I saw you at work, and it looked really stressful, and I'm worried about you."

"That's blackmail."

It was, and I felt a pang of guilt for even mentioning it, but it was my mother's happiness on the line.

"It would be blackmail if it was a big deal," I said. "But it's not like she's going to stop loving you or cut you off from a huge inheritance. Worst case? She'll send you meditation tapes and crystals."

He glanced over my shoulder again. I knew they were watching from the kitchen and pretending they weren't.

"I'm not worried about my mother's love," he said. "Manipulation is beneath you."

He seemed disappointed, which shouldn't have bothered me. What did I care if he was disillusioned? His opinion of me hadn't mattered in years. Why should it now?

"Okay," I said, deciding I cared and it didn't matter why. "Forget that. No blackmail. Just for me, because I'm asking."

"Plan a wedding. Just because it'll make you happy?"

My first instinct was to minimize. Call it nothing. Say the plans didn't have to be big. We could just say we were getting married in city hall in three years.

But I was committed to the pitch, and that meant no backpedaling.

"Yes. The whole thing. A hall. A band. A long white dress. A honeymoon in Paris. It's all talk, but if we're going to talk, we might as well talk big."

"You really want to do this?" he whispered.

Did I? No, I didn't. But even though it was an insane lie for an intangible result, something about it felt ambitious. As if dating him was fine and dandy but faking a marriage was reaching for the stars. Thinking small hadn't gotten me anywhere. Somehow, this was going for the glory.

Leaning in to me, he breathed on my cheek. The arm he'd draped over the railing stroked my hair. His lips moved to my jaw while he caressed the back of my neck.

"Let's do it," I said. My brain had become completely untethered from my body. I would have said yes if he'd promised me a plate of chicken.

He kissed me, and for a second I didn't kiss him back. I was too stunned at his gentleness. I was a feather pillow, bending under him, barely holding my shape.

I was going to regret this. He was handsome. He was a wonderful person. I wanted to kiss him. A little pucker. A little change in the angle of my head. A taste of his tongue on mine. A little groan I had no control over before we were in full make out.

Oh my God. My body was praying for more, and my mind was reminding me not to get attached because in the end he was still a guy I was attracted to, and guys I was attracted to broke my heart.

"Gross!" Tiffany said from the driveway. Not expecting to hear her so close, we yanked apart. "You're eating her face, dweeb."

She rolled her eyes so hard I could only see the whites.

"You came out here to criticize how I kiss my fiancée?"

I coughed.

"No, I came out here to tell you Ace is playing the Smell. You can hire him for your wedding or whatever."

"You go to the Smell?" he asked.

"I'll tell him to put you on the list." She turned to head back down the driveway, waving her phone. "Bye, Rachel."

"Bye, Tiff."

"Yeah," Sebastian called. "Thanks for the pointers."

"Anytime, dweeb," she called over her shoulder.

"If we break up," I said, "I'm going to tell her you were the best kisser I ever had."

I didn't mention that I wouldn't be lying.

CHAPTER 21

SEBASTIAN

The party started in an hour, and I was already set.

Seema's kids were at Westbrooke, the snazzy private school behind the twenty-foot hedges on Olympic. Expensive birthday parties were required, and Tijaan, who was in second grade, had made a special request for the entertainment. The cartoon guy. Me. Again.

It was a pretty small event, but the kids always loved it when I brought AnimaThing. I'd hook it up to the flat-screen TV, and the kids transformed themselves into superheroes, easily doctoring their costumes, faces, and bodies to be whatever they could imagine. They were a total gas.

"Do you need anything?" her husband, Teddy, asked. He was a white guy who played golf and did accounting for Overland Studios and who kept them in a huge house with a pool and original art on the walls while his wife took big risks at Sync Inc.

"Nah."

"Any improvements since last year?" He handed me a cold beer.

"Haven't had the time." Any updates were free-time projects. Pixar had bought the software and shelved it so it wouldn't compete with something they had going.

“They’ll still love it.”

“Where are Tijaan and Mindy? They need to test it out.”

“Seema sent them with Nanette for haircuts. Tijaan was starting to look feral, and Mindy can’t let him go for a cut without her.”

“Don’t blame her.”

“You’re really something with them. They love you.”

“They’re great kids.”

“Seema says you’re getting married?”

I almost choked on my beer. He slapped me on the back, laughing.

“Don’t act so surprised, dude. You know she tells me everything. So. Childhood sweetheart?”

“It’s complicated.”

“Well, congratulations. Marrying Seema is the best thing I ever did. This”—he tipped his beer to the high windows overlooking the huge backyard, the pool, the overall seven-million-dollar house—“all of it means something because of her. So good on you.”

We clinked bottles. He thought he was clinking to my happiness, but in my mind, I was toasting his.

“Teddy.” Seema came in wearing a flowing floral dress over bare feet. “The food’s here. Can you get them set up?”

“Can do!” He hopped away, kissing his wife before he passed.

“You need anything?” she asked me.

“Nope. You told him about Rachel?”

“I tell him everything. Did you not want me to?”

“No. It’s fine.”

My phone dinged. Seema went back to the kitchen when I fished my phone out of my pocket.

It was Rachel.

—Hey, Seb? You there?—

—Yeah—

—I've thought about it—

Oh, shit. I finished the beer. If she was kiboshing this, Seema and Teddy had Japanese whisky I might have to hit. I didn't realize how much I wanted to keep to the wedding plan until Rachel told me she'd "thought about it."

I waited for her next text. I didn't want to encourage her. I wanted her to be my fiancée for another five seconds. I wanted more time to dig out that girl who had changed me into a man.

—You don't have to do this—

Was she letting me off the hook or telling me what she wanted, the way a person would say, "I know you're busy," when they want to get off the phone?

—There's not much in it for you. And as favors go, this is pretty huge—

It was ridiculously huge. If I were a guy who hadn't wanted her since I was a hairless whip of a kid, it would have been outrageous. But this "favor" was all I could think about. She'd done so much for me, even before we got suspended together. I bet she never even gave any of it a second thought.

I called her, and she picked up on the first ring.

"Hey," she said. "I mean it. No hard feelings."

"I want to tell you a story," I said, putting the empty bottle on a coaster. "It's from when we were in middle school. Seventh grade. You were on your trip to Washington, DC."

"Eighth grade," she said. "I'm sure it was eighth. Did you not go? Wait, you weren't there."

"Right, eighth. I went with the group in the spring."

"Right, right."

"I had to walk home by myself, and Scott and Bobby saw me."

"Fucking Cletus and Jeb. I hated them."

"Me too. But anyway, they found me, and that went about as well as could be expected."

She didn't add anything. I could hear her breathing and no more.

"So I was crying like a baby when I got to Mandarin Lane. Dad was already"—I stopped myself from saying *dead*. I wasn't here for sympathy—"gone, and Mom was working at the preschool. Tiff was in day care, thank God. I had . . . uh . . ." I really wanted that scotch now. "Head wounds bleed bad, right?"

"Oh . . ."

"It looked worse than it was. My pride was really what they hurt. They kept saying stuff about my girl bodyguard and calling me a fag."

"Their parents were assholes too."

"Your mother saw me coming down the street and . . ." I stopped, remembering my uncontrollable idiot blubbering as I'd explained to Mrs. Rendell what happened. She'd wiped the blood and tears from my face just like my own mother would have. "She took care of me," I continued. "She cleaned up my head and let me watch MTV until Carol got home. She said something that stayed with me. She said, 'It gets better.' She said that over and over. And you know? It did get better, but only because I believed her. So when you talk about a favor I'm doing for you, sure, that's true. But I'm doing it for your mother too. If she's sick, and this makes her feel good, then fuck it. No problem. We'll be engaged until she's through this."

Rachel cleared her throat. She sounded sticky and wet.

"Are you crying?" I asked.

"No. Fuck you," she said, pretty much admitting she was crying. "But thank you. Really. Thank you."

Outside, Teddy showed the caterers their space, the outlets, the kitchen in the guesthouse. He seemed so *set*, and I felt like a driver in the rain.

"And we're dating on the sly anyway."

"Yes," she said. "We are."

"Okay, now that we're on the same page, let's talk about a ring."

"I was thinking of grabbing one from the prop room."

"They have diamond rings?"

"Fake. Cubic zirconia or whatever, but they look real enough."

"Yeah . . . no."

The kids were home. I could hear their pounding feet, Seema's admonition to put their shoes in the closet, their squeals as they headed for me and the AnimaThing.

"Seb. Give me a break."

"I'll pick you up Saturday at ten."

"Really . . . no!"

I hung up a second before Tijaan jumped into my arms, and I made him, his sister, and all their friends into superheroes.

CHAPTER 22

RACHEL

Sebastian's text came in at 9:45 a.m. on Saturday.

—I'll be there in fifteen—

I'd gotten up early because, in the space between wakefulness and sleep, I'd found a gaping plot hole in my script.

Not the viral video script.

That wasn't happening.

It wasn't right. I wasn't going to be responsible for shoving a terrible thing in this woman's face, whoever she was. And I wasn't going to tell Sandra because she'd give it to someone else, which would make it all a wash.

Maybe if I rewrote "Broken Promises" until it was so perfect it glowed in the dark, they'd shelve "Viral Love."

Maybe, just maybe they wouldn't fire me. But first, "Broken Promises" had to be perfect.

And it wasn't.

Our heroine-left-behind's friends and neighbors hadn't contacted the hero all those years just to make conversation, and he'd never asked about her. The issue had come up when she was telling him she didn't think their love was written in the stars because the stars had moved, but he hadn't changed.

Which begged the question of why she didn't know that.

And on and on until I wrote it down so I could get it out of my head. I'd woken up at five so I could carefully lift the second act out of the script as if I were removing the funny bone in a game of Operation.

The idea of getting out of my apartment and leaving the story's guts hanging out was pretty appealing, except for the gaping plot holes in my life. Sebastian was on his way to me so he could buy me a diamond ring. I had lots of thoughts; most of them involved second-guessing the whole plan. I texted my doubts to Sebastian.

—This is a lot of money for a fake wedding—

I'd dreamed of a sparkling ring so hard that after Bruce and I had broken up, I'd started a savings account to buy my own freaking diamond. It had two hundred dollars in it.

Sebastian texted back.

—We can return it. But you need a rock or they won't believe it—

—OK a small one though—

—We'll see—

"No Porsche today?" I asked when I met him by his Audi. I didn't want him to see my scrubby apartment because I was 100 percent sure he lived in a palace.

"We don't need to go that fast." He indicated the laptop I was hugging. "Why do you have this?"

"In case I think of anything."

He held out his hand. "Give it."

"Why?"

"I'll put it in the trunk. Come on."

I gave it up, and he wrapped it in a blanket before slipping it in the back. It was better protected than I felt without it.

He opened the door for me, and I got in. The seats were leather, and the car was new and clean. Mine still smelled like cigarettes and dog hair from the previous owner.

"Okay," he said, starting the car. "I got us an appointment at Harry Winston."

"What?"

"I refuse to give my sister the satisfaction of going to Tiffany."

"There's a jewelry store in the mall."

He turned onto Wilshire. "Are we doing this or not?"

"Fine."

"Try and have fun with it."

"Noted. Fun. Got it."

"Who was the last guy you wanted to marry?"

The last guy? As if there had been a string of them. I filtered out the offense and assumed his best intentions.

"The last guy was Bruce Geraldo."

"The development VP at Overland?"

His profile revealed nothing.

"You know him?"

"I read the *Hollywood Reporter*. I like to keep up with who's developing animation projects. But go on."

"Right. Well. He was really supportive. He got me meetings and acted like he believed in me. Maybe he did. But he also believed in flashing around his Amex Black. One night we were out, and this guy he worked with told me his parents were visiting from out of town. He wanted to know if I thought getting them a bungalow at the Beverly

Hills Hotel would be too ostentatious. And, like, how would I know that? I played along until I realized he thought I'd been there with Bruce numerous times."

"He'd expensed the rooms?"

"Yeah. And I never saw the inside of one. So. There was that. My 'boyfriend' made some excuses about renting them for visiting talent and then . . . only then . . . started talking about what kind of wedding I wanted. I played along, but it wasn't the same."

"When did you break up with him?"

A short laugh escaped my throat. "That's the thing." I could have sugarcoated it or made it seem as if I had some agency in the relationship, but I couldn't give him anything but the truth of how pathetic I was. "He heard I found out and dumped me like"—I snapped my fingers—"that. It was like he was getting in front of it. He had to deny me the satisfaction of breaking up with him."

Sebastian drove, and I let him understand the sheer depth of my wretchedness. He could judge me. He *should* judge me. But I knew he wouldn't.

"What do you think he's going to do when he finds out?" he asked.

"If this were a romance, he'd show up at the end of the second act asking for me back, and at the climactic moment, you'd beat him up to prove your caveman love." I rubbed my eyes. I shouldn't have said that either.

"What's real-life Bruce going to do?" He stopped at a light.

I shrugged. "Probably call me. Try to get me in bed and break us up to prove a point, then dump me again."

He looked at me in disbelief for a second before the light went green. "That's spiteful."

"I guess I'm just imagining the worst."

"Well, let's get a ring on that finger and see what he does."

Sebastian and I sat on a velvet couch and inspected a tray of rings. They were all gorgeous, and none of them had price tags.

I was wearing a two-and-a-quarter-karat round cut because it was the smallest one they'd brought.

"It's nice," I said.

"Here." He took his phone out and held it in front of the ring. "I'll tag it 'Harry Winston.' It'll make Tiff insane."

"Such an asshole move," I said as he sent her the picture. The saleslady came back with a leather folder of paperwork as I watched the ring flash. Would I have to get manicures from now on? Maybe. No one wanted scrubby hands with a ring like this.

A call came in on my cell, and since Sebastian was busy with the saleslady, I picked it up.

"Hi, Dad."

"Hey, sweetie," Dad said. "I was wondering if you remembered, back two years ago? More or less? Do you remember the doctor we got the second opinion from?"

After the second positive biopsy. You didn't get a second opinion on a clean bill of health.

"The one on Beverly Glen?" My voice was too loud. The ring was too showy. I was too big in the space.

The second opinion had been worse than the first. It confirmed there was no mistake.

"No," Dad said. "The lady who did the second treatment opinion."

I froze with my right hand tugging my left ring finger. Was the Tuesday biopsy with Dr. Gelbart a second? Were they already on treatment?

"Why?"

Dad paused for a second too long. I shot Sebastian a look. He read my face like a book and went from smiling to concerned in a heartbeat.

"The insurance company wants more paperwork. I forgot the doctor's name."

I stood, my life a tunnel leading straight to my mother at her sickest and all the times I'd thought she couldn't fight it anymore.

"I filled out every fucking form," I growled. He was lying. Flat-out lying. That treatment was taken care of. She was getting it again and not telling me. Was it her lymph nodes? Her bones? It could be anywhere.

"Dad, what's going on?" I'd walked out to the main area, a hushed, ambiently lit temple to jewelry.

"I'm up to my ass in forms, Rachel," he snapped. "Do you remember or not?"

"I'm coming down there right now."

The guard stopped me as I tried to walk out. I paced back in, obeying him and ignoring him at the same time.

"I just need the answer, please." Dad sounded tired. "Not drama."

Sebastian showed the guard a slip of paper, which I thought nothing of, because I wasn't thinking.

"I'll give you drama when I get there," I said. This time, when I stalked to the door, the guard held it open.

"I can't wait. Now can I have the name?"

"Ramsaroop," I said. "Dr. Ramsaroop."

And that was how I walked out of Harry Winston with a two-and-a-quarter-karat engagement ring.

"It's fine," Sebastian said as we crawled up San Vicente.

"How can it be fine?"

"Sync Inc. has an account."

"And this is a business expense?" I held my hand up so he could see the massive boulder he'd just bought.

"I'll take it as a disbursement."

I put my face in my hands. I could feel the weight of the ring as I rubbed my eyes.

"I don't even know what that means." I lowered my hands as he got off the freeway. "And don't tell me, Mr. Stealth Finance Guy. I don't c—wait. Where are we going?"

"My place."

"No! I have to get my car and go to San Diego."

"From what you told me, your father doesn't need you there."

"He does whatever Mom tells him, and if she tells him, 'Don't tell Rachel the cancer's back,' he's not going to tell me."

"Then he's not going to tell you there either."

"It's harder to lie to someone's face."

"Okay, so if he tells you all the things you think he's not telling you, then what?"

"I'm going to be there for her."

"If she doesn't want you there—"

"Shut *up*! If I'm willing to go through it again, she has to." Before the words were fully out of my mouth, I knew I was wrong. I hadn't thought before speaking.

Sebastian stopped the car in front of a nondescript apartment building in the foothills and pressed a button over the visor. The gate rattled open. He didn't correct me or tell me I was being selfish and immature. He just pulled into a spot in the shade of a jacaranda tree and cut the engine.

"I should go home," I said. "I have a ton of work to do."

"Bring your laptop in."

"I don't want to bother you."

"I'll ignore you."

"You don't need to babysit me. You talked me out of it."

"Good." He opened his door. "Come on, already. I'm hungry."

I thought he'd have some kind of mansion in the hills, but it was a small apartment of four in the building. It had a killer view of the LA Basin, an open kitchen/living space, and a separate bedroom with a half-open door I peeked into for a second.

"Set yourself up wherever," he said as he opened the fridge. "I have chicken salad, leftovers from Loteria Grill, PB and J, and . . ." He closed the door. "We can do Postmates. The world is our oyster."

I opened my laptop on the counter and slid onto a stool. The cursor blinked, asking for my code.

I really did have a lot to do.

I closed it and laid my arms over the lid. "Peanut butter and jelly."

"Excellent." He pulled the ingredients out of the door shelves and gave a carton of milk a sniff. "Still good. You in?"

"For milk with PB and J? Hell, yes."

He arranged plates, utensils, jars. To my right, the walls were made of glass. A tripod with a black cylinder on top was set in the corner. It had the proportions of a soda can, but it was huge.

"Is this what you traded your old telescope for?" I asked as he poured the milk.

"This is a dozen upgrades later."

"What can you see?" I bent to look, but the eyepiece was capped.

"From here?" He walked over and handed me a glass. "Not much. Planets mostly, if it's clear. If I go out to the desert, though? I can watch the girls in the International Space Station take a shower."

I laughed, and he smiled with me.

"Did you look in my room when we were kids?"

"Never once."

"Really?"

I don't know why I expected a different answer. His telescope had been set on the other side of his room, and I didn't think much about it until I asked. But I was still surprised he never peeked.

"The lens was too strong to focus across the street. Also, you were beautiful, but I think I knew I needed you as a friend."

"To boundaries." I held up my milk glass, and we clinked.

He went back behind the kitchen bar to finish making the sandwiches, and I slid onto a stool across.

"I like your apartment. Most guys would get a big house to impress women."

"I don't like women who are impressed with big flashy houses."

He laid down a smooth layer of peanut butter on all four slices of bread.

"Are you going to tell your mom this is fake?" I asked. "Not the ring."

"Obviously." He screwed the peanut butter lid back on.

"The wedding, I mean?"

"So she can run across Mandarin Lane and tell your parents?" He spread the jelly on one side and closed the sandwiches.

He was right, of course. The whole thing would explode if any of them knew.

"I guess we can't tell anyone," I said. "But I told CJ."

He slid my sandwich over the counter. "I'm sure it's fine."

When I bit the corner of the sandwich, the huge rock changed the landscape of my vision and the weight of my hand.

"I can't stop looking at it," I said, watching the stone catch the light.

"It's amazing on you."

"Are you sure you can bring it back?"

"Yup."

Everything was perfect. Handsome guy. Sparkly ring. Happy family. We ate in comfortable silence.

"Since we're engaged," I said, "can I ask you something insulting?"

"Is that what happens when you're engaged? You get insulted?"

"No, you don't get insulted. You get asked insulting questions."

"Oh, now that I know how to react—"

"It's okay to ask?"

"Hit me with it." He popped the last corner of his sandwich in his mouth.

"You and Tammy broke up almost two years ago."

"Yes?"

"You haven't even mentioned an ex who might get upset you popped the question to me and not her?" I took stock of his expression and his posture and calculated he wasn't insulted. "Much less a current girlfriend, which is weird."

He stopped the glass of milk halfway to his lips. "Weird?"

"Look at you." I held my hands out, elbows straight, pointing out something incredibly obvious that anyone could see.

"What?" Sebastian just looked at his shirt as if he were checking it for splattered jam or dribbling milk.

"Oh, criminy. Really?"

"You're saying I have no girlfriend, so you're pointing out something wrong with me?" He gathered the plates. "Is that the insulting part?"

"Have you met you?"

"Every morning." He was chewing his sandwich as if his brain were made of super-high-density concrete.

"You're gorgeous! I mean, to tell you the truth, you're a little thick in the head right now. But you're very hot, so I have no idea why you've got space in your life for fake engagements. Which"—I held my hand up to stop him from saying what he'd never say anyway—"I'm super glad and grateful, but your singleness is a little too convenient."

"Convenient? You think I'm lying?"

"No. But if I wrote a fake fiancé episode, the guy would either be coming off a breakup or be a real ladies' man doing it to inherit the family business, because no one—and I mean no one—would believe you were single. It would be unrealistic, and we'd have to change it."

He nodded, hands on the counter.

"I could be gay?"

"A gay man wouldn't have kissed a woman the way you kissed me."

"I think you have this all wrong." He came around the kitchen island and sat on the stool next to me. "I have impossibly high standards."

Of course. He'd want the most successful, high-powered, runway-model-gorgeous woman he could get.

"There are dating services for your type," I said. "You'll find her." I faced my sandwich so I could shove it in my mouth to gag back something less kind.

"There are no dating services for my type of woman."

"You sure?" The peanut butter was stuck to the roof of my mouth. I washed it down with milk.

"My type does the right thing. Not because she has to or because it's expected. It's her first reaction. And she's ferocious about it. She fights tooth and nail for people she loves. The world's a better place because of her."

Slowly, he put his finger on the corner of my mouth to stroke away a milk moustache. I snapped up a napkin and wiped it.

"Sounds like she's in trouble a lot."

"She doesn't care, and neither do I."

I slid my laptop toward me. "I should call a Lyft."

"You can work here if you want."

"I can't. I . . ."

I couldn't write about the fictional high school sweetheart who mysteriously had Sebastian's voice and looks while the actual voice and looks were right in front of me.

"I was just going to watch a movie. You can sit over there."

"What were you going to watch?"

He shrugged. "You have any suggestions?"

"It's usually helpful if I watch something similar to what I'm writing."

"You're watching it with me?"

"It's kind of like working." I tapped my laptop. "Have you seen *Sweet Home Alabama*?"

"The one where Reese Witherspoon leaves her high school sweetheart and comes back rich and famous?"

"Yeah."

He clicked a button on a remote control. Panels slid back to reveal a huge TV.

"You're on."

I launched onto the couch, ready to watch a second-chance romance where the hero didn't look or sound like Sebastian Barton.

CHAPTER 23

SEBASTIAN

In the middle of the movie, Rachel announced that she had to make a bathroom run.

"Through the bedroom on the left," I said as the lights went up.

"Thanks." She slid off the couch and headed over.

"You want popcorn?" I asked.

"Sure."

I checked my messages. Tiffany had texted.

—Carol wants 2 know what dates r good 4u4 the wedding

Hello? Dweeb?

They just picked something—

I went out to the patio and called her.

"What the heck, Tiff?"

"Okay, dude, they've lost their minds. Like, utterly lost it."

"They picked a *date*?"

"So they saw your IG post."

"*My* IG post?"

"My post but your picture. And they were standing out there talking when Samantha came out with her little Tory Burch bag all like, 'Oh, did you see that ring?' and they were all, 'Yeah, we're so excited,' and Sam was all, 'Did they set a date?' and they were all, 'No but we hope it's soon,' and Sam was like, 'Tony had a cancellation in March, but—"

"A cancellation where? At Cotillion?"

Our neighbor owned a party hall. A weekend in junior year rarely went by without a Cotillion sweet sixteen the class dweeb didn't get invited to. Then came the graduation parties I pretended I didn't want to go to.

"Duh," Tiff said. "Cotillion Arms by the water, which is so hard to get a space, apparently. So she was all, 'You have to book it now,' and they were all, 'OMG, that's so great, let's call them,' and then Tony came out and said he got a call to book it, but he hadn't responded, so if they got it in the next hour, he could tell the new people they missed out, and they were going to call Rachel, but before they got her, he offered a neighbor discount he made up, so they booked it. It's supposed to be a surprise, so don't say anything."

By the time she finished, I was sitting on the edge of a patio chair with my hand over my face.

"When am I getting married?"

"March eighth. Congratulations, dweeb. When you have babies, I want to be *Aunt* Tiffany, okay? No first-name-basis crap."

Inside, Rachel came back from the bathroom. I had popcorn to make.

"I have to go," I said to my sister. "Do not let them do another thing."

"'Kay, bye."

Rachel was in the kitchen with a bag of popcorn in her hand. "I found this—hope it's okay." She tossed it in the microwave and set the timer.

"It's fine. So . . ."

"How do you like the movie so far?"

"Fine." I sat on the stool she'd been on before the movie, ready to break the news. "Bowls are above the toaster." She reached for them, hiking her shirt enough to show me a few inches of her skin.

"The snappy dialogue is so era specific," she said.

"I think it was a way for them to hide their feelings," I replied.

She tapped her fingers on the counter and spaced out for a second. "I think that's good. I think I can use that to make it less shitty."

The microwave beeped. It was the perfect time to tell her, but she added something when she opened the door.

She flung the hot bag to me. I caught it, bouncing it in my hands twice before letting it drop. I opened the bag and filled the bowls. All I had to do was tell her, but she'd gotten very pensive and faraway, as if she was shutting out distractions.

"Rachel?"

"Hmm?"

"Is that your concentration face?"

"Oh." She waved her hand. "Yeah. Sorry."

"Don't be. It's kind of cute."

"Bruce hated it." She picked up the bowls. "Always made it a point to interrupt because I wasn't paying attention to *him*."

I wasn't going to do that. Our wedding date could wait another hour. We went back to the couch, but this time, she brought a notebook and sat in the middle instead of at the end. As the story unfolded, she scribbled in her book.

I leaned over. I couldn't understand a word of it. "What are you writing?"

"Dumb romance—obviously. I'm going to have to fix act one."

The movie was fine, but the real show was Rachel. I could practically hear the gears turning in her head. At one point, she put the book to the side and leaned in to me. I put my arm on the back of the couch, and with a sigh, she let her head fall against my chest during a dance number.

"Happily ever after in one hundred nine minutes," she said when it was over, leaving her head where it was. "You can set your watch by it."

"It was fun. Are you hungry? Do you want dinner?"

"I should be getting back."

But she didn't move. We sat together. I took a deep breath before touching her shoulder. She stayed, so I ran my thumb along the skin below her short sleeve.

"I have to admit something," she said.

"Okay."

"I thought you'd laugh at me."

"Why would I do that?"

"Because I work on a romance show."

My fingers got jealous of my thumb and joined in touching her. I wanted her to keep talking.

"I have friends from USC making real movies."

"They laugh at you?"

"Not to my face. They're super nice to my face. But I know . . . well . . . to be fair, I don't know. I assume they're giggling and rolling their eyes behind my back. So it's mostly me laughing at me, I guess. And Bruce didn't laugh as much as he used it against me."

Before I could press her to continue, she went on as if a dam had broken.

"He said that for a romance writer, I didn't know how to be romantic. He said I was all locked up. He kept telling me to let go, and I tried, but I didn't know how to do it enough to make him happy."

"Have we established that you're too good for him?"

"That's what my mother said. But I can't get with the idea that a person's too good while another isn't."

I could have pointed out that she acted as if she weren't good enough, but she'd deny it. I'd remind her of how she was when we were kids, and she'd shrug.

"I stopped drawing," I said, taking my fingers off her shoulder. "I stopped making art to do what's safe. I never let go enough to take the risk of committing to what I was really good at. You never compromised. That's what I love about you."

The last sentence slid past filters and common sense. We were different people. I couldn't love her without knowing her, but the man had stepped aside to let the boy speak. I clamped my mouth shut too late.

She sat up straight. "What time is it?"

"Almost four."

"I should get going."

"Probably a good idea."

She tucked her laptop under her arm and got out her phone, where she'd see notifications from her mother. "I'll get a car."

"I'll take you."

"No, it's fine."

"If I don't see you to your door, your father won't forgive me."

She pocketed the phone.

"If you insist."

I got my keys before she could change her mind.

She flipped through my playlists, quickly finding the indie rock selection.

"Hey." She pointed out the windshield at a bright dot in the sky. "What's that?"

"Venus."

"Which is going direct, apparently?"

"Who knows? Astrology calculations were off by fractions of a second a hundred years ago. The problem compounded every year. They're all wrong now."

She leaned back, looking out her window as I headed south on Fairfax.

"So we're not meant to be?"

"I didn't say that."

She paused long enough for me to regret suggesting we were somehow fated to be together.

"There's a partial lunar eclipse with Venus in opposition," I said. "On Valentine's Day. It's supposed to be spectacular."

"I'd like to see that," she said. "Can you remind me to look out the window, Mr. Barton?"

"I will."

"You should make art again."

I turned onto her street, trying not to get whiplash from the change in subject.

"You were really good."

"I had a teacher once who said, 'If you're able to quit, you should.' A real artist can't quit." I pulled up to her apartment building. "I'm not like you."

"A failure?"

"Shut up. If you got busy with something else, you wouldn't stop writing. You wouldn't know how. You're a real artist. I was a kid with talent. There's a difference."

"Maybe." She hugged her laptop and shouldered her bag. "I'd invite you in, but the place is a mess, and my roommate might be home."

"It's fine. It was great seeing you."

"And, uh, thanks for the diamond ring?"

"Yeah. About that?"

Her face fell. She touched it as if she was going to have to take it off.

"About that," I repeated. "I talked to Tiff while you were in the bathroom. It seems our parents set a wedding date."

"They what?" she exclaimed. "When?"

"Today."

"No, when's the date?"

"March eighth."

"Oh God." She was horrified, but it seemed born out of something bigger than inconvenience. "Oh God, this is terrible."

"I'll talk to Carol. We can push it back."

"No . . . it's . . . I mean, yes, sure. But do you know what this means?"

"They can get their deposit back."

"It means she doesn't have long." She hugged her laptop tighter. "She's rushing to get it done before she dies."

"No, Rachel. They got some kind of discount at Cotillion. You know how cheap they are."

"Bullshit. Bullshit times ten." She got out her phone. "I'm calling her, and she's going to tell me everything."

"Wait." I put my hand over the phone.

"What now?"

"If she doesn't want you to know, pushing is going to upset her, and she still might not tell you."

Her mouth tightened to a thin line, and her breathing was so deep her body rose and fell with it.

"I am *so mad*. So mad. And worried. Seb, I don't want her to die."

She looked at her engagement ring. I didn't know what it represented to her, but if it started reminding her of cancer and death, I was going to throw it away.

"Maybe it's not what you think," I said. "Maybe they just love you."

"Maybe." She was looking down, so I couldn't see her face. But her voice was shaking. I pulled her into my arms, and she fell into me, arms still wrapped around her laptop. I buried my face in the spot behind her ear, where I could breathe in her strawberry shampoo.

"Let them be," I said. "I think they just want you to enjoy your wedding."

She laughed to herself. "I've had my heart broken so many times. I bet they suspect it's on the horizon."

"Maybe *you* suspect it's on the horizon."

"It's just as inevitable."

"Except this time." This time I was going to get my heart broken, but she didn't need to hear that. "You're safe this time."

"That feels nice."

Did she mean my face in her hair or the safety of not getting hurt? I heard a sniffle before I could ask.

"Don't let them see you cry," I said into her hair. "Pretend you don't suspect anything. It's what they need."

"Okay." She took a few deep breaths and sat up. "No crying."

"Good. Now go finish that script."

She opened the car door. The light went on.

I got out and met her on her side of the car.

"I'll walk you to your door."

"I go to my door alone all the time."

"Not on my watch."

She didn't shrug. Her smile wasn't resigned. It had the warmth of an invitation.

Following her up the steps, I wasn't sure what I wanted out of her besides a few more minutes. I wasn't ready to drive away with something unfinished.

Under the dim light by her door, she shuffled her laptop to one arm and dug around in her bag for her keys.

"Hang on," she said, pressing the laptop between her elbow and hip. "I need another arm."

I slid the computer away.

"Thanks." She dug freely and came out with her keys like a buried treasure. "I'm such a mess."

She isolated the key and put it into the dead bolt lock, leaving the key chain hanging without turning it. Her eyes glinted before she spoke.

"You said you loved me."

I knew I wasn't going to get away with letting the boy speak.

"I was a little infatuated with you in school."

"I know. But what I was thinking was . . . maybe if there's a part of you that loved me, the wedding isn't such a lie."

"You didn't feel the same."

"Well, no, but . . ." She took a step closer to me. "I'm kind of developing an unhealthy crush on you."

"Unhealthy?" I leaned in. We'd already kissed once for show. Another time, poorly, in a bathroom.

"I'm rebounding."

"Obviously." I touched her face and slid my hand behind her neck.

I kissed her with my entire body, wrapping my free arm around her waist. The damn laptop kept me from holding her with both arms, but what I lacked in bilateralism, she made up for. She put her arms around me. It wasn't our first kiss, but it felt like the first one we had for ourselves.

Someone came up the steps, and she pulled away, looking past me. It was a guy with a sleeping toddler draped over his shoulder. Her chubby arms were slack, and her thick black lashes pressed against her cheeks.

"Hi, Oscar," Rachel said.

He waved and gave her a thumbs-up with his keys pressed into his palm. He stopped at the adjacent doorway. I handed Rachel her laptop as he went inside.

"God, that's a cute kid," I said.

"You should see her riding up and down the balcony on her tricycle." She mimicked the back-and-forth motion and made a *gujj* noise that represented speed. We laughed together for a second before our eyes met, and we were caught in an uncomfortable silence.

"I'd invite you in," she started. "But—"

"Too soon."

She turned the key and opened the door a crack before stopping. "Seb," she said.

"Yes?"

"Come with me."

"Where?"

"I was going to wait until you drove away. Then I was going to get in my car and go to Mandarin Lane. But I don't want to go alone, and I don't want to go with anyone else. I know you think it's wrong to ask her directly if she doesn't want to be asked, but I have to. I just have to."

A simple choice. I could be there for her, or I could argue that I was right.

I reached in and closed her door. "Let's go then."

CHAPTER 24

RACHEL

Sebastian didn't fight me. More importantly, he didn't try to cheer me up. I hated fake, upbeat platitudes, and I was in no mood for small talk. He just drove and held my hand all the way to San Diego.

It was after ten when he pulled up in front of my parents' house. He let go of my hand to put the car in park.

"Should I go in with you?"

"Yes. Just . . ." I opened the door but didn't get out. "Just let me do the talking."

"All right."

We got out and went to the door. Dad answered in sweatpants and an old T-shirt. Behind him, three guys at a desk were yelling about sports as if everyone should care.

"Rachel. It's late."

I brushed past him. Sebastian followed. I saw them look at each other, my dad asking what the hell was going on without words.

"Where's Mom?"

"At a movie with her reading club. Is this about Dr. . . . what's that on your finger? Holy heck."

"Forget the ring. And yes, it's about Dr. Ramsaroop."

Dad sighed and brushed his hair back.

"I want to know," I demanded. "I have a right to know."

My father went to the dining room table and picked up a stack of papers.

"This," he said, "is the form I had to fill out."

I snapped them away, calling his bluff.

"Look at the dates," he said. "Two years ago."

He was right. The insurance wanted verification because there was a day's discrepancy in the forms.

"Believe me," Dad continued, "I'd rather you filled it all out, but we're trying not to bother you. Trying real hard."

I handed him the papers.

"What about the second biopsy?"

That was a risk. I had no proof they'd gotten another and no idea if they'd do two on a woman who'd already had cancer.

"What about it?"

Confirmation of the worst-case scenario. I couldn't be mad. I wanted to be. Anger was a great balm for sorrow, but I couldn't gather enough of it to shout at him. I looked at Sebastian, and he took my hand and sat on the couch, pulling me next to him. Dad sat in his chair.

"Why didn't you tell me?"

"There's nothing to tell yet."

"When you know, I want you to call me right away."

Dad smiled, but there was no joy in it.

"Princess, you're just like your mother. You push to make the world what you want. But it doesn't work that way." He paused, tapping the arms of the chair, then looked to Sebastian. "You want a beer?"

"Driving."

"Good man. Rachel? Beer? Water?"

"Don't change the subject."

Dad clicked off ESPN and tossed the remote back on the side table.

"You know what you're getting into with this one, Sebastian?"

"I do."

"Maybe you do. But I don't think so. If you think you love her now, you just wait until you need her. She'll move heaven and earth to make life right for you. I thought I loved her mother until she showed me what it was like to be loved *by* her. Was like a revelation. Raised the bar. Fighting for her life every day, and every day she found some way to show me she loved me." He focused on me. "Maybe that's not what you want to hear about your parents. But it's a playbook for how you're going to be with him. And your kids. And it's the reason I'm not telling you a thing your mother doesn't want you to know. That's how you love someone. You prioritize their happiness. And if you want to make her happy, you won't ask."

Dad had picked me up and dropped me right back in my place. Sebastian put his hand on my back. I'd never been so grateful for another human's silent presence.

"Just tell me she's not giving up."

"My wife?" He chuckled. "That'll be the day."

As if he was seeing how serious I was for the first time, his laugh fell away. He scooted himself forward on his chair and leaned toward me with his elbows on his knees.

"Look at you." He took my chin in his hand. "We couldn't be prouder of you. Both of us. You're talented and ambitious and hard-working. But I have to tell you, when I held my baby girl in my arms, I didn't pray for any of those things. I prayed you'd be a good person, and my prayers were answered."

"Daddy." My voice cracked. "I'm scared."

"Don't be. It's going to be fine. Come here."

I leaned in to him, and he hugged me. I rested my cheek on his shoulder. He smelled of Old Spice and comfort. Skinned knees and broken hearts. Holiday dinners and yardwork. He was petty fights and wise words.

"You sent her out to a movie because you knew I was coming."

"I made a few calls," he said when I pulled away. "Get out of here before your mother gets home."

"I don't know how to feel," I said after an hour driving in silence. I faced Sebastian. "How do you feel?"

"Like your dad's a rock star." He glanced at me before putting his eyes back on the road. "I don't envy you, though. You'd hate not knowing something's wrong if you could do something about it."

He knew me better than anyone.

"I'm glad you're here," I said.

"I'm glad too."

Dull words in short sentences. Platitudes and sentiments. I would have deleted the last two sentences as boring and meaningless.

I would have been wrong.

Some words were repeated between people over and over because they were the only way to express the complexity of feeling between them.

I was glad he was with me.

CHAPTER 25

RACHEL

"Oh. My. God." CJ stopped dead in her tracks when she saw me. Not me. The rock on my finger. I was waiting for her and Sandra outside the production office.

"Like I told you," I said, tucking my hand under my arm. "Fake."

"No, honey." She sat next to me and tapped my arm until I held my hand out. "This thing is real."

"I mean the wedding."

"Irrelevant." She sat back and crossed her arms. "Do you have a date?"

"March eighth. It's crazy, but our parents are so gung ho. And my mom is so happy. And things are happening."

She crossed her arms. "You like him."

"I like him too much to marry him, if you want to know the truth."

"Girl, you've got to write this story."

"It's not going to have a happy ending." I handed her a stapled sheaf of papers. "The outline for 'Viral Love.' Do you want to read it first? It's terrible."

She shook her head and waved the outline away. "Let me tell you my own story. This is too good. Real life. This is when I was dating."

She was always dating, even when she said she wasn't.

"Like, when?"

"Two, three years ago. Doesn't matter. I met this guy through a dating service. Really tall. Handsome. Had these big green eyes. House up in Bel Air. You cannot believe this house."

"What did he do for a living?"

"Lawyer. Shocking. He invites me to this big charity event for, like, legal scholars or something. Ruth Bader Ginsburg was there. Anyway, he picks me up in a black-on-black Range Rover, and so I'm like, hey. This can work. I can get with this. And he tells me right out of the gate, his ex-wife is going to be at the event, and he wants me to wear an engagement ring."

"To make his wife jealous."

"Exactly."

"How mature."

"Yeah, also, he was, like, forty-five, so he has no excuse except . . . the ink wasn't even dry on the divorce, and she was already engaged. Bringing her fiancé. The whole deal. So mind you, he's still driving when he leans over and pops the glove compartment. Points to a little velvet box and says, 'Try it on,' like nothing. Like he was handing me a hat. And I take it out. It's massive. His wife is going to see it across the damn room. I put that thing on right away. Wild horses couldn't have stopped me. Trust me. And then, this guy I knew for five minutes? I suddenly felt *attached*."

"Stop."

"I did. We got out of the car. I put my arm in his, and it was like I owned him, and he owned me. I said, 'Point her out,' and I made sure she saw that ring, because I wanted to spite her . . . for him."

"Did he win her back?"

"Hell no. But I was with him for five months, and I wore it all the damn time. Things happened. We were fake engaged, and things . . . emotional things . . . just started happening between us like crack, crack, boom. I could feel it."

"Then what?" I was hugging my laptop to my chest, wedding and ring forgotten.

"Then one day I woke up and was like, 'Nah.'"

I sat back. "That's a shitty ending."

"Truth." She flipped through my outline, speed-reading it.

"But it was real," I said. "It happened."

"Happy endings happen too." She picked up her red pen and clicked it.

"It's too long. I know."

"This kiss needs to move here." She drew an arrow in the margin, making it sooner.

I'd spent the weekend running on caffeine, typing an ending to the outline for "Viral Love" and lovingly crafting "Broken Promises," as if it would ever be made.

"Nice ring." A hand came from behind me and pulled the pages away. Sandra didn't even break her stride getting into her office. CJ and I followed her in as if we were debris on her tide.

"Thanks."

"Who's the lucky guy? Bruce Geraldo?"

"No."

"Thank God." She held up the outline without even looking through it. "This is long."

"The first act needed two extra scenes," I said. "To show how she got over being used like that. I had to make it real."

Sandra opened to the middle and read, flipped to the second page and scanned, then went to the end.

"It's cohesive," she said, snapping a piece of tape off the dispenser and sliding it to her pinkie. "New guy beats up the ex on Facebook Live. Good. Thematically strong. She's a waitress who becomes a lawyer. We have too many waitresses and interior designers. Make her a photographer all the way through." She let the papers fold together and addressed

CJ. "Work on tightening the first act with her. We're casting Tamara East. She's twenty-four, not thirty-two."

"Got it."

Back to me with another snap of tape. With practiced dexterity, she maneuvered it between her thumb and index finger.

"Start writing it. Real is fine. Real is great. Real needs to happen before the commercial."

"Okay."

That was it. I should have been thrilled, but I wasn't. I'd made it crap, and she still wanted me to write it.

"Can we talk?" I asked.

"Sure."

"See you at morning breakout!" CJ spun on her heel and walked out, closing the door behind her.

Sandra folded her hands over my pages and gave me her attention.

"So," I said. "You remember my mom?"

"Never met her, but I assume you have one."

"Okay. So. You met with me because you liked 'Barista Diaries.'"

"Still do."

Why the hell was I talking about the spec? My God, I should get fired for not knowing where to start a story. "I wrote it while Mom was getting chemotherapy, and my dad didn't know how to use the washing machine, so I was living with them."

"Right. In San Diego." Snap. She ripped and looped another inch of tape and started balling them all together.

Of course, I'd told her this. Everyone knew. Our personal experiences were daily story fodder.

"I think the cancer is back."

"I'm so sorry." She stuck the tape to her desk blotter. "Do they know what stage?"

"No . . . I . . . it's me. I think it's back and she's not telling me because she doesn't want to interrupt my career. I found these meds, and my dad called me with this weird question . . . I don't want to bring it up in the room."

"I understand."

"But if I have to split in . . . I don't know . . . March? Sooner? Later? For a month or a day—I don't even know. I just don't know."

"Wait." She rolled the tape with a flat hand. "So the oncologist didn't tell you that's what's happening?"

I couldn't tell her about every little signal, but I couldn't deny the reality of them either.

"No," I said firmly. "But I know my parents."

"All right." She leaned back, put her elbows on the arms of the chair, and laced her fingers over her chest. "I'll tell you what. If you go, we have to hire another room assistant. That's just the reality. But if we're renewed, and we have a space—which we will—I'll consider you for staff"—I gasped, but she didn't slow down—"on one condition."

"What?"

"It'll be easy." She tossed the tape ball into the trash. "You get this"—she tapped my outline—"into shape so we can shoot it while you're gone."

"You're on." I oversold my enthusiasm for the project, but Sandra either didn't notice or didn't care.

"And you come back from hiatus with a staff job."

A staff writer. Quarter million a year and a career path. A reel. I could get meetings more easily. Pitch pilots. I'd have an actual credit. It didn't even matter if it was a *Romancelandia* episode about a viral video. It only mattered that I had the credit.

I stood up. "I can do it."

"Great."

"Thank you!"

As I headed for the door, she called out, "Congratulations on getting engaged."

I waved and ran off to the breakout session.

CHAPTER 26

RACHEL

I still hadn't gotten used to the ring. I stared at it in the shower, turning it this way and that, trying to find the most glittery angle. It caught in my sweater, and when it spun around so the diamond faced my palm, I made a fist so I could feel it against the tender webs of my fingers. I'd given myself a quick manicure so my nails would be worthy of it. I'd cut the edges round and painted them a deep red.

The Wednesday Sebastian and I were supposed to see Tiffany's boyfriend at the Smell, he reminded me, because I'd completely forgotten.

—He goes on at 11. Don't dress up—

—Don't these people work?—

—I have no idea what Tiffany does for a living—

—IDK if this is a good wedding band unless we want to have a mosh pit at our reception—

It didn't matter, of course, because we were finding a way out of this. Somehow.

—We don't have to hire them. We just have to act like we're looking, remember?—

He was right.

VIOLET

When you look at me like that, I flinch inside. I feel you getting under my skin, and I'm afraid.

VINNY

Maybe it's time you stopped thinking everyone is out to exploit you.

"My God, Vinny," I said to myself as I deleted his line. "You're an asshole."

The video script was a disaster. The more I wrote, the more guilty I felt. The more guilty I felt, the more I wanted to do right by the "Delete It" girl. The more I wanted to do right, the worse the script got. And when it got that bad, I distracted myself with a story that was coming along nicely.

JAKE

I know I screwed up and left, but maybe you screwed up by staying here.

AMY

Living in a big city doesn't keep you from being a screwup.

JAKE

You were given a talent, Amy, and you're responsible for it. Maybe I ditched you, but you ditched yourself.

—I'll pick you up at 10—

How had it gotten to be eight p.m. already?

—Parking's terrible. We should Lyft—

—You're right. I'll swing by you—

Actually, I didn't want that. I wanted to finish this. I wanted to cut it close and write in my notebook the whole way there, because Jake came to life when he gave her back her agency, and it changed the entire tenor of the fictional relationship.

—I'll meet you there at 10:30. I'm writing—

—OK—

Wow. He said okay without a fight.

That was a pleasant surprise.

Bruce wouldn't have agreed to that. He was always afraid I was going to be alone in public and someone's dick was going to fall into me. It was ridiculous for a bunch of reasons.

One, that he was just so freaking ridiculous.

Two, that I tolerated it.

I'd thought his jealousy made him devoted, but it didn't. It took away my ability to choose to not let someone's dick fall into me. It made me into a child.

AMY
You're right.

I wore nice jeans and cowboy boots. A little makeup. Hair up. Black button-front blouse that made my waist look trim but was probably too uptight for the venue.

The Lyft pulled up to a gritty warehouse Downtown. A line of punks, hipsters, and cosplayers wound into a back alley.

Sebastian, in a button-down shirt and sports jacket, was waiting at the curb.

"You said not to dress up," I said, flicking Sebastian's lapel.

"It's a jacket. And look at you. You did your nails."

"The color was called 'Blood of My Enemies.' I'm not made of stone."

He smiled and put his arm around me, leading me down the alley, past the line. A rivulet of water flowed along a drainage trench, and a subtle reek of garbage and fish emanated from every surface. I held my diamond in my palm, but the crowd seemed pretty harmless. We didn't fit in, but they ignored us, puffing on vapes and cigarettes, adding fruit and tar to the smell.

"Shouldn't we go to the back of the line?"

"Tiff put us on a list."

"What's the band name? They seem pretty popular."

"Shittbird, with two *t*'s." He pointed to the back door of the club as it came into view. The band names were spray-painted by the door. *Shittbird* was painted biggest.

Two bouncers stood by the door. Both were huge and bald with goatees, wearing biker jackets. One was Latino. One white. That was the only difference. They looked like they'd coordinated everything else like synchronized swimmers.

The Latino guy pointed to us and opened the rope. We went in, and once we were past the door, the stench was overwhelming. Yes, a hint of fish and garbage, but also cigarette ashes, spilled beer, and marijuana. The red carpet was stained, and the walls were plastered with a decade's worth of show posters. The walls vibrated with loud music and a singer who growled.

"Hey," a pale woman in a red dress said. She had black pigtails, tattoo sleeves, and a welcoming smile. "You're on the list with Shittbird?"

"Yes," Sebastian said. "We're in the VIP room."

"Awesome!" she exclaimed as if she was truly thrilled at our amazing luck.

She led us down a back hall and up a flight of stairs to a lounge overlooking the stage. Most of the tables were occupied. I was relieved to see we hadn't overdressed. Clear plastic tubes stuck out from the centers of their tables like deep-sea tentacles.

"My name is Tempeh," she said, taking a Reserved sign off a table overlooking the stage. "Can I get you guys a bong? The base can have plain water, vodka, or cognac."

I looked at the table next to us. The clear plastic tube had a bubble of thick amber liquid at the bottom. A bong. Right.

"Uh . . ." Sebastian looked at me. I wrinkled my nose.

"Makes me paranoid," I said softly.

"No, thank you," he said to the waitress. "I'll have a Heineken, and she'll have . . . ?"

"Same."

Downstairs, customers bounced on folding chairs on either side of the long tables. The bongs were shorter. The band howled, and the guitars made a wall of sound.

I felt someone sit next to me. Tiffany. She had Egyptian eyeliner and multiple eyebrow piercings.

"What happened to your face?" Sebastian asked.

"What happened to your life?"

"The first six years were great."

She stuck her tongue out at him.

Our beers came in cans with two stacked plastic cups. Tiffany put her arm around me and held her phone in front of our faces. I smiled.

"Show us that ring, honey," she said. I flashed it for Instagram.

"I'm glad we're up here," I said after Tiffany left, tapping on her phone.

"Definitely quieter."

"I guess that means we're grown up now."

He poured beer into a plastic cup and pushed it to me. "I don't feel grown up."

"That surprises me."

"Why?" He poured his own.

"You seem so together. Sold a company. Started another. Nice apartment."

"My partner? Seema? House and two kids." He leaned forward when the music started. "Tuition payments and a husband. That's grown up."

"You can't get a house? You didn't make a gazillion selling AnimaThing to Pixar?"

He smiled around his beer.

"What?" I said.

"I live in that apartment because it's all the room I need. But I own the building."

I put the cup to my lips because I didn't want to laugh at him. That was the most adult decision a person could make, and he still didn't feel grown up? Give me a break. I was the thirty-year-old child here, in my beige-walled-and-carpeted Hollywood apartment. The discount granite countertops were window dressing.

We watched the band, which meant I didn't have to talk about this anymore. I was caught between resentment at my own failures and admiration of his accomplishments. Not the money or the car or the hard work he'd done on his body. But his ability to think clearly about his path.

"The other night?" I said with the beer going right to my head. "At the end? By my door?"

"When I kissed you?"

"I kissed you back."

"Yes." He raised one eyebrow. "You did. So?"

I cleared my throat and swirled my beer in its plastic cup.

"I *should* say we can't do that again. Because for a clear-thinking, mature person . . . that would be the smart thing."

"Are you a clear-thinking, mature person?"

I shrugged and took a gulp of beer, putting it down like the period at the end of a sentence. "Nah."

He looked down at the band. Would he be clear thinking and mature for me?

"They're not bad," Sebastian said, pointing downstairs. The tables had stayed upright with cups and new bongs. A miasma of vapor and bong smoke hovered between us and the floor below.

"Maybe we can hire them instead of Shittbird."

He laughed and nodded, and just as I was about to get up to pee, he lazily slipped his hand into mine. That touch was so right, just then. In the middle of a hard rock show with lyrics I couldn't make out, my hand in his felt like a pull toward who I was going to be.

Then I saw Tiffany talking with a guy in a short haircut and tux, and I knew why he'd taken my hand. Not to tell me I had a way forward but to convince his sister we were real. I couldn't even be mad at him. He was doing this for me.

"Bathroom," I said, taking my hand out of his. I walked toward Tiffany.

"Rachel!" She grabbed me and introduced me to the guy in the tuxedo. Clear peach skin. Big blue eyes. Crooked smile. Scar on his chin. Romance-hero good looking. "This is Ace!"

"Hi, Ace. Nice to meet you."

"I hear you need a band," he said.

"Uh . . ." I glanced at Tiff as I shook his hand.

"This is him! He's the lead bird in Shittbird!"

"Oh. Yes." I tried to hide my surprise. "I can't wait to see you play."

"Gonna be cool."

"Yep, hey, where's the ladies' room?"

"Through this hall, downstairs, and to the left." She took Ace's hand and leaned in to him. "Get back quick, or you'll miss him."

I didn't know why she thought I'd miss anything until I saw the line. I got behind a woman with a shaved head and a skull piercing. The band ended their set, and I was still in line. Damn, I really had to pee now. By the time I was second in line for the door, I was bouncing up and down like a toddler, checking social media to distract my mind from my bladder.

I found myself on Instagram, flashing a Harry Winston diamond. #sisters #thesmell #ShittbirdRULES #itsreal.

"Hey, Rach!"

Man's voice. Familiar. Not Sebastian. I turned, and for the love of all that was holy . . .

"Bruce." He would have fit in perfectly in the upstairs room with his polo and chinos, but here he was, downstairs with the plebes. My ex-boyfriend from my ex-life, back like a bad penny. His dark hair had grown below his ears, and he'd gained a few pounds. He still had nice hands and a generous mouth, but all things being equal, Sebastian was better looking. He wasn't mine, but Bruce hadn't been either. Not really.

"I just got here, and I saw you on IG." He held his phone up to the picture of Tiffany and me. Same one. #itsreal.

"What are you doing here?"

He smiled as if this was exactly the question he was hoping for.

"Doing a little thing with Brad Sinclair, and we need music. Heard about these guys." Shrug. "There's no rest in this business."

Someone brushed by, and I got one space closer to relief.

My ten-pound rock was turned around, pressing into the inside of my knuckle. It felt warm and pulsing, as if it wanted some fresh air.

"Yeah, well, have fun at work."

"What brings you here?"

My brain was being run by my bladder. I was first in line. I didn't have time for explanations.

"With people."

"Still liking that job I got you?"

The jab was delivered with such élan, such confidence, such an air of "this is just how people talk," that I almost said, "Yes, thank you."

Almost.

"Still a second-rate executive without a produced credit?" I asked.

He didn't answer. Just smiled.

"I recognize this." He waved his finger at my little dance. "You always waited too long."

God, that smile. I'd fallen right for it a hundred times. What a stupid girl I was. I'd fallen for the coolness. The insiderness. The admiration of a guy who could make things happen.

The bathroom door opened. One of the two women who came out held it open for me.

"Yeah, bye."

"Hey." He grabbed my arm, and the effort to hold back from punching him meant I almost pissed myself. "I'll put you and a plus-one with my party upstairs."

"Bye, Bruce."

He let go, and I bolted to the bathroom.

I spotted Bruce and his all-male revue of douchebags as soon as I got back upstairs. He waved me over, almost knocking over one of the six bongs at the table. I waved back, then made a hot left to sit next to Sebastian.

"As soon as they're done, I want to go," I said.

"You okay?"

"Yeah. Fucking fine." I bent my neck to see my ex, and Sebastian followed my gaze.

"Is that Mr. Beverly Hills Hotel?" he asked.

"Ugh." I turned back to the stage below. Shittbird was about to start. Ace was still in his tux, looking like he was going to croon us horizontal.

Sebastian put his arm around my shoulder and drew me close. "You're with me."

Looking up at him, I couldn't help but smile. Bruce wasn't an emotional threat if I was with Seb. That was the only kind of threat I was worried about.

Before I could thank him, the music exploded. Ace roared. The guitars screamed. I opened my eyes wide and shook my head, mouthing *No way.*

Sebastian shrugged and said into my ear, "I already hired them."

CHAPTER 27

SEBASTIAN

Her mouth dropped.

Ace and my sister had sat down with me while Rachel was in the bathroom, and he'd given me his bona fides. Opera, with a specialty in Italian phrasing. Colburn School. Seven instruments. I'd tried to wait for Rachel, but she'd taken forever, and Ace was a pretty convincing guy.

"Don't worry."

It was too loud for a long explanation, and it wasn't like I'd signed a deposit check or anything.

Below, Shittbird started the second song, and Ace ripped his jacket off as he sang, leaving it in a metal bucket. Then the shirt and tie went in. Dude was tattooed like a biker and ripped and greased like a bodybuilder. Someone flipped a table and bounced like a pogo stick as Ace grumbled and snarled.

This guy was dating my little sister?

From my high vantage, I could see Tiff front and center with her phone out. Live streaming? Photographing? Two guys slammed into each other and bounced, and one hurled straight at my sister. Rachel gasped. I got halfway out of my chair. He missed her by inches, and from what I could tell, she didn't bat an eyelash.

"That was close," Rachel said.

"I'm not sure I like Ace."

"We should—"

The rest of her sentence got cut off by three guys sitting at our table as if they'd been invited.

"You've got to be joking," Rachel said.

"Bruce Geraldo." He held out his hand, leaning forward so I could hear him. I shook it. His high school ring was on his pinky finger.

"Sebastian Barton."

"These are my friends—"

"Yeah—Bruce?" Rachel said, pointing to an empty table in the corner that must have been theirs. "Nobody cares. Go sit." She was right handed, but she pointed with her left so he'd see the rock I'd gotten her. Good girl.

Bruce's knee bounced under the table, shaking the surface of our beers. He was taking more stock of me than an index fund. Meanwhile, downstairs, Tiff was unaware of another near miss, and Ace was setting his bucket of fancy clothes on fire.

All this together turned the knob on my adrenal glands up to eleven and a half, because normally I'd ignore guys like Bruce and his buddies. I wouldn't run like I did in school, but I wouldn't get puffed up with them. But in that room with Rachel to protect, I was ready to flip a table.

"You heard her," I said, half hoping he'd give me a hard time. I was sure I'd get the living shit beat out of me, but when he took too long to move his ass, I couldn't let it go. I snapped my fingers in his face until he looked at me. "There's someone waiting for you. Go figure out who they are someplace else."

His friends laughed at him, and Rachel squeezed my hand, covering her mouth with her left as if she had to keep from joining them.

Bruce knocked on the table and got up. His two buddies did the same. They just stood the hell up and went back to their table. My mind was a complete blank as I tried to process new information. It was like putting a boiled egg in a pan and cooking it raw. The results of what I'd done were that far from what I'd expected.

"Thank you," Rachel said, putting our clasped hands in her lap.

I couldn't even look at her. Not yet. I was still reviewing the events of the last two minutes as the adrenaline drained from my blood.

"I still got it," I said.

I hadn't had to defend myself from bullies in a long time. Back in high school, when we got back from our three days of exile, we were ignored. The torment stopped. It was bliss. I never had to deal with anyone like that again. Still, bullies were my area of expertise. Being humiliated by someone they considered beneath them was a trigger.

Down below, the bouncers were having an impossible time of it. Tiff was still holding up her phone, unmolested. It was as if she had a force field around her. Only one table remained standing with a few bongs upright. They were dead, with brown sludge at the bottom. The table had been pushed flush with the front of the stage, the only thing between her and Ace, who was now in nothing more than his sweat-stained Jockeys.

"He's got presence," I said. "I'll give him that."

"I hope my aunt Polly passes out."

Ace stepped over the front of the stage and stood on the table, shouting into the mic, and with one clean motion, he leaned down to kiss my sister. She had the presence of mind to move the camera phone so it caught the messy mack down. Then Ace rose to a crouch, screamed a couple more words, and grabbed a bong. He tipped the tube to his lips and . . .

"Oh!" Rachel cried. "No! Gah!"

. . . drank the bong water.

I glanced back at Bruce and his buddies. They pointed and clapped at Ace as if he'd done a quadruple flip.

"Okay, well." I slapped the table. "I think we've seen what we need to see."

"Yeah." She stood with me. "No bongs at the wedding."

Hand in hand, we walked down the hall, Rachel in front of me, the back of her neck exposed under a messy high twist. I knew what she smelled like now. I'd held her and kissed her. I'd whispered in her ear.

This Rachel.

My Rachel.

My blood pumped with new chemicals. Aggressive, hot substances that turned everything into mush except her body and mine. I could take that neck in one hand to hold her still and say things she'd never heard before.

The exit spit us out farther down the same alley as the entrance. The back wall was right behind the stage. Ace's howling was loud and throbbing when Rachel looked back at me and opened her mouth to ask me a question.

"Where—"

I kissed her so forcefully and so accurately that I would have surprised myself if I wasn't so fucking high on endorphins. She clutched my shirt, kissed me back, took my tongue, let me push her against the chain-link fence. Our legs twisted, and my erection brushed against her. Yes. Yes to all.

And then, like a piece of stray code that shut the entire system down, I was pulled backward, and *bam*—that old familiar feeling of being punched in the mouth.

"Bruce!" That was Rachel a million miles away but right in front of me, protecting me like she always had. God bless her, but fuck that. I sidestepped. Bruce was all smiles and confidence, adjusting his lapel like he wanted to look good when he beat me up.

He was red.

Everything was red.

The adrenaline was back, activating the surface of my skin, the bones underneath, and everything in between. I didn't even think about calculating the distance between us; my body knew I had to take a half step, curl the fingers of my right hand into a fist, pull my shoulder back, and hit him in the face.

The crack of his nose under my knuckles was the most satisfying sound I ever heard.

"Sebastian!" Rachel cried. "No!"

Another half step. Bruce had his hands over his face. They came away blood streaked. I only had that second, and something in me knew it. I hit him again with my left. *Pop.*

Ace roared for the both of us.

Everything slowed down. Bruce bent over. His friends were coming at me, and Rachel was trying to get between them.

I'd kill them all.

Rip them to shreds.

It was all choreographed perfectly until a mostly naked body thrust itself between me and the three guys I realistically couldn't have beaten in a fight. Then more bodies and confusion as Ace, wearing nothing but underwear and tattoos, wireless mic in hand, leaned against the chain-link fence and—without losing the rhythm—vomited brown bong water and pizza.

It didn't sound that much worse than the song itself.

"Ace, baby!" Tiff cried, still filming. Her blue Tiffany case looked out of place in the alley behind the Smell. The crowd had followed them out, moshing and slamming in the alley. My sister saw me and, not moving the camera, said, "What the hell happened to you?"

I was yanked away before I could answer. One of Bruce's cronies. Had to be. They were going to use the cover of the alley mosh pit to beat the hell out of me. I twisted to look for Rachel. I didn't want her getting in the middle of this, but I couldn't find her. I took a big step, almost tripped, gained my footing, and surrendered to the pull of whoever was navigating me through the flying bodies by my shirt.

It was Rachel, and we were running.

Without breaking stride, I took her hand off my shirt and held it. We coursed through drunk night birds on Spring Street; crossed against the light; turned left, still running; clambered uphill; and slipped into a packed parking lot.

We slowed down and, as if we were of one mind, skirted cars to get to a dark corner between an old Buick and a brick wall, panting as if we'd run a marathon.

"Jesus," she gasped. "You . . ."

"I did."

Her chest heaved. Nipples hard in the cold. Sweat shining on the skin above her collar. She wiped blood off my lip with her thumb. "Then . . ."

"I'm not . . . ," I said, pointing my finger while I caught my breath.

"You're not." She read my mind, but I still had to say it.

"I'm not a dweeb."

"You were . . ."

I kissed her again. It was the perfect continuation of the alley, but I was even bolder. I wanted to eat her alive. I tasted sweat on her cheek and neck. Felt soft breasts through her shirt, her heartbeat under my hand.

"You were never a dweeb." She finished her sentence, tugging my hair as I bit her neck.

She was wrong. Dead wrong. I was everything they'd said I was, but now? I pinned her to the hood of the Buick, and when she wrapped her legs around me, I pushed against her as if I could dent the steel into the shape of her body.

"I want to rip your clothes off and fuck you right now."

Shit. I said that.

I said it, and it was the truth, and it felt like a rush of blood everywhere.

I kissed her before she could answer. If she felt the same, I was going to come right in my jeans—and if she didn't?

If she didn't, I would have been shocked to the core because she was kissing me and pushing against me like it was her job.

"I want to take you home," I said into the hot corner behind her jaw.

"I like that plan." She pushed into my dick and slid down it.

There was so much I wanted to say. So many words a dweeb wouldn't have the right to utter. But I wasn't that person anymore.

"I can't wait to get between your legs," I said into her ear. There were things I should tell her first, but she tightened her fist in my hair. I had to stand straight and think about hedge funds before I got any closer.

Stretched on the hood of the car, elbows behind her, legs apart, with a look in her eye that was sexier than the dirtiest word. If she said one . . .

"Not before I—"

I put my hand over her mouth.

"Save it. Please."

CHAPTER 28

RACHEL

His lip was split, but I'd stopped tasting blood a long time before he'd kissed me against a lamppost while we waited for the car. He kissed me in the back seat with his hand between my legs, pressing against the seam of my jeans. We were a raging twist of hands and lips.

This was a bad idea, overall.

The adult side of my brain knew that we were entering some kind of hormone-fueled phase where putting me in a wedding dress was going to complicate what could be a normal relationship progression. But I didn't have much practice listening to the adult side of my brain. Not where men were concerned. Not with him pushing me against the wall by his front door and my legs wrapping around his waist.

All those years, Sebastian hadn't had a dick. In my mind, he'd been a friend. A sexless male of the species. And now my entire world revolved around the hard length under his jeans.

He got the door open with his fingerprint or a code or something I couldn't see through the kissing and the groping. We tumbled into his apartment and landed on the floor, rolling around like we were on fire. He kicked the door closed, cutting off the light. A lamp by the side table went on automatically. Reaching under my shirt, he got under my bra, and when he touched my nipple and then gently and expertly squeezed it . . . I released a metric ton of arousal into a thick groan. He sucked in a breath and looked down at me.

I reached for his belt buckle, fingers brushing his hard bulge.

"I need to tell you something," he said, taking his hand off my breast.

"I'm on the pill." I pulled the leather through the loop.

"Not that. Thank you, but not that."

"Later." I yanked the hook out of the notch and was about to slide leather against metal when he licked the bloodless split in his lower lip, and I knew he meant it.

"Tell me."

"I want to tell you two things. You're so . . . so everything. I don't know if I'll make it past the first."

"One thing." I held a finger in front of his face. "Then we do it."

"One thing."

"Okay, go."

He bowed his head so I couldn't see his face.

"I've never . . ."

I waited, but he didn't finish. I waited more. Nothing. He kept his head bent down.

"Seb?"

Up on his elbows, he made a couple of hand gestures that may have meant that whatever it was, wasn't a big deal. Nodded. Seemed to go from dismissal to a death knell to admitting a momentary lapse of judgment.

"Tell me later," I said.

"I never . . ."

"Whatever."

"Did it."

"It?" I knew what he meant. There was only one "it," but I needed confirmation.

"It. The thing. Sex. The complete, consummated act."

Knowing what he'd meant by it didn't keep me from being caught between disappointment and shock.

Disappointment, one, because he'd put the brakes on a nicely speeding train.

Shock, one, because . . . duh. Who wouldn't be shocked?

Shock, two, because his touch hadn't been clumsy or amateurish.

"I'm sorry," he said.

"Okay, so . . . I'm thinking . . . not tonight?"

He rolled off me and onto his side with his head resting on his hand.

"You don't want to know why?" He ran a finger from my throat to where my top button was fastened.

"I do, but my brain is mush."

He pinched open the top button.

"It's not a great time to bring up exes, and personally, I've had enough of them tonight." He popped the next button. "But the primary reason is Tammy wanted to wait until marriage." Pop. "And I agreed because I respected her." Pop. "And before her?" Pause. Then pop. "I guess I just didn't get around to it."

"Five years together with no sex? You're a ninja."

Pop. Last button. "We did other things." He opened my shirt with the assurance of a man who was adept at other things. "But not the final act."

"I don't want to rush you then," I lied.

He pushed my bra over my breasts.

"I don't want to rush *us*."

"You're so mature," I joked just before he locked his lips around my nipple and sucked it. The arousal flowed back but with less urgency as he teased slowly, unbuttoning my jeans.

"Rachel," he whispered, blowing his wetness off my nipple. It twisted into a hard knot. He got up on his knees. "The second thing."

"Door number two. I can't wait."

He pulled my leg up and slid one boot off. I offered him my other foot, and he pulled the boot off from the heel.

Laying his lips on my ankle, he stopped and considered.

"Let's open door number two later."

"Okay."

He reached for my waistband and pulled down. My jeans came off inside out. He seemed relieved that he didn't have to talk about the second thing.

He pulled his shirt off. The boy I'd known now had a dusting of hair across a torso that no man achieved without work. He was tight, defined, with a happy trail between his abdominals disappearing behind a half-undone belt. I reached for him, but he picked up my leg and kissed the inside of my knee, and I was tilted back again, doing nothing more than feeling his tongue and teeth inside my thighs.

He breathed against my underwear, pressing his nose against my clit, then his teeth, their sharpness dampened through the fabric.

"You're such a tease," I groaned.

"You have no idea."

He pushed the underwear to the side and spread me open with two fingers. Everything he did he waited a torturous extra second to do so that by the time the very edge of his tongue found the very edge of my clit, I was on fire.

He looked at me from below, watching my reaction to his gentle kiss.

"Do it, please."

He stiffened. Took a long blink. Did he not like being told what to do?

No, it wasn't that.

It was something I didn't have a moment to think about because he did what I asked, sucking between my legs for a second, leading me to another plateau, then stopping to kneel between my legs. He helped me wiggle out of my underwear.

"What do you want?" he asked.

"Do that again."

"Say it. Say everything you want."

I wanted sex. The whole thing. I wanted to demand it, but that wasn't what he meant. He slid his hands between my thighs and to the center.

"I want you to put two fingers in me."

He sucked in a breath as if the request alone turned him on, then slid two fingers in me, bending down until I felt his breath. "What else?"

"Your mouth. Like you just did."

"My mouth what?"

"Suck my clit."

"How?"

I wasn't used to this much talking. I usually just took whatever was given.

"Gently."

"Like this?"

"Yes," I squeaked. "Then harder."

"Say when."

It wasn't long before I was at a plateau and needed a little more.

"When!" He didn't do it, not until I said, "Suck harder!"

He did it harder. Exactly right harder. I came on his living room floor, and he slowed down until he was killing me. It was murder. He was killing me, and I was dead.

I yanked his head away. He crawled over me, shiny faced and smiling like a sexy former dweeb virgin murderer-by-orgasm.

"Okay," I said when I got my breath back. "Now you. How do you want your 'other things'?"

"In the bed." He kissed my throat. "Will you stay tonight?"

"Work tomorrow." I looked at my watch. "One more hour."

He got up on his knees. "We can do a lot in an hour."

The 10 was empty at that hour, and the Audi coasted along. I was drained from Sebastian's affections yet still unsatisfied.

"What time do you have to get into work?" he asked.

"Early. I have things to fix before everyone gets in."

"Like what?"

I sighed and watched the city flow by at a consistent speed.

"I'm working on a script they want and a script they don't. The script they want is one they asked for. So it'll be made for sure. I don't have to pitch it. It's a guarantee. Once that happens, I'll get a staff job, and it's smooth sailing from there."

"That's great!"

"It's icky."

"Icky?"

"We fictionalize real-life stories. 'Ripped from the tabloids,' et cetera. Mostly, they're really general, or we change them a lot, or if it's a celebrity . . . so whatever. But this one? I don't know." I shook my head, debating how much to tell him. "It's about someone who was betrayed in such an ugly way. She's a real person. And no matter how much I change it, I can't stop feeling like . . . if they run it . . . it'll hurt her."

"Ah."

His *ah* was more than a breath of affirmation. It wasn't even for me. He was affirming something to himself.

"What?" I asked.

"What are you going to do?" He glanced at me as he got off the freeway in Hollywood.

"I don't know." I rubbed a speck off my laptop. "If I don't write it, someone else will. So I should probably just do it and get right with the world later. Let Mom be confident I'm fine and making headway in the world. Then I can . . . I don't know."

"Mm," he said, and again, his hum was more than an elongated consonant sound.

"Mm, what?"

He stopped in front of my building and put the car in park.

"I'll walk you up." He took his keys out of the ignition.

"No."

"I know you're capable but—"

"I'm not leaving this car until you tell me what the *ah*s and *mm*s are about."

Finger through the ring, he clinked his keys against the side of his hand.

"The girls at school didn't like you," he said. "You got invited to parties, but you were never part of the 'in' crowd."

"They were bitches."

"They were. And you could have been the most popular girl in school. You were pretty enough. You wore the right clothes, and trust me, the guys all thought you were hot." He tapped the bottom of the steering wheel. The moonlight made his hands look carved out of marble. Long fingers made of angles instead of curves. Wide at the palm. The kind of hands that I imagined when I imagined being touched.

"But being popular wasn't about that," he continued. "You also had to be mean and manipulative. You weren't. You could have been at the top of the food chain. Instead, you did what was right every day, even when it kept you down."

"But I'm not that girl anymore."

"That's too bad." He opened the door, leaving me with the feeling that I'd said something terrible. When he walked me up the steps, his hands stayed in his pockets. I fished for my keys. Was I imagining the sudden distance?

"Sebastian," I said at the door. "What do you want to do?"

"I think . . ." He took a second. "I think I made it this long. I want to wait for marriage."

I laid my hand on the knob.

How the ring managed to sparkle in the dead of night with the nearest streetlight half a block away was a mystery only a jeweler could unravel. But it didn't matter why or how. What mattered was the fact that the ring was a lie built on a foundation of my mother's happiness.

"Fake or real?" I asked. "The marriage."

"Real."

I would have been disappointed if he'd said *fake*.

"You're a better person than I am."

He cupped my face in his hands.

"No, I'm not," he said, kissing me softly, letting his lips lie on mine as if he were stamping a truth on them, then gently letting them part. "I am who I am because of you."

"You were always strong, Seb. You just didn't know it."

"So are you." He kissed my nose and let his hands fall away. "I had a good time. Drank a beer. Punched a guy out."

I laughed. "Nearly got puked on."

"Success." He cleared his throat. "You still want to go through with the engagement? Even with the new date."

"I feel like she's rushing for a reason, so let's keep going until I can figure it out."

"What's next, though?" He counted on his fingers. "We have a band. A hall. A date."

"Invitations. Dress. Tux." I put my key in the lock.

"Food," he added, taking a step backward.

"I guess I'll be seeing you soon."

"Bye, Rachel."

"Bye, Seb."

Once I closed the door behind me, I leaned against it with my heart pounding.

CHAPTER 29

SEBASTIAN

I was a thirty-year-old millionaire who still didn't know people.

I had contracts to look over. An algorithm to tweak. A lunch meeting with some hedge fund assholes who would order Japanese whisky and ogle the waitresses while they pulled their cuffs back to make sure I could see their watches.

They were easy to figure out. They wanted to win at all costs. The stakes for them were obvious.

Rachel wasn't as simple. When we were in school, I knew her. Or I thought I did. She was a righteous fire who stood up for the little guy. In a secret sketchbook, I'd drawn her as a warrior with a flaming sword, seen from below. Eight feet tall, towering over anyone who would do wrong.

Maybe I'd oversimplified.

I found a pencil in the back of the drawer and flipped to the blank back page of a contract. I hadn't done more than doodle in years, but there was something about her that was too complex to get my head around, and I was having a hard time compartmentalizing. My mind kept pushing to unravel it.

After so many teenage drafts, my hand knew what to do. The powerful body. The forward-lurching posture. The challenge in her face.

The clenched hand. Her hair blowing back in the wind. She took up the page, corner to corner as she always had, but it wasn't her anymore. Even as I drew her, she was a stranger in two dimensions.

Maybe I wasn't much of an artist anymore.

A knock on the glass door made me flip the page as if I'd been drawing porn. Which, for lack of a better word, had been exactly what it was.

Wade came in. "You down for drinks?"

"I think I have to work tonight."

"You won't be thirsty?" He threw himself into the chair across from my desk. "Come on, man. What's going on? That girl dump you or something? Forget her."

"No." I leaned back. "We're getting married."

"What? When?"

"March."

"You knock her up?"

"Impossible."

"You wanna fill in the blanks for me, or do I gotta grill you?"

"It's happening. That's all you need to know."

He rapped his knuckles on the desk. "Okay, right here. Right now. You love her?"

Wade had asked a question my fiancée never had. I answered truthfully.

"I don't know."

"You what?"

"I loved her when we were kids. But we didn't see each other for years, and we're not kids anymore."

"When you first saw her again, you loved her or nah?"

On Christmas Eve, the first time I'd seen her in years, she'd been doing the pee-pee dance in the hallway. She'd come off a long drive. Her hair had been half out of its ponytail, and she'd looked tired.

"I did," I said.

Wade put his forehead on the desk and stretched his arms across it, laying his hands flat on the surface.

"You all right?" I asked.

"I am so happy, my man." When he sat up, his hair was askew. He smoothed it. I felt like shit for not giving him the whole truth, but Rachel and I had a deal.

"You're not going to try and talk me out of it?"

"Why would I do that?"

"It's a little quick."

"Nah. That first moment? That's what counts. My parents met in Vegas at a bachelorette party in 1986. Married in an Elvis chapel the next weekend. Still together."

"Your father was at a bachelorette party?"

"He was stripping." He said it with zero shame or defensiveness. "Dude was ripped. My ma was a personal trainer. She'd seen ripped dudes before, but the minute she saw him, she said she knew. Dad too. He said it was like . . . seeing her was like coming home."

Rachel and I had a longer history, and our wedding was for more complex reasons, yet the moment I'd seen her on Mandarin Lane, I'd come home.

"You just described the feeling perfectly."

"Good. I got a tailor off Rodeo. Make you a custom tux you can keep, so long as you don't gain seventy pounds." He stood and went to the door. "Classic cut. You'll wear it to your daughter's wedding. You know what? I'll make an appointment right now. Fix you up."

Wade worked for me, but he was the only guy friend I had, and he wasn't a bad one.

"Wade."

"Yo?"

"You're all right."

"I know, dude." He rapped his knuckles on my desk again. "See you at lunch."

He left me with the conversation lingering in the air.

Coming home.

She'd changed. Or maybe the world had changed. Or I'd changed.

I flipped to the next blank page and started a new drawing without thinking about what I wanted out of the sketch. I drew her not as I remembered her but as who she was. The female equivalent of Clark Kent. Jeans and sneakers. Hair up. Realistic curves. She was hugging her laptop and looking right at me.

I held the paper at arm's length and scrutinized the expression I'd given her. It wasn't quite the battle-hungry-warrior look I'd always drawn as a teen, but it wasn't meek or reserved either. The few pencil strokes that made up her face stared right at me, daring me to unleash the superhero she still had inside.

Art revealed what the mind couldn't process. The expression could have been the result of rusty hands, but it wasn't. I knew it as soon as I recognized it.

Rachel didn't need a husband. She needed a superhero.

Wade had gotten an appointment with Benito the tailor after work. Squeezed me in, apparently. I was still disconcerted and more and more convinced I couldn't be what Rachel needed. We could go through with the engagement, but in the end I'd fall short.

I watched in the mirror as he pinned and tugged, mumbling instructions to his college-age assistant in English and his seamstress in Italian.

"You look sharp," Wade said, leaning on the doorjamb. "Real sharp."

"I look like a pincushion."

"You have no aesthetic vision." He pronounced *aesthetic* as if he were chewing on a wad of gum.

"I went to design school on a full scholarship."

"Whatever, dude. Whatever. You oughta go classic. Black on black with the satin collar. I got mine with a charcoal pinstripe, but that's not your style."

"Mother-of-pearl buttons," Benito added. "Smoke color."

"That's what I got," Wade confirmed.

I shifted my shoulders in the canvas jacket. It did look good for a pincushion. It wasn't the jacket that didn't look right. It was me.

"Are you wearing it?" I asked Wade. "To the wedding?"

"Of course. I'm the best man, right?"

I hadn't thought to ask anyone to be best man because we were going through the motions of a wedding without planning to actually get married.

"I don't want to string you along," I said. "But if there's a wedding, you're best man."

"If? You getting cold feet?"

"No, but plans might change. That's all."

"Is it because of . . . the thing?"

"The thing?"

"She gotta test the merchandise before she commits?" He smiled and punched me in the arm. "Or did you already . . . ?"

"No, we didn't."

"You need some pointers?"

"No. Please, God, no."

"Good man!" Benito said as if he knew exactly what we were talking about. "Save it for your wife."

Wade cackled, and I closed my eyes, wondering how much longer he'd torment me with my virginity.

Rachel had hung up the *Cast Away* poster over her couch. She'd answered the door in sweatpants and bare feet and led me to the kitchen table, where she'd set up her precious laptop, legal pads, and rows of colored pens.

"I have water." She flicked the collar of my cardigan. "Ruth keeps every kind of soda in the world in here, if you like that."

Her hair was up in a loose bun. The back of her neck was a sheet of paper drawn with loose dark curls.

"Water's fine." I sat at the table kitty-corner from the laptop and watched her get two bottles from the fridge. The woman still moved like the girl I'd loved, with extra nervous flourish and little hums when she found what she was looking for.

I was watching her body so closely that the water bottle was midair before I saw her toss it. I caught it with one hand.

She threw herself in her seat, curling her calf around the chair leg and bracing her toes against the hardwood floor as if she wanted to launch herself into the job. Her toes were perfect. I wanted to kiss each of them.

"I got a tux," I said.

"Oh, wow. You're committed."

"Needed one anyway."

"Okay," she said. "The price of the hall goes up after eighty guests. My parents gave me a list that's forty-three, but we have some overlap, so I think we'll be fine."

She cracked her water open.

"I want to show off," I said, opening my bottle. "Can we invite Brock and Scott?"

"That would be delicious, but no."

I took out my phone, found my mother's email, and forwarded it to her.

"I have a lot of cousins on my father's side. They're optional."

Her email dinged, and I watched her intensity as she opened it, scanning the spreadsheet. She could have been doing her math homework or planning out all the steps of her life.

I wanted this to be real, but I had to be honest with myself. We needed more time.

"Did you find out if the date was moveable?" I asked.

She looked at me over the screen.

"I did."

"And?"

She closed the laptop.

"She said sure. Whatever I wanted. Then she launched into 'I'm sorry I'm pushing.' Then it was 'I'm just so happy to see you settled.' And I got nervous, so I chickened out and said it was a perfect date."

"We need to figure this out before it goes too far."

"I'm a coward."

She wasn't a coward, but she was convinced she was. I didn't know if I could shake her assumptions away. I slid my chair around so I'd be next to her and opened her laptop. The spreadsheet flickered on.

"Heather McNulty?" I said, leaning in to her with my arm on the back of the chair. So close I could smell her strawberry shampoo. She turned to face me. "Wasn't she your archenemy?"

"Healthy competition for the essay prize." A hint of peppermint was laced in her breath. She'd just brushed her teeth. "Also, she's in my mother's book club." I put my eyes on the screen before I kissed her. "If she was terrible to you, she's out."

"She's fine. Four kids. Wow."

I faced her. I was in her apartment ten minutes, and I already wanted to drag her onto the couch. "Lucky lady."

"Should we give the kids their own section?" She sorted them on the spreadsheet. "We have like two dozen."

"Sure." I moved a little closer to her cheek.

"I was at my friend Tanya's wedding, and she hired people to keep an eye on them."

"I want to put my lips on every inch of your skin."

Her eyelids fluttered.

"We're waiting."

"We're waiting." I kissed the place right below her ear. "There's a lot we can do while we wait."

"It's a weeknight." She groaned as my mouth worked its way down her neck.

"Yup." My hand found its way inside her thigh.

"We have to finish this. Seating. Chart."

"Mm-hmm." Up her leg, where she was warmest. She stood when I got to the place where her thighs met, tipping the chair.

"Seb."

"Rachel." I leaned over to right the chair.

"I want to, and we can't, and I just . . . God. When you touch me, it's like you know just what to do."

"And that's bad?"

She sat and scooted her chair back in.

"I'm not as strong as you. So let me do this."

Tapping, typing, dragging names into little sections, she worked furiously. So sexy. She thought I was strong, but I wasn't really. The wall between my desire and my determination to wait was paper thin.

I was about to feel her thigh again when she looked away from the screen.

"Do you want the Garcias on your side or mine?" she asked, all business. I knew that tone, and I knew that look on her face.

She wasn't resisting for herself. She was resisting to make it easy for me.

I leaned back, grateful and a little awestruck.

"Mine."

She nodded and moved them around.

Somehow, with her help, I managed to keep my hands off her body and my mind on the invitation list.

CHAPTER 30

RACHEL

Sebastian and I met when we could to manage the little tasks of planning. I tried to meet in public so he wouldn't be tempted to break his promise to himself. Also, to be honest, so I wouldn't be tempted to let him. We'd have lunch in a little park in Culver City to work on the seating arrangement, which never seemed to be right. Or we'd meet for dinner to discuss the processional song. I'd make sure to drive myself so he wouldn't walk me to the door, where I'd be tempted to invite him in.

Our meetings weren't even about the wedding anymore. We were really dating, and I was really falling for him.

But the date was getting closer, and we weren't there yet.

We weren't quite real.

Mom called while I was at work.

"I sent you an email about the catering, and I forgot to mention a dress," she said.

"I'll get it at David's Bridal. I'm not a custom size or anything."

"Carol wanted me to tell you that she could make you something."

It didn't matter one way or the other, and frankly, I didn't want to spend a ton of money on a real wedding dress for a fake wedding. But

I could tell she was sour on the idea, and since this was all about her, I went with it.

"She shouldn't trouble herself."

"Making a bridal muumuu shouldn't take more than a minute."

I laughed. "I can throw a belt on it."

We laughed together, but the worry crept in like the Santa Ana winds.

"Ma?"

"Yes?"

"You're okay?"

"With what?"

I had an opening, right there. I could have asked her directly and gauged the truthfulness of her answer by its tone. I could have given her a chance to tell me everything, but I discovered something about myself inside that opportunity.

I didn't want to know.

"With me getting married so quick?"

"Oh, my dear! Of course! We all knew it was going to happen eventually. The only two people who didn't know were you and Seb."

"Really? You believed Carol's charts?"

She laughed again. If she was sick, she was covering it up really well.

"The way he looked at you when you were kids and when we saw you at Christmas? It was so obvious. It's faster than we thought, but you know . . . love doesn't have a speed limit."

We worked through lunch so the staff could write in the afternoon. I checked my phone on a bathroom break. A line producer chatted with the casting assistant at the mirror, and the toilet flushed in the stall next to mine. Notifications showed the email Mom had mentioned—subject line: *caterer?*—and a text from Sebastian. I was relieved to hear from him, then surprised at my relief, then disappointed in it. I was supposed to be keeping a clear head, but I couldn't wait to talk to him.

I opened his text first.

—Sunday ok for food tasting?—

He must have been cc'd on Mom's email, which I still hadn't opened.

—Sure. Time?—

—It says 2pm—

Of course he'd opened the email. Sitting on the toilet seat, I tapped to my mother's note. Sebastian hadn't been cc'd.

> Rachel,
>
> Hello, sweetheart. Dad and I are going to Tahoe for the last two weeks of February, so we need to pick the menu this weekend. Sunday at two works for us. Can you and Sebastian make it then?
>
> I heard you hired Tiffany's friend. I have a list of songs we think are very romantic. Do you want to approve before I give it to her?
>
> Here's a link for beautiful engraved invitations! I ordered them. We have 24 hours to cancel or change, so let me know.

We are all so excited for you!

Love always,

Mom and Dad

The bathroom got quiet as everyone filed out.

Two weeks away with Dad?

Dad hadn't taken more than five days of vacation in a row in his life. Was it a bucket list trip? Or was it a round of chemo she didn't want to tell me about?

Maybe it's just a damn vacation.

I texted Sebastian back.

—2pm is ok for me—

—Rachel. This is fun, but we need to make sure we're rushing for the right reasons—

—I'm pretty sure—

I wanted to dump everything on him. I wanted to beat him down with worry over my mother, but he was already doing more than enough. I wanted him to make me feel better, but that wasn't his job.

—Pretty sure? Should you talk to your father, maybe?—

I wanted to be mad at him. At his doubt. At his vacillation. But he was being sensible, and I was being ridiculous. It was one thing to tell a big white lie to make your mother happy. It was another to rent a hall.

—You're right—

After breakouts, the writers had all gone to their respective corners to work on their shows. Sandra sat at the end of the long table with my sex-video episode work in front of her. Multicolored Post-its stuck out from the sides like tongues. I was to her left with my laptop open. CJ was to her right.

Sandra folded her arms over the script and looked at me as if I were on the 101 when she'd specifically told me to take the Cahuenga Pass.

"What is this?"

"It's the first act and outline of 'Viral Love.'"

"It's a revenge thriller. All we're missing is flying bullets."

"I . . . I couldn't let him get away with it. She needed closure to move on."

CJ flipped her pen between her fingers, looking as if she'd prefer a painless death to another minute in that room.

"It wasn't rational," I said nervously. "Just . . . the stakes seem too high. This wasn't about her ex not respecting her or treating her badly. It's right and wrong, and I don't believe she'd just move on from that. They have to act real. I have to believe it."

Sandra worried a Post-it from the stack. She didn't pull it out, but I could tell the temptation to put the sticky side on her skin was killing her. Getting control, she laid her hands flat.

"Love is not rational. Romance, in particular, is not. We're selling a fantasy."

"I don't . . ." Deep breath. "I don't believe that."

"Really? Tell me why we can't have them kissing by the middle of the second act."

"When I put it sooner, it felt forced." I threw myself into my chair and leaned toward my boss as if I wanted to crawl into her lap. "But it's worth it. It's just worth it, and I don't know how we can physically get to an HEA in fifty-nine minutes, but when she takes his hand and looks at him"—I put my hands on my heart—"and she says, 'I'm scared,' it broke me. It freaking broke me, and I wrote it. But if it happened on page thirty, I'd be checking my phone in front of the TV because who cares? And we should care, because she's scared he's the same, and she's scared he's different. She's scared she's going to make a mistake and ruin her life."

Sandra turned to CJ.

"What do you think?"

"I think she's selling it."

"She really is." Sandra pushed her markups to me. "But she's stuck on morals, and no one cares."

"People care!" I interjected. "They do! And if they don't, I'm going to make them care!"

"Don't make me think you're right," Sandra said. "Make me feel it."

Back at my desk, I opened "Viral Love." I knew where the trouble spots were.

All I had to do was add feeling where thinking had been.

Easy.

Maybe "Broken Promises" had the same problem.

Maybe I had the same problem.

My "Viral Love" outline was meaningless even with the changes. The whole thing was like a rock in my shoe. I just couldn't bear knowing there was a real story out there I wasn't telling.

Why shouldn't I tell it? If I wanted the audience to feel it, I had to feel it, and I was only going to feel it if I believed it.

With that realization, I decided not to call my father. I pulled onto a side street and parked so I could call Dr. Gelbart's office.

"Hey, Arianna." My hands were shaking. "I'm, um, calling to check and make sure about my mother's appointment . . . next week?"

I didn't know if she had an appointment next week.

"I don't have her down," Arianna said. "Not until she's finished with Dr. Friedman."

"Finished with . . ." Dr. Friedman administered chemo. My heart turned into a molten lump. "Last two weeks of February, right?"

"You'll have to ask him. Are you okay?"

"I'm fine."

"Do you need his number?"

"I have it. Thanks."

I hung up and stared at my phone, then called Sebastian.

"Hey, what . . . ?" he said.

"Here's the plan."

"Okay."

"I called her doctor. She's getting chemo end of this month. She's not telling me. She gave me a song and dance about taking a vacation. So we plan the wedding for March eighth. After the chemo we postpone it or cancel it or whatever."

"That sounds good."

A woman pushed a stroller, talking on the phone. Laughing. The baby shook a stuffed squirrel. Normal people doing normal things.

"If I'm settled, if she thinks I'm doing all right, it's going to be easier for her. Everything's going to be just easier and more successful and better."

"It's good, Rachel. Just take it easy."

"I'm mad at her. So fucking mad. But I want her to be happy when she's in chemo—then I'm going to give her a piece of my mind."

"Until then . . ."

"Until then, everything's normal."

CHAPTER 31

RACHEL

By the time I got home, I'd calmed down out of necessity. I checked Mom's link to the engraved invitations.

"Those are nice," Ruth said, looking over my shoulder. She'd just gotten out of the shower. Her hair was up in magenta clips that matched her floral robe and flip-flops.

"I wish I knew how much she was spending on them."

"Probably expensive," she said with her head half in the fridge. She got out a Diet Coke and tapped the top before popping it.

"Are you coming? You can bring Mario."

"You're so sweet." She put her arm around me and watched me poke around the website. "I'd love to. What are you doing for a cake?"

"We got it with the catering."

"Click that." She pointed to a dropdown that said *special pricing*. "Maybe there's a clearance section with prices."

"Good thinking." But no. It was the exact opposite. "Forty percent extra for a rush? What a racket."

"You're already paying it," Ruth said, tapping her gel nail on the screen to count weeks on the little calendar.

She was counting correctly. I closed the laptop.

"She's out of her mind," I said, referring to my mother.

"She wants you to be happy. So." She clapped her hands. "No bridal shower?"

"God, no."

"Bachelorette party?"

"No. Please, no."

"Night out with the girls? Come on. Don't be such a dud."

"That I can do."

She squeed and jumpclapped. I couldn't deny the obvious. Weddings made people happy.

"No strippers, Ruthie."

"What's your problem with strippers?"

"They're paid to act like they want to fuck us, and they don't. It's all lies."

Ruth was already on her phone. "What's your mentor's email?"

"I'll text it. Hey, so . . . ," I started, getting up my courage. "The woman in that video? 'Delete It?' You implied you knew her."

"She was a client."

"Was?"

"She quit when it came out. Quit everything."

If I didn't write this thing and do it justice, one of the staff writers would. I had to stand between her and a fake HEA.

"I think I need to meet her."

"Let me make a few calls," Ruth said. "You free Saturday?"

"Yes, but if you get strippers, I'm walking out."

She cut the air with her hands and put a very serious look on her face. "Absolutely not." She made the Girl Scout sign. "Scout's honor. No strippers."

CHAPTER 32

RACHEL

Seven male strippers lined up in front of the stage and made their pecs do a rhythmic flex and pop to the classic seventies music. Trays of lemon-drop shots appeared at the table one after the other. Ruth put another one in front of me.

"How much is this costing you?" I shouted after I slammed it back. The world was swimmy and generous already, but the lemon drops were sweet and refreshing.

"It's on the WDE agency." She flashed her corporate Amex.

My mother was at the edge of the stage, stuffing a five into the G-string of a guy who was definitely not named Max, no matter what the MC said. Tiffany was clicking and posting. A few girlfriends from USC were laughing with CJ. They'd all met me here for a surprise. I could have walked out, but even I had limits to how rude I was willing to be.

The whole thing was stupid. It was exactly like I'd said. The strippers were paid to act as if they wanted us, but they didn't. The guys knew it was a campy fake exercise, but to my surprise, the women did too. We all knew, and we all played along.

Even me.

Max pulled my mother up on the stage and said something into her ear. She nodded and laughed, and all seven of them gathered around her. They kneeled in a sweaty circle around her, worshipping her by putting their hands half an inch from her body and moving them up and down. She raised her arms and shimmied her hips. Turned and shook her bottom.

My mother with her reconstructed breasts, living fully.

I loved her so much.

I was on my feet applauding, laughing so hard my face hurt. Someone said something about a lap dance. CJ put her arm around me as Ruth fed me another shot. Tiffany pointed her blue phone at me because if there was no video, it didn't happen.

"Lap dance!" CJ cried.

I knew what a lap dance was. It was where a woman stuck her tits and ass in a guy's face, and he wanted to touch her but couldn't, making it a profitable exercise in frustration. It wasn't what was happening now, which was my friends pushing me toward the stage.

A Latino with perfectly soft skin on a perfectly hard body reached down and took me by the wrist, hoisting me up.

"You can call me Dirk," he said. "What's your name?"

"Rachel, but I'm really not—"

"Our first bachelorette lap dance of the night!" the MC announced.

"Rachel!" Dirk told him.

"Raaaacheeellll!"

My friends cheered and clapped.

"But—"

I was being placed in a chair before I could finish.

"If you want to tap out, snap your fingers," Dirk said in my ear. "Relax and have fun if you don't." He smiled reassuringly at me and gave a quick nod. I gripped the sides of the chair.

The music started, and Dirk waved his ass in my face. I was ready to snap my fingers. I didn't want to fuck this guy. I didn't even want to touch him.

"Come on, Rachel!" I heard from the crowd. Looking over, I found my mother kicking back a lemon drop and a dozen women I respected with their hands up and their bodies swaying.

What the hell. It was a show. If my mother could live a moment like this without apology, so could I.

I pretended I was cupping his ass and turned to the audience with an "ooh, nice" face, and when Dirk turned around, I gyrated against my chair. When he kneeled in front of me, I pretended I loved the way he made like he was nuzzling my breasts.

Mom was talking and laughing with Ruth. She had tears streaming down her face.

This was actually awesome.

I was done letting Dirk call the shots. I stood up, turned around, and bent over the back of the chair. Screams from seventeen tables of people I didn't know. I shook my ass as a stripper pretended to fuck it. I could barely gyrate I was laughing so hard.

Blinking the tears away and facing a completely different direction over the back of the chair, I saw the other side of the room, where Sebastian was standing with the guy from New Year's—Wade.

He gave me two thumbs up.

I pointed to him with two fingers, then pointed at my eyes, then back at him. He made the same motion.

I see you.

Dirk dropped to his knees and ate out my ass. I made a cartoonish surprised face, which made Sebastian and his friend buckle in laughter.

"Let's give Rachel a round of applause, everybody!"

I stood up. Dirk and I took a bow.

"You were great!" He patted me on the back. "I thought you were going to snap out."

"Glad I didn't!"

The MC led me off the side of the stage, where Sebastian and Wade stood.

I jabbed Wade in the chest harder than I would have if I'd been sober.

"Ow!" he said, twisting away. "Hey!"

"He is not a dirtbag or a dweeb. You say you're sorry."

"Who?" He jerked his thumb toward Sebastian. "This dirtbag?"

I punched his arm, and he laughed.

"Uncle! All right! He's not a dirtbag; he's a . . . whatever. I don't know."

"Hunk." I slid my arm around Sebastian's waist. "He's a totally hot hunk."

Wade put down his drink and held up his two pointer fingers, asking me to give him a moment. Then he turned to face his friend.

"I'm sorry, Seb, but she's right." He swiftly locked his hand on the back of Sebastian's neck and planted his lips on his mouth. They were laughing so hard the kiss only lasted a second. I couldn't hold a grudge against Wade if this was how their friendship worked. I kind of even liked the guy.

"Now youse are even," Wade said. "You both been touched by another guy tonight."

Sebastian wiped his mouth. "She got the better end of the deal."

"I don't know how you don't punch that guy out."

I shook my head. "It's all just fun. It doesn't have to be a big serious thing."

I was telling myself as much as I was telling him.

"You remember Wade," Sebastian said. "Met him at Stanford."

"I was in business," Wade said, elbowing his friend. "This dork was in design, and he's my boss. You go figure."

"Awesome," I said, grabbing Sebastian's arm. "But he's still not a dork, unless you want to get punched again." The room was tilting, and my mouth was so dry it burned. Only one thing would cool it down. "I need another lemon drop."

"How about water?" Sebastian put his arm around my shoulder, and I wrapped myself around his waist.

"Oh, sure. Killjoy."

"And fresh air."

"I'm gonna go keep the ladies company." Wade excused himself. On stage, three more bachelorettes were getting the dance treatment.

"Come," Sebastian said, guiding me someplace, then someplace else. I held on to him as if he were a buoy in a constantly shifting sea. Then, with a cold blast of air, we were on Hollywood Boulevard.

"Whoa!" I said when a guy in a Spider-Man costume appeared in front of me. Sebastian pulled me away. The crowd was made of chaos and noise. Vendors with light-up toys had set up tables at the curb, and the smell of bacon filled the air.

"Yes, please!" I shouted when I saw the portable grill with bacon-wrapped hot dogs.

Sebastian got out his wallet and ordered one. "You sure you're going to keep this down?"

"Cast-iron stomach."

We turned onto a quieter side street. He kept me straight as I bit into my hot dog.

"So good," I said around a mouthful. "This is so good. Do you want a bite?" I held it up to his face. He went to take it, but I pulled away, losing so much of my delicate balance I had to grab a parking meter. "Bite," I said, holding it up again.

He took hold of my wrist and bit it, leaving his hand on my skin.

"Not s'posed to touch, Mr. Barton."

He swallowed and smiled, letting his hand drift down my arm before letting me go.

"You're cute when you're wrecked."

"You're cute when I'm wrecked." I took the last bite. The salt filled in the burning spaces on my tongue until my mouth felt numb. "Also when I'm not wrecked, if I remember right. You're really hot then too."

"Come on. Let's walk it off."

I took his arm and let him guide me around the block.

"You're going to make someone a great husband one day," I said. "You're a gentleman, but not like you think I'm weak or frail." I tried not to slur and failed. "You have a nice way about you, and you didn't act all weird with the lap dance."

"I knew you didn't want Dirk."

"But lots of guys would be jealous."

"I didn't say I wasn't jealous."

"You want a lap dance? No touching!"

"No, you know what I want?"

"I don't know if I'm in any condition for that right now."

My weight shifted with the moving sidewalk, but he kept me straight until I thought about his last text. I grabbed a railing and stopped us.

"I want to remember you like this."

"Drunk?"

"Just having a good time." He put his arm around me. "Not worrying if you'll measure up. Not stressed about your mother. Not trying to write something you don't want to. Just being Rachel."

"I'll try to be me more often."

He took my shoes off and put me in my bed fully clothed, stretching the blanket over me.

"There's water and Advil on the night table."

"Mmph."

"I'll call you tomorrow."

He leaned down and kissed my cheek.

"Are you going to take advantage of me now?" I asked.

"Nope."

"Then do it again."

He leaned down, but his lips didn't touch me. His breath warmed my ear as he whispered, "Good night, Rachel."

"Seb?"

"Rachel?"

I patted the bed. It tilted when he sat on the edge.

"My feelings are confusing me," I said. "I'm not strong."

"Yes, you are."

"I used to be strong. Now I'm just a nobody who has to play the game or get crushed."

"Are we talking about us?"

"I have no idea what I'm talking about."

He moved a strand of hair from my cheek and tucked it behind my ear.

"You're not nobody," he said. "You're a warrior for what's right in the world. I think you just forgot that."

"Can you remind me?"

"When Sadie Hahn was sick for a week and Heather Birman gave her the wrong math assignment out of spite, you switched the names and took the F. Mrs. Trulio yelled at you in front of everyone."

Heather was mean and smart, but Sadie was just a little smarter, which made Heather meaner.

"You took it like a trooper," Sebastian continued, "because you had to do what was right."

"It would have been right to switch Sadie and Heather's names. I didn't have Heather's paper."

"You made it as right as you could."

Nothing had been made right. Heather went to MIT because her father was an alum, and Sadie went to UC Merced because her parents could afford it.

"Can you stay with me? I just—" I got my elbow under me, but the room spun so fast I dropped down again. "If I puke, I'm going to wish I was dead, and if I talk to someone, I might fall asleep, but if I do puke—which I might—I don't want to be alone."

"You don't want to wish you were dead by yourself?"

It was more than that. Sure, I didn't want to be alone, but even more—I didn't want to be far from him. He'd make it all right. If my cast-iron stomach bent and cracked, it would be ugly and painful, and I was just drunk enough to want what I wanted without shame.

"Drunk logic," I muttered.

"All right."

He took his jacket and shoes off, turned the lights out, and stretched out next to me. I scooted next to him and turned to my side, facing the window.

"I like that we're friends again," I said. "Like we were. But with jobs instead of school."

With a laugh, he turned and put his arm around me. Between his body and the steadiness of the moon outside, the spin of the room slowed.

"Do you ever feel bad about lying to your family?" I asked. "About the engagement?"

"Do you?"

"Tonight, I did. Because it made them happy, and it was a lie."

He said something, but it was muffled, and sleep hit me on the head like a boulder rushing down a hill.

CHAPTER 33

SEBASTIAN

Rachel had asked me if I felt guilty about lying to my family about the engagement, and I wondered if she'd remember what I'd said before she'd fallen asleep.

"In the end," I'd said, "I'm marrying you. Now. Later. Whenever. The only lie is the timeline."

She texted me the next morning.

—Thank you for last night—

—I hope I kept you from puking. You seemed all right when I left—

—Woke up fresh as a daisy at six. Been working. You should read this script I'm writing since no one else will—

—Why?—

—Because it's not about us but it's about a guy who comes back home after getting successful and dealing with the girl he left who never went anywhere—

I could have told her all the ways we were different from the story, starting with the girl who never went anywhere, but I came at it obliquely.

—No, I mean why won't anyone else read it?—

—Because they only read what they ask for, and they always ask for crap—

—You're not capable of crap—

We spoke every day the week between the bachelorette party and the Cotillion tasting. Every day, I reminded her of who she was. Every layer she shed revealed a little more of the girl I'd loved.

If she heard me tell her I was going to marry her now, later, or whenever, she never mentioned it.

I felt like I was in high school again, except this time I'd had a taste of her. By the time I met my family at Cotillion, we were a week into being friends, and all I wanted to do was be alone with her.

"So I did the chart for the date," my mother said. We were on the Cotillion veranda, waiting for Rachel and her family to arrive. Tiff was huddled in her hoodie, swiping her phone. The short beach was on the other side of the gazebo, where we were supposed to make our vows. We'd been given wine for our empty stomachs.

"What do the stars say?" I asked, even though I didn't really care. I couldn't believe I was finally sitting in the Cotillion Arms, and it was total trash compared to where I took clients for lunch. It was clean enough but ragged at the edges and decorated to do no more than avoid offense.

"Saturn's going into Sagittarius. Travel. Definitely overseas travel. You need to do it a week earlier."

"It'll be fine."

"Can you talk to her?"

"No. I'm not going to tell her you want to change the date because Saturn's going into my sun sign."

"Is everything okay at work?"

"Yeah, why?"

I poured myself more wine while she pulled a folder from her bag.

"Money's flowing away from you." She opened the folder. My chart. I was used to looking at it but was more impressed by the aesthetic of the lines and shapes than its ability to tell me anything about my life. "I want you to get this timing right, sweetheart."

"Carol," Tiffany said without looking up from her phone, "maybe the stars are bullshit."

"They have something to say whether you believe it or not, young lady."

"Hey." I pushed Tiffany's leg with my foot. She looked up. "Tell Ace no puking at the wedding."

"It was a vodka bong. You would have puked too."

"What—" Carol was cut off by Mrs. Rendell, who shuffled in with her hair up in a twist.

"Sorry we're late!" She slapped a stack of printed card stock in the center of the table. "But look at this."

She sat next to her husband. I turned, looking for my fiancée, and found her behind me with her hand on the back of her chair. I leaped up and pulled the chair out for her. She sat.

"Oh, dear," Carol said, looking at a card. I took one off the top. It was our wedding invitation.

"My name is backward," I said.

"Naitsabes," Tiffany read it. "Kinda cool, actually."

"We're getting a refund," Rachel's mother said. "But in the meantime, I don't know what to do."

As they argued about the invitations, Rachel leaned in to me and whispered, "They redid the banquet space since we were kids."

"You mean it looked worse?" I grumbled.

"You don't remember?"

"I've never been here."

"You never wanted to come to any parties."

"I was never invited."

She stared at me with her mouth open.

"It's a sign," Carol said, spreading three charts on the table. "Now we can change the date."

"Give it a rest," Rachel's dad said. "I'm hungry."

"Yeah," Tiffany said, putting her phone on the table for half a second.

"We're all here!" Tony appeared from nowhere, clapping his hands for attention. He was tall, with a slicked-back widow's peak and nine a.m. shadow on his cheeks. "I am happy to welcome you to Cotillion Arms!"

We all gave our most gracious thanks. Rachel's left hand was on the table, the flash of her diamond blinding even in the shade. Her manicure had worn off, but the hand looked no less perfect. She glanced at me. I must have been giving her some signal I didn't intend. She slid her napkin onto her lap and left her hand there.

"First," Tony said with another clap. Two waiters appeared with trays of greens. "A selection of salads to start. Caesar, green, and greek. We also have a Cobb that's a little heavier and a composed fruit salad that's a little lighter." The waiters dropped little piles of salad onto each of our plates. Another waiter placed a card and a stubby yellow pencil by our water glasses.

"Please rate your experience with each dish," he said. "The bride and groom will make their choices, no matter what you think. But we like to know."

"Honeydew," Rachel muttered, wrinkling her nose when the fruit salad was put next to her plate of greens.

"I like honeydew," I said.

"You can eat mine." She forked her Caesar and wrinkled her nose when she tasted it. "No anchovy."

"I'm sure they can add it," her mother said.

"I hate anchovy," replied her father.

"Who even eats the salad?" Tiffany said, leaning over to check her notifications.

"So," Mrs. Rendell said, "have you guys decided on a honeymoon yet?"

Rachel put down her fork and wiped her mouth.

"Not yet," I said.

"I have to wait until hiatus in July anyway," Rachel said.

"Well, Hawaii's right out then," her dad said. "Too hot."

"They won't give you time off work?" Her mother.

"No, Ma."

"Rachel always had a thing for Paris," Mrs. Rendell said.

The waiters came back and removed plates. We rated our salads. I leaned over to look at Rachel's. Fruit salad was a big no.

"Quit it," she said with a smirk, covering her paper. "No cheating."

"What if I want honeydew?"

"There's a supermarket around the corner."

Tony appeared.

"I am overjoyed to see you two together, all grown up and so in love." Tony beamed at us as if he hadn't chased us out of his driveway a dozen times. He picked up a spoon to tap a water glass. "Everybody clink!" Glasses clinked. Everyone was delighted to do it. Rachel and I exchanged a glance. "Come on, lovebirds!" Tony exclaimed. "On your wedding day we will tap until you kiss!"

Of course they would.

When she pressed her lips together after she sipped her wine, a wet line of pink was left between them. I could practically taste it, cool and stinging before it yielded to the rough warmth of my probing tongue.

Her face in profile, the whorl of her ear, and the hair tucked behind it tapped the memory of those days we'd walk home, side by side. The way she laughed at my jokes or scowled back at Scott and Brock. I'd never been comfortable in my own skin, except when she was with me.

She put her glass down. I put my arm around the back of her chair and put my mouth close to her ear so she could hear me over the clinking glasses.

"You smell like honeydew," she whispered.

"They're going to clink until we kiss." I laid my lips on her cheek.

I felt her nod. She looked around the table at the expectations of our families. She angled her head differently to whisper back.

"I'll get you new pants."

The clatter of glassware was immediately followed by a wet feeling on my thigh.

"Damn!" Rachel jumped up. "I'm so sorry."

My pants were splattered in red wine. Waitstaff descended on us with napkins as parents cooed and cried out laundry tips. Tiffany hugged her phone. Carol picked up her charts, though only one had been reddened at the edge.

"It's all right." I put my hands out to calm the fray. "I'm just going to—"

"Bathroom's this way," Tony said. "Let me show you."

"I have it." Rachel grabbed my hand and pulled.

"She has it," I said to Tony before I was yanked into the restaurant and through the kitchen with its clanking pots and white coats. She strode like she knew the way, which she did because she'd been invited to the full experience of high school.

We pushed out the back door and stepped into a small, shady yard with a table, a stack of plastic racks, and a water heater. She let go of my hand and leaned against the wall, under a corkboard with a staff schedule tacked to it.

"Sorry," she said. "I freaked out."

"About?"

"This whole fake thing. When those glasses started clinking, I looked at them all, believing this fat lie we told them . . . and I started to feel too guilty to kiss you."

"Rach." I reached for her, but she put her hands up.

"Don't. Seb. Please. I like you. I'm scared."

"What are you scared of?"

"You."

I was standing over her, too close, too tall, too demanding. But it wasn't me she was scared of. No. Not with her big brown eyes searching mine so directly. It wasn't me.

"What are you scared of?" I repeated. I couldn't believe how cool I was playing it on the one hand. On the other, my confidence wasn't about me. It was about Rachel—who she was and how she made me feel like a smitten kid. She was an ache I'd never cured.

"Me." She looked past me for a moment; then it was back to home base. "I'm scared of me."

On the other side of the fence, a horn honked, but it didn't break the moment. I was pretty sure a bomb could drop on the Cotillion Arms, and we wouldn't have budged.

"What if . . ." She swallowed before she let a rueful smile curl her mouth. "You know . . . what if? We start pitches like that. 'What if a prince falls for a maid?' And that's your hook."

"What's Rachel's hook?"

"Mine are never commercial."

"You only have to sell it to me."

She tilted her head, and after a barely discernable shrug, she put her hands on my arms.

"What if I'm just a mess? What if inside I'm just ugly and sloppy and raw? What if you bring all that out, and I lose myself . . . and I'm sentimental and emotional? They clink those glasses, and it's so tacky and contrived. But I liked it, and I wanted it to be real. I wanted their happiness to be real. But it's fake. I'm fake. We're fake."

I had to admire the brutality of her honesty.

"Right here," I said. "Just us. Alone. Is it fake?"

"I don't know."

"My feelings for you . . . they're real. What about yours? Fake?"

"I don't know. I can't tell if I like you or the idea of getting married."

She never pulled a punch, even when it hurt. But I'd always known where I stood because I could see the meaning past the words.

"I like the Rachel who doesn't always know what's right but tries anyway."

"See? I'm a mess."

"I like the Rachel who pulled my hair when she came."

"Stop." She drew her hands down the front of my shirt, running the pad of her thumb against the crease of my placket. "I didn't pull it hard. Did I?"

"You did. I like the Rachel who pushed her pussy against my mouth when she wanted more. Who told me to suck harder and opened her legs all the way so I could get my tongue inside her. You tasted like heaven. You tasted beautiful and sloppy and raw."

Her neck and cheeks had broken out in pink bumps, and her lips parted. I leaned over her, lips close to her forehead but not touching.

"When did you get so confident?" she asked.

"Being a dweeb means you find out who you are early, because everyone tells you."

"I wish I could separate how I feel from this game we're playing."

Lips close to her cheek. Close enough to feel the tiny white hairs on her skin. "How does this feel?" My lips didn't make contact with her throat. They didn't need to. She smelled like berries as red as the blood rushing to the surface of her skin.

"Real."

"Tell me what you want." I brushed my lips against her throat, along her jaw, moving my hand over her rib cage.

"We should get back," she said, making no move to do so.

"I want to make sure you're not confused first. What's on the other side of that door is playacting." I reached behind her and snapped the lock.

"What are you doing?"

"On this side of the door is what's real."

Sliding my hand up her shirt, over her arm skin, under her bra, I watched her cheeks flush and her lips part. She moved forward to kiss me, but I pulled back. I wanted to see her face when my thumb found her nipple.

Her eyelids fluttered.

"You've been so good," I said, "trying not to tempt me. But now that's fake too."

"We can't," she whispered. "The staff will want to come through."

I kissed her cheek, her neck, her ear, and breathed four words.

"Pick up your skirt."

When she reached down and lifted it, my dick stretched my wine-soaked pants. My mouth opened on hers. My tongue entered her. My hands reached behind, over her ass, between her legs, while she opened my fly and released a raging hard-on desperate for a place to land.

When I pushed her underwear away and found her slick and warm, my mind went blank with need. And when her hand wrapped around my dick, I couldn't pay attention to the kiss. I buried my nose in her hair and brought my hand around front, four fingers on her clit.

"Real enough for you?"

She didn't answer. Just looked at me and brought her hand to her mouth, licking it.

"Yeah." When she fisted my dick again, her palm was slippery.

"Yes," I growled through my teeth, pushing her against the wall. Two fingers deep inside her, heel of my hand on her clit, matching her rhythm.

"Seb." Her voice wasn't more than a husky breath. "You're so good. Yes."

"Come."

She picked her shirt up.

"You too?"

I anchored my hand to her so I wouldn't stop.

"Yes."

She clenched around my fingers, head back, mouth open, hand squeezing pleasure out of me until we were both left panting.

"That was so romantic," she said.

I laughed and stood straight. Her shirt was pulled up, and her belly was covered with my orgasm. I plucked a rolled-up napkin from the cart and let the silverware spill out.

"You can put it in the director's cut." I wiped her up and pulled her shirt down.

"That's one way to get fired." She took the napkin and wiped my fingers, then tossed the napkin in the hamper.

"Can I admit something?" I said as I unlocked the door.

"Only if it's true."

"If I'm going to make fake marriage plans, there's no one I'd rather do it with."

"That's the closest I've ever gotten to a real proposal."

I kissed her, and we went back to the table.

CHAPTER 34

RACHEL

We'd decided on the chicken marsala, broiled salmon, and the beef wellington because it was my favorite. We agreed to get invitations from the store and handwrite them in one fell swoop, together.

Then Mom was going to get her secret chemo.

Then we were going to call off the wedding, but not *us*. We were a real thing.

"You can sit wherever you like," the hostess said as she blew past me in a black polo shirt. Her Denny's name tag said *Ximena*. She was in her twenties, rushing from dining room to kitchen and to her tables with a look of cold urgency. When she got to a booth with a couple and took out her pad, then she smiled and took their order as if she had all the time in the world.

Watching Ximena kept me from doing what I was supposed to be doing, which was making things right.

I'd watched the video again to memorize her face. Her name was Zoe, and unless she was in profile in the throes of ecstasy or heart-sinking horror, I couldn't pick her out of a crowd.

Hi Rachel,

Sure, if you want to meet we can. Ruth says you're ok and I trust her.

I already know you don't need permission to do a show with the basic plot of what happened. So, I'm not quite sure what you want to talk about. I won't sign anything without my lawyers. I don't want to go too much into it, so I may not answer all your questions.

I'm a dental hygienist. I'll make sure to wear pink scrubs.

—Zoe

I found her in the smaller dining room in the back. She'd cut her hair and dyed it dark brown. Over her mauve scrubs hung a lanyard with a laminated tag and buttons with toothy smiles. She had one arm curved around a white mug and the other stretched to the center of the table, scrolling her phone.

I started in her direction.

Softly, she laughed at something on the screen. A cat video. A meme. An inside joke from a friend. Scrolling, she kept her smile.

And here I was, about to sit down so she could relive something so painful she'd quit acting. A dental hygienist had a dream she kept alive. She had the talent to land an agent at WDE, but she didn't have the money to quit her day job.

She gave up out of shame.

A shame I was going to make her relive over lunch and again on cable TV.

She put her phone down and sipped her coffee, scanning the room for me.

Fuck this. I knew right from wrong, and this was terribly wrong. Before her eyes landed in my direction, I turned around and left.

I emailed her from the parking lot.

> Hi Zoe,
>
> Hey, I'm sorry, but I have to bail.
>
> I've decided not to use your story.
>
> Thank you so much for agreeing to meet me anyway.
>
> —Rachel

I wanted to say more, but there was nothing else to say. Not to her. She didn't need to hear my reasoning or what I was giving up. She didn't need my friendship or my condolences. She needed to be left alone.

Sitting in my car, I took a deep breath. Maybe I'd always known I couldn't write this script. Even so, this was the moment I accepted it. That meant no job in the fall. No produced credit. Square one. Thirty years old and nothing to show for it.

I should tell CJ so she could fail at talking me down from the ledge.

And Sandra so she could fire me.

I should tell my mother so she'd know that if she had cancer, I could take care of her again. The illness wasn't going to interrupt my career or anything else.

I didn't tell any of them.

I texted Sebastian.

—Hey—

I didn't know what I wanted out of him, but he was the only one who wouldn't overwhelm me with the consequences of my actions.

—I was just thinking about you—

—Really? Was it about the beef wellington?—

—It was about the honeymoon. When did you say you went on summer hiatus?—

It didn't matter when the show went on hiatus because I wasn't going to have a job. I was a loser. Forever. I'd had a couple of big breaks, and either life stepped in the way, or some sense that I was too good for my job stopped me.

And this poor guy thought he had a real prize on his hands. What he wanted was a real Rachel with achievable ambitions, and what he had was a self-saboteur.

—Dude. This is all fake. There's not going to be a honeymoon—

—Think of it as a trip—

I wasn't going to think of it at all.

—I'll see you Saturday for the invitations—

I put my phone away and drove back to my job.

CHAPTER 35

RACHEL

When I pulled up to Mandarin Lane, Sebastian was high on a ladder leaning against his mother's house, unhooking the string of lights under the roof gutters. I jogged across the street with my arms through the handles of bags of invitations.

"Hey," I called up, dropping the Papyrus bags of blank wedding invitations at the base of the ladder. "You ready to write your name eighty times?"

He leaned and shook a length of lights, but they wouldn't unhook. "I wish my name was Bob or Ted."

His mother ran out. "I called Roy!"

"I'm fine," he said, trying to whip the lights off the hook and failing.

"There's plenty to do on the lawn. You don't know how to use the ladder."

"Are you kidding me?"

Behind us, a truck screeched to a stop, blocking the driveway. Roy was out in ragged jeans and a beard starting to grow under his moustache.

"Goddamn it, kid!" he shouted.

"Roy! Get him down!"

He stood at the base of the ladder. "You trying to get yourself killed?"

"First of all," Sebastian said, "I'm not a kid."

"Well, you should be smarter than one."

Sebastian shook his head, leaning farther as if to prove a point.

"Son, ya gotta move the ladder!"

Sebastian shook the string of lights harder. They came off the hook, but he lost his balance. Both Roy and I grabbed the bottom of the ladder to hold it steady.

"Sebbie!" his mother cried.

"This is what I'm talking about!" Roy yelled.

Sebastian came down, and when his feet were firmly planted, he stayed at the bottom and looked at Roy.

"I'm fine."

"By the grace of God you are. I've been putting these lights up and taking them down five years now. Can I show you how it's done?"

"No," his mother said with her hand on Roy's arm. "He doesn't need to know."

"Of course he does. Stop treating him like an incompetent." He kept the ladder where it was and put his hands on either side. "Follow me up."

The aluminum ladder creaked and bent with every step Roy took. Carol was a hand-wringing mess.

Sebastian watched.

"I have to tell you something," I said. "Later."

"Is everything all right?"

"No, but I don't want to talk about it."

We stared at each other for too long.

"Come on up, kid," Roy called down from the roof.

"Off I go." Sebastian put his foot on the bottom rung.

"Have fun."

Up he went.

"Rachel!" my mother called from across the cul-de-sac. "Did you get the pens?"

"Ye—" I froze in the middle of a single-syllable word.

Mom was in the doorway, just pretty as you please, as if there were nothing unusual at all with how she looked. Nothing to see here.

Just a haircut.

Another few minutes came off the end of my life, because it wasn't just a haircut. It was a parted-on-the-side, feathered, swept-over thing that was too damn short by a mile.

She'd been so proud of the way her hair had grown in. There was only one reason she'd cut it that short, and it wasn't because she thought it was cute. She cut it because she expected to lose it, and short hair made less of a mess.

The fact that I'd figured out she was sick again didn't make the confirmation any easier. I was frozen with my hand on the ladder asking myself what I'd do if I didn't think she was sick. I'd mention it. I couldn't *not* mention it.

If I were a character in an episode, and I were writing myself as a character, not having seen the pill bottle or helped my dad with insurance . . . what would the dialogue be?

I picked up my bags of invitations and started across the street. "Why?" I asked Mom when I was close enough.

"Don't you like it?" She turned, modeling the back for me.

"Not really."

"Why not?"

"It reminds me of when you were sick." I passed her and went into the house. Yes. That was exactly what I'd say if I didn't know the cancer was back.

Mom left the door open but closed the screen door. I put the bags on the dining room table.

"I thought Dad liked it long?"

"Your father got used to the drains being clear. To be honest, I'm not a young girl anymore. I can't be bothered taking care of long hair." She patted it as if it were out of place. "This suits my lifestyle."

She was in tight yoga pants and a ribbed tank under a zip-up hoodie she kept open just below her breasts. Her flats had bows on them. She was taking time with how she looked. She cared. She wasn't giving up.

It was time to stop making it about me. I dumped a bag out onto the table, shrugging, because it wasn't my head, and if I were a fake character in a fake show, I'd get over it.

"It suits your face shape too."

"I agree." She sorted through the stuff I'd dumped and held up a pack of black calligraphy pens. "Perfect! These are exactly the ones."

Every little bit of delight I could deliver to her made me unreasonably happy.

I focused on that. If I could maximize those moments, my work would be done.

—

Fast.

Cheap.

Good.

When blocking out the production for a show, you got two out of three. If you tried to do it fast and good, the budget would explode. If you wanted to do it cheap and well, you had to leave more production time.

I discovered this went for wedding invitations as well. Carol came over in loose pants and a flowing shirt, her crystal necklaces down to a casual half dozen. Dad poured Mom wine and offered beer. Tiffany passed out cards she'd written with the correct spelling of everyone's name, the date, and the location. We had enough time and enough people to get it done fast and cheap.

Good went right out the window once the wine kicked in, which was right about when Sebastian and Roy showed up, not a broken bone between them. Carol moved so my fake fiancé could sit next to me. He kissed me on the cheek, and I couldn't help but breathe a little deeper to appreciate his lemon-and-leather scent.

"We're inviting Laci Strong?" I asked.

"She sent casseroles when your mother was sick," Dad said. He'd given up on the calligraphy pens and moved to ballpoint. No one objected. Fast and cheap were the priorities.

"They were terrible," Mom said, using her fancy pen to swoop the *S* in *Sebastian*. "But the thought counts."

"Do we have to seat all three of her kids?" Tiffany asked. She was also using the calligraphy pens, but with less clear results. "My friend Esme had a wedding. No kids allowed."

"Weddings are better with kids," Sebastian said.

"Everything's better with kids," I said, thinking nothing of it until I caught Sebastian's gaze next to me. His eyes were positively glinting.

"You two better get started!" Carol said, and I felt my face turn red hot.

"Classy move, Carol," Dad grumbled.

"Class has nothing to do with it. I ran their charts."

"No need to rush," Mom said, putting her latest on the pile. "Rachel has a career to think about."

"Okay." Tiffany jumped in. "I do not need to be thinking about my dweeb brother making babies."

I put my pen down and took her phone.

"Hey!"

"Say you're sorry."

"For what?" She reached for the phone, but I held it away.

"He's not a dweeb or a nerd or anything like that."

"He totally is."

"Look at him." I looked, and Sebastian looked right back at me, Rolling Writer in the middle of my name, waiting. "He's gorgeous and cool and . . ." I hesitated because of the company but decided to sell it because I believed it. "Sexy as hell."

Tiffany looked at him for half a second, said, "Ugh!" then went back to her half-assed swirly *C*.

"Say you're sorry for lying."

"Keep the phone."

Dad snickered, and then everyone broke out in laughter. Watching Mom laugh made it all worth it.

We got done just before eleven o'clock. When the game came on, Roy and Dad surrendered their pens and kept each other company. Roy had touched Carol's shoulder as he passed, a gesture that wasn't lost on Sebastian. I kicked him under the table.

"Grown woman," I whispered.

"He called me *son* a dozen times up there."

"I think he likes you."

Tiffany took my distraction as an opportunity to slip her phone away from me.

Mom and Carol shooed everyone away so they could stick on the return address labels "the right way." Sebastian and I went onto the back deck for fresh air. The winter night was cold by Southern California standards, meaning we needed sweaters.

We sat together on the patio couch. I stretched out, putting my foot on the table and leaning my head back on the cushions, looking up at the stars. The wine had made me good and loopy, and I followed the flashing red light of a plane crossing the sky.

"Everyone needs to do their invitations by hand," Sebastian said, shaking his left hand.

"That would put a whole industry out of business."

"But it made your mother happy. I could see how that affected you."

"Was I that obvious?"

"Little bit."

"She cut her hair."

"I like it."

"Dad likes it long. *She* likes it long, except when she's going to lose it. When it's all going to fall out, you cut it so it doesn't clog the drains."

He didn't argue or try to bring back my happy moment.

"You haven't asked me what I wanted to tell you."

"Figure you'll get to it."

I crossed my arms, winding them tightly against the chill.

"I don't think I'll have a job after this season."

"Why's that?"

"They wanted me to write something I didn't want to write."

He turned away from the sky. "Artistic integrity is important. I admire that."

"Yeah, well, it wasn't artistic integrity." I didn't continue until he turned back to the sky. "They wanted me to write about a specific situation." I thought I saw a shooting star, but it moved steadily. A satellite. "Have you seen the 'Delete It' video? Where there's a couple going at it—then she sees he's been making a video the whole time?"

"Heard of it."

"It's terrible, but we dramatize real stories, and this one was put in my lap. I either tell a story I have no right to tell, or I lose my job."

"And?"

"Fuck that job."

"She's back," he said.

"Excuse me?"

"You can see the North Star," he said, pointing. "Pretty unusual with the light pollution."

"I can see it all the time." I leaned close to him and pointed to one of the brightest stars in the sky. "There."

"No. That's Alioth."

"But it's in the Big Dipper, right *there*."

"That bright star at the end of the handle points to it. Follow and it's right"—he moved my hand left—"there."

"Really?"

"I don't lie about stars."

"I can't see it."

"The whole northern sky revolves around it. You can be anywhere in the world and know the right direction based on where she is."

"I bet she has a narcissistic complex."

He laughed, leaning closer to me, shoulder to shoulder.

"My father took me out to the desert one night to show me the Leonid meteor shower. Got me up at one in the morning. Shooting stars whipping across the sky."

"That sounds amazing."

"He was pretty amazing. Carol talks about him like he was a boring guy with nothing going on. But he wasn't. He was interested in everything. Even my mother's crazy spiritual stuff."

"You miss him."

"All the time."

I pointed to a light moving across the sky.

"Where do you think that plane's going?"

"Uh. Hmm. Someone's honeymoon?" He leaned closer.

"Thank you for offering Paris," I said.

"I shouldn't have pushed, but I could use a vacation."

"I want to stay at a cheap place on a narrow cobblestone street. The windows should have flower boxes, and there should be a little balcony with a cast-iron café table."

He sat up and pressed his right thumb into the center of his left palm.

"Even if we cancel the wedding, we can still go on a trip."

Not if I couldn't pay for it. And I wasn't letting him pay.

Sitting straight, I took his hand and put it in my lap. "You have a writing cramp."

I massaged the center of his palm in circles and worked outward.

"I'm fine."

"Shush. It doesn't work if you talk." He had good, strong, masculine hands, and as I kneaded the cramp away, I found myself imagining them on me. I turned it over. The back of his hand was no less appealing, nor his wrist, which also needed attention.

"My mother reads palms . . . try not to be shocked," he said, turning his hand so I could see the creases on the outside of his pinkie. "I'm having four children, apparently."

"That's why she wants you to get started." I turned his hand back to where it was. "Just relax. A cramp isn't just in the hand—it's the entire forearm."

He sat back and let me do my thing, which I was making up as I went. I didn't know anything about hand cramps, except that I'd had plenty as a girl writing stories in legal pad after legal pad. My mother had rubbed the tight muscles and given me Advil to ease the pain.

As I worked his muscles, the diamond ring glittered with every movement. It must have been the wine that was making me so maudlin and goopy, but I was deeply grateful that I got to wear such a beautiful thing for as long as I had.

"Thank you," I said. "You doing this—it means a lot to me."

"It's not that big a deal."

"It is. I'm taking up space in your schedule. Costing you money."

He shot out a little laugh. "Dating's never free."

"Still." My hand pushed a path up his forearm. "There's an opportunity cost."

"There's an opportunity cost to *not* being your fake fiancé too."

I pressed my thumb inside his elbow and worked my way down.

"Yes, well, the opportunity to get cramps handwriting wedding invitations doesn't come around every day."

"Or seeing our names together like that."

Our names.

I could guess what he meant, but I didn't want to. It was all too muddy.

When I got to his dry palm, I was done. He grabbed my hand before I could pull it off.

"Rachel. Look at me."

I did it, because when he asked for something, he was hard to refuse. Half his face was yellow from the kitchen lights. The other half was moonlight blue. He was angular and beautiful, my high school charge, the boy I'd stood in front of a dozen times because he was my friend and neighbor and because I cared about him.

"Do you remember door number two?"

Door number one had been his virginity. His sexual inexperience informed his sexual dexterity.

Did I want to know his other secret? What would that inform?

Out of sheer curiosity, I wanted to know. But no. No, I did not. What I could see of his expression told me volumes. It was a deep, raw thing I wasn't ready to hear. I knew too much already.

I stood like a shot, releasing my hand from his.

I put my fingers on his lips.

"Not yet. Please. I'm not ready."

He pressed my fingers to his lips and kissed them. His eyes closed as his lips lingered, sending a shot of arousal down my spine before he let me go.

"Not yet, then."

CHAPTER 36

SEBASTIAN

Not yet.

When, then?

Let's face it.

Never was the answer.

"You look tired, honey," Carol said, packing the stuffed envelopes in a box. "You should stay the night." Rachel came in with a cloth to wipe the wine crescents from the tabletop. Mom addressed her. "Don't you think?"

"Yeah. Probably." She stretched to get the surface end to end, and all I could do was stare at the way her body moved. "Even with no traffic, it's ninety minutes."

"You guys going to make it home all right?" Rachel's father asked as he entered from the kitchen.

"It's late," my lovely fiancée said. "I'll leave in the morning."

Her dad gave me a nice bit of stink eye. I'd grown up across the street from him and knew him well enough to know that thirty years old or thirteen years old, his daughter and I were not married. His look said loud and clear, *Not under my roof.*

"Do you two want to sleep in our basement?" Carol asked. "The couch pulls out into a queen."

Rachel looked at me with eyes wide, frozen at the table's corner.

"No," we said in unison.

"She has work to do," I said at the exact same time as she said, "He has to get up early," which exacerbated the problem by implying we'd be fucking so much she wouldn't be able to get any work done and I'd be too tired to get up in the morning.

The suspension of voices was so sudden and complete the only sound in the room was the crickets outside.

"Well, then," Carol said, hoisting the box. "You two figure it out. The mailbox place on Hartford is open Sundays. These should go out first thing in the morning."

"No taking it back once the invitations go out," her mother said.

"Better get backsies now," Tiffany said to Rachel.

Rachel halved the wipe between her hands and halved it again, giving me a smile and then glancing at her mother before she answered.

"Better send them before he changes his mind."

I tried to catch a glance, looking for a moment where she committed to this because she had feelings for me, but when I saw her face, I knew she'd answered to send Tiffany a message. She turned, keeping her head down as she went to the kitchen.

Rachel was an open book with a single word on the page.

Fear.

She was afraid for her mother. That was clear. But there was more. For a while, I couldn't tell if she was afraid of being stuck with me or if she was afraid she really liked me enough to go through with it. Then I couldn't tell if she was afraid I'd back out.

Behind door number two was the reason I wasn't afraid.

She was the same Rachel I'd always wanted to marry. From day one, when I was eleven and her family had moved in, I couldn't believe my luck. This gorgeous creature, right across Mandarin Lane. And soon after, her family showed up at my father's wake. She was the only kid from school there. She'd let me cry on her shirt and didn't leave my side for a minute. She made her parents bring her to three wakes and a burial so I'd have a friend around.

I loved her then. I loved her through high school. I loved her even when I was with Tammy, who couldn't change me no matter how hard she tried. Rachel would never ask me to change, but she was so far out of my league I'd never dared to dream she'd want me.

Alone in my old room with the desk lamp on, I stared at the ceiling like I had in high school, thinking about Rachel sleeping across the street. Her bedroom light had gone out an hour ago, but she sat at her desk by the light of her laptop, pounding her dreams into words.

There was a soft knock on my door.

"Yeah?"

Tiffany poked her head in.

"You're up."

"You knocked because you thought I was sleeping?"

"Whatever." She came in. "Hey. Look." She sat on the edge of my desk chair with her phone dangling between her hands. "Uh. I'm sorry."

"For what?"

"Calling you a dweeb all the time."

"It's all right."

"No, it's kind of not. I was talking to Ace—who really likes you, by the way—"

"Is that his real name?"

"Yeah."

"Wow."

"Anyway. I was bitching about Rachel getting on my case, and he said she's right. Which . . . I got mad at him at first, but he's got a point." She rolled her eyes. "Which is whatever, but he said it's not nice, especially in front of your fiancée. He said I was being alpha and staking out territory I felt like she was invading. He said you're not my territory, and if I wanted to piss on something, I should piss on him."

"Whoa . . ."

"Not literally, asshole."

"I know that. I mean, that's kind of romantic. At least . . . from a guy who screams and drinks bong water for a living."

"I guess it is." She flipped her phone around between her hands. "The thing is, like, I'm twenty-four, and I still live here, and I feel like I'm keeping it together. The family. You were living in NorCal for a long time, and you came back, but you're still gone. It's just me and Carol. And I felt like . . . if you were a dweeb then, you'd still be my brother. Maybe you'd come back, and we could be all together like always."

I sat up. "Is this Ace talking? Or you?"

"It came out when I talked to him. He's a really good listener. He's getting his PhD in psychology from USC."

"Wow again."

"But anyway. I'm glad you're happy. And you're worthy of being loved." She rolled her eyes. "Those were Ace's words, but I don't have better ones, so that's fine." She stood up. "Deal with it."

I stood before she could leave.

"Can I have a hug?"

She sneered but threw her arms around me. I ruffled her hair when I let her go. "You're all right, Tiff."

"Whatever."

After she clicked the door behind her, I was ready to resume my view of the ceiling when I caught sight of the laptop light in Rachel's bedroom window. It was one in the morning, and she was still at it.

I was worthy of her love.

She knew I was going to tell her I loved her, and she'd avoided me.

What was the point of being worthy of her love if she didn't know how to accept mine?

CHAPTER 37

RACHEL

JAKE
I've been lost all these years, but whenever I looked at the sky, I knew you were there. Everything pointed to you. You're the still point at the center of my universe. You're my North Star, Amy, and I love you.

"Viral Love" was in the trash heap of my mind, but "Broken Promises" was on fire. The first and only romance I'd ever written was getting as sharp and clear as any unproduced, invisible script would ever be.

Sebastian's light went out at one fifteen or so. I tapped out a few texts to him but, in a show of Herculean discipline, deleted them without sending. I was supposed to be writing, not fucking around.

I fought sleep but collapsed sometime after three. In the morning, I checked my phone right away. No texts.

Sebastian's car wasn't in Carol's driveway. Neither was hers. She'd sent the invitations out.

No backsies.

"Seb left without saying goodbye," Mom said, pouring me coffee. "Did you guys have a fight?"

"No, I just . . ." What could it be? Bad enough we hadn't braved a ride home to sleep in the same bed. "He had something to take care of at the office."

"On a Sunday?"

"Foreign markets." I blurted out the most logical lie for the guy I knew but a terrible lie for the animator she knew. "Anyway, I like your hair. I didn't tell you."

She smiled and patted it. "Eggs for breakfast?"

I called Sebastian once I was on the 5.

"Hey," he said into my headset.

"You left."

"Carol was making millet toast for breakfast, and I decided to avoid it."

"Good call."

He didn't add anything else. Just silence.

"I told a fib about you," I said. "To my mother."

"Like?"

"I told her you went home early because of foreign markets."

I was hoping he'd tell me why, exactly, he'd run out.

"It's fine."

He wasn't talking as if he wanted to get off the phone, and he didn't sound angry, but I knew when a guy was being distant.

"Is everything all right?" I asked.

"Yeah."

"You sure?"

"What's the next thing we have to do?"

I scanned my internal calendar.

"We're meeting the minister on Friday evening."

"Great. I'll see you then."

Was he going to hang up? My deep well of panic bubbled.

"Wait."

"Yeah?"

What did I want out of him? A little warmth, at least.

What was I entitled to?

I wasn't sure. I was an old friend and a fake fiancée with a four-pound diamond on my finger.

"We should meet before then," I said.

"Why?"

Okay, that was it. Something was off with him. He was being defensive. I replayed the previous night and couldn't find a reason for it.

He waited for an answer. No filler. No small talk. Six lanes of traffic were Sunday-morning clear, and I couldn't think of why I wanted to see him, except that I did.

"Seb, can you just tell me what's on your mind?"

From his side, I heard the suck and whoosh of a screen door opening, then the chirp of birds. He must have moved onto his patio.

"Door number two is on my mind."

"Tell me, then."

"You didn't want to know."

"If I knew it would bother you, I would have wanted you to tell me."

After a pause, he said, "Secret number two has nothing to do with one."

"Okay."

"It's the scariest one."

"Don't be scared."

"I'm not scared. You are."

"You know what?" I clicked my blinker and moved toward the freeway exit. "I can't do this while I'm driving."

"Do what?"

"Show you I'm not scared." I got off the 5 at Dana Point. "I'm going to pull over. Give me a second."

"You're a piece of work, Rachel Rendell. Do you know that?"

"I've been told."

I parked the car by the beach. The marine layer hung over the horizon like a screen. A couple walked on the beach, circled by a loping hound chasing birds. A jogger huffed along the concrete path.

"Okay," I said, getting out of the car. The air was damp and cool, but the fog kept it still. I sat on a bench overlooking the water and put my feet on the iron railing. "I'm here. Give me door number two."

"I didn't want to say this over the phone, but maybe it's for the best."

"You can say it again when I see you."

He cleared his throat. "So."

"So."

I didn't fill the space anymore because he needed it. I listened to the chirp of birds on his side of the phone and the squawk of seagulls on mine, but I didn't say another thing.

"So," he said, finally, "when you guys moved in across Mandarin, I was probably the most miserable person who ever lived."

I had a million snarky responses and a few preferable uplifting things to say. With more discipline than I thought I had, I kept my mouth shut.

"I had no friends," he continued. "I had to outrun Scott and his gang both to and from school. But you showed up, and you were interested in me. Even when you made other friends and you could ditch me, you didn't. I kept waiting for you to turn your back on me, and you never did."

He was making me into a hero, and I wasn't. I'd just been a lonely person with a few friends. I'd enjoyed his company, but I'd stuck by him because he'd made me feel useful. That wasn't noble motivation.

"Rachel, are you there?"

"It wasn't a big deal," I said. "I'm not a saint."

"No, you weren't, I guess. But to me you were. And you were beautiful on top of it. So I did what any kid like me would do."

Another long pause. Another jogger passed. The dog chased the birds. A truck passed on the 5.

"I fell in love with you."

I wasn't shocked by the news. We'd been adolescents. He was a nerd, and I was the only girl who gave him the time of day. I was a natural object for his urges between eleven and eighteen. So no, I wasn't shocked he'd loved me then. I was shocked by the gravity with which he delivered the news at thirty years old.

"I don't . . . ," he started, then redirected, talking faster and more convincingly with each phrase. "I never stopped loving you. It went dormant when we were apart, but when I saw you again, it was still there. I'm going through with this wedding because I never got a chance to make my father happy before he died and because your mother means a lot to me. But it's also because I love you. I've always loved you, and the problem . . . the real problem . . . is that you don't love me."

I was caught with my mouth open, waiting for the right words to come out. I was facing the sea and the people on the beach, but I didn't see them. I was searching my mind for words and coming up empty.

"I just scared you," he said. His screen door whooshed and slapped, cutting off the birds. "I'm sorry, but not really."

"No. I'm fine."

I was fine in that I was breathing, but I was detached from a decent human reaction to what he'd just told me.

"I need some time to think," he said.

I was supposed to say something, but I didn't know what it should entail. Comfort? Love? Hope? Potential? How could I know what to say if I wasn't sure how I felt?

"I'll be at the meeting with the minister," he said.

"All right."

"I'll see you then."

"Yeah . . ." I was going to say his name and stop him from hanging up. Just put this whole conversation on a slower track. I felt like I was grabbing at dollar bills in a wind tunnel. "Seb . . ."

He'd already hung up.

CHAPTER 38

RACHEL

I hadn't seen Sebastian in years before Christmas, but that week felt just as long. My mother collected RSVPs and assured me that they'd be ready to hit the ground running when they got back from Tahoe.

"Are you sure?"

"Of course I'm sure!"

She sounded way too chipper. I thought the lady was protesting too much, but I let her think she was fooling me.

"I haven't seen your new pages on 'Viral,'" CJ said over lunch, picking the cheese out of her salad.

I shrugged. "It's not ready."

"I don't expect it to be."

"I—" The rest didn't come out. She looked to me with such complete interest and attention, like always. CJ had invested her time and reputation in me, and I was about to disappoint her.

Not today.

I changed the subject.

"How's 'Hedging His Bets' coming?"

One thing about writers: we loved stories. We thrived on picking them apart and rearranging them. We could do it all damn day.

"Okay." She popped a forkful of feta in her mouth and chewed while she thought. "Enemies-to-lovers trope. He gets a court order to hire a diversity specialist, and she's the first applicant."

"Because he doesn't really care."

"No, because he put it off, and the deadline is the next morning."

"And she hates him."

"No, he was her high school crush."

"So he makes her job impossible."

I was breaking a cardinal rule of etiquette. You could interrupt to encourage the conversation, but not to second-guess the writer.

"No. Rachel?"

"I'm sorry." I straightened, ready to listen. "Go ahead."

"Later." She waved her fork at me. "It's not ready anyway. What's going on?"

"It was a lie." I pushed my sandwich away. "The wedding and everything around it. Tell me your pitch. I'll shut up."

"Mm, nope." She got to the lettuce, put a big forkful in her mouth, chewed, and swallowed, leaving me in suspense. "The hot guy and the fake wedding. Let's hear it."

"I can't. It's too icky."

"Pitch it to me." She twirled her fork. "Out with it."

Taking another bite of sandwich, I used my chew time to put it together. It had a sense but—obviously—no ending.

"So you got the part with the marriage contract, and they were friends when they were kids?"

"Yup."

"Her heart's been broken a hundred times, so she's not looking for a guy, but she asks him to do the planning because her mother wants her to be settled so bad. So they figure, they make all the plans; then when her mom goes into remission, they call off the wedding. He agrees to it because he cares about her mother and because his dad died when he was little, and he felt like he never had a chance to make him proud. At least that's what he says, and it's true enough. So they do all the things. They hire a band and get a hall. They're . . . intimate." My face burst into prickly heat. "And she likes him. He's so honest. There's zero bullshit."

"That's a fresh take."

"No joke. This is new for her. She doesn't have to be a detective or pick apart every word. It just is what it is. I mean, it's all a lie, but a straightforward one. She's getting into it, but that kind of honesty is a little scary, you know? Because she has to reciprocate, and that means she's setting herself up to be hurt. Again."

"I'm assuming your set pieces are getting the wedding together? Renting the hall, getting the band, et cetera?"

"Yeah. Exactly. But, so, at one point he tells her in this completely forthright way that he's going along with it for all the reasons he said, but also because he loved her from when they were kids, and he still loves her. And this is where it goes wrong because in romance, *he's* supposed to run away scared. But no. She's the one who loses it."

"That's fine. You're still in trope."

"And—God. I want ice cream. I'm realizing what a cliché this is."

"You mean that when he pulls away, you realize that you love him?"

"I don't know if she loves him yet, but she wants to love him, and she knows she could love him if it wasn't all based on lying."

"But he's pulling away, and now you have to win him back?"

I shook my head. Not because CJ was wrong. She was spot on about how it would work on TV, but in reality?

"That's too easy," I said.

"Not when it's your life, honey." She jabbed her salad until her fork was loaded. "When it's your life, easy is the goal. What's the next set piece?"

"We're interviewing the minister."

"When's the wedding?"

"Four weeks, give or take."

"Hmm." She chewed thoughtfully. "Last of the second act. It'll get worse before it gets better."

"Great. Just great."

I knew the tropes inside out, but in real life, I wasn't sure I could stand it getting worse.

The happy couple met at the Episcopal church on Grove. Sebastian was already in the office, across the desk from Father Jamie, laughing at a joke I hadn't heard. My fiancé wore a dark-blue jacket and jeans, clean pressed, neat, like he wanted to make a good impression.

He stood when I entered, put his hand on my arm, and kissed my cheek. His cologne was astringent and clean, and I found myself leaning in to him to take another breath. When he broke the kiss, he didn't look at me.

We made our introductions. Sebastian didn't make eye contact when he scooted my chair out to sit.

Jamie insisted we call him by his first name. He was in his fifties, with rich dark skin and a slightly musical Jamaican accent. We had to convince him we were real. A pitch. I wasn't in the right headspace for the con game, but I didn't have a choice.

"So," he said, "I like to get a sense of the couple before I officiate. Why don't you tell me something about yourselves. How did you meet?"

"We lived across the street as kids." I twirled my lying diamond. "Walked to and from school together."

"Rachel saved me from a few of the class bullies."

"It wasn't that big a deal. It's what anyone would have done."

"No one did it before her."

"Anyway," I interrupted, "he went to school in Palo Alto. I went to NYU. Blah blah. Time and distance."

I looked over at his profile. I'd seen him from that angle a hundred times walking home, and it was the same but different. Sharper. Sexier. Even clean shaven it was more masculine. I could love that jawline. I could bury my face under his chin and take in that cologne until I fell for him completely.

I was swooning. I didn't swoon. Swooning was gross, but for once I didn't resist it. Swooning kept me from thinking about my impending job loss.

"We saw each other again at Christmas," he said. "And for me at least, I loved her the same as I did when we were in high school."

He turned to me, and I saw a profound sadness. I turned back to Jamie.

"The rest is history."

The pause was like a water balloon filled under a dripping faucet. I didn't realize what I'd done until it was near bursting.

"Have you thought about your vows?" Jamie said, finally. "You going to write your own?"

"The standard's fine." Sebastian's voice was tight.

"Yeah," I added, glancing at his profile, then back to Jamie. "That's fine."

The pastor leaned back and knotted his hands over his chest.

"I've married thousands of couples," he said. "And I can tell on the first meeting who's going to make it." He pointed back and forth between us. "You two have something. You're going to be together into your dotage."

My reaction was unscripted. An unwilling signal from my heart to my mind. I burst with a happiness that filled my chest and stretched an involuntary smile across my face.

Sebastian cleared his throat. "Can you excuse me?"

He spun out of his chair and walked out. I looked at Jamie, not knowing if we could continue the interview without him.

"Go," he said. "Go to him."

I thanked him and followed Sebastian. He'd gone outside to a little garden courtyard with a Saint Francis fountain and stone paths around flower beds.

"Seb!" I rushed to his side. "Are you all right?"

"I'm fine. I just needed some air. We can go back in now."

He started back to the door, but I wasn't ready to go back to that room.

"Did you think?" I asked. He stopped walking, his back to me, shoulders straight, hands down. "You said you needed time to think. Did you?"

He turned.

"Yeah."

"What did I say that hurt you?"

"'The rest is history'? And then you come out here and ask about what's right in front of you? I know you got screwed over. I know you've been dumped and hurt. But you don't get to use me to make yourself feel better."

"That's not . . ."

I stopped my denial.

Was he right?

"No," I said. He wasn't right. "You're a lot, Sebastian. You go right for the guts, and that's fine, but my guts aren't used to being exposed and prodded all the time. Which is a disgusting analogy. I'm sorry. But I don't have another one right now."

"It was easier to love you from afar."

"Yeah, well, everything's easier from afar."

In two steps, he was toe to toe with me.

"I loved you when we were friends. I love you as my fiancée. I'll love you when we cancel the wedding. But when I think about the fact that you don't love me . . . it doesn't make me happy. That's all."

Maybe him walking off before I could answer was an act of self-preservation, but it hurt all the same.

CHAPTER 39

RACHEL

"Hello?" Ruth snapped her fingers by my ear. "You're melting."

Shaking the fog out of my head, I jabbed my spoon into the vanilla. It went right in. I'd been staring into space long enough to turn rock-hard Häagen-Dazs into a thick paste.

Ruth was next to me on the couch, poking at her phone with one hand and eating ketchup-flavored Pringles with the other.

"You were talking about Zoe," I said.

"She said when I contacted her, she jumped at the phone. It reminded her that she loved acting. So—"

"She's acting again?"

"We're sending her on auditions again."

"Wow, that's awesome."

"You did good," she said, shuffling the chips to the top of the can.

"Totally unintentional. But maybe she'll put in a good word for me when she lands a role, since I won't have a job unless I hand in 'Viral Love . . . ,' which I won't."

"What's happening with Sebastian?" She had a shade of suspicion in her voice, as if losing my job wasn't quite ice cream worthy.

"He's been weird."

"Like tinfoil-hat weird?"

I sighed and put the container on the coffee table. I couldn't explain his weirdness without explaining my own. I grabbed a pillow and hugged it.

"Our engagement is a lie. I'm sorry. It was . . . is all a big lie."

She put her phone down. "What kind of lie?"

"My mother's cancer is back." Tears formed and fell in a single blink. "And we felt like getting engaged would make her happy."

"Oh. My. God."

"Please don't be mad."

"Rachel."

"I loved the bachelorette party."

"No. Your mother."

"I know." I wiped tears off my cheek. "But did you see how happy she was? Sticking a five in a G-string like she didn't have a care in the world?"

Ruth bounced off the couch and came back with a roll of toilet paper. I unspooled a length and blew my nose.

"I'm so sick of crying about it," I said. "But then there was him, and I didn't have to cry. He made me happy."

"So you broke up?"

"Not yet!" My voice cracked. "I mean . . . no. But he thinks I don't love him, and I'm not sure anyway, but I probably maybe do."

"Probably maybe?"

"Why isn't that good enough?" I balled up the paper and tossed it on the coffee table. "I don't even know what I'm crying over. Him or my mother."

"So." Ruth tucked her pedicured feet deeper into the cushions. "The fake-wedding thing is a little crazy."

"Totally crazy."

"But it makes sense now. You know how I met Mario?"

"He was your personal trainer." I unrolled more toilet paper to get at the last of my tears.

"He was my personal trainer when we were trying to get my sister into rehab," she corrected. "She almost killed herself twice with opioids, and we were like this." She crossed two fingers. "But she hated me because I wanted to 'put her away.' So on the outside I was this." She indicated her perfectly made and polished self. "But inside, I was a mess twenty-four seven. Mess. I was like a lobster they cut down the middle, spread open, and put on a plate meat side up. And one day I was working out with him, and he pushed me too hard with the sit-ups. I broke right in the gym. Like, bam. Crying and yelling. Right in front of him. He carried me to the locker room. It was so sweet. I fell in love with him right there."

"So you're saying I'm upset about Sebastian because of my mother? That it's not real?"

"No. I'm saying when you're open like that is when you can let someone in. And it's real. Really real. The realest." She plucked a couple of Pringles from the stack. "These things are gross."

"I don't know what I feel."

She stuffed the two chips in her mouth without losing a crumb.

"You love him."

"I do?"

"When you got a lap dance, he thought it was funny and cute. He trusts you. You trust him. Your face lights up like the Sunset Strip whenever you talk about him. Please." She pressed her finger against the inside of the can to pick up the dust. "I don't even care if the wedding is fake. Everything else is real." She kissed the flavored crumbs from the pad of her finger. "Mm. So bad and good. What are you going to do about your mother?"

"Nothing, I guess. Keep her happy until she's better."

"Wrong."

"Wrong?"

"Wrong. You let her live her life, and you tell Sebastian you love him." Ruth waggled her perfectly shaped eyebrows. "Valentine's Day is in two days!"

She was right. The most romantic day of the year was the perfect time to win him back.

CHAPTER 40

SEBASTIAN

Valentine's Day with Tammy had usually started with church and ended after a heart-shaped dessert shared by her entire family. I could count on getting a couple of dirty words out of her at the end of the night, but it was never hearts and flowers. If she got roses, everyone got roses. Rules.

So I hadn't given the Valentine's loop much thought. I knew it was happening from the dozen roses on Seema's desk and the gold heart balloons on the back of her assistant's chair. But even after Rachel texted, I didn't connect Valentine's Day with having anything to do with me personally.

—Are you in the office today?—

—Yes—

The one-word answers without follow-up questions such as "Why do you ask?" were hard to maintain at first. But if I distracted myself right away, I could resist the urge.

The flowers came at lunchtime. One dozen reds with balloons in the shape of Xs and Os.

"Well, well," Seema said when they arrived on my desk. "That's romantic. Rachel, I assume?"

"It's nothing," I said, figuring the gesture was to be shared with our families so we could continue this ridiculous charade. I opened the card.

Dear Sebastian,
Happy Valentine's Day!
Rachel

I'd been right. The gesture was empty. For show. No more than a signal to the world at large.

"It's nothing." I folded the card away.

Rachel's text came in a few minutes later. I was alone in the office.

—Did you get the flowers?—

—Yeah. I'll put them on IG later so Tiffany sees it and shows Carol who will show your mother—

She called.

"Hey," I said. "What's up?"

"You don't have to IG them."

"What's the point otherwise?"

"I—" The vowel came out like a hiccup before she cut herself off. I continued working, clacking keys to put in a rush order of two dozen roses and a basket. "I was trying to be romantic."

"I know. I get it. We're good." I was already on the Forgetful Dude website. "I'm having roses sent to you. You like chocolate, right?"

"Duh. I'm human."

"I'll take that as a yes."

Click. Large box of chocolate.

"I thought you'd like them," she said.

"It was a sensible idea under the circumstances. Thanks for reminding me."

Seema came in with her phone tucked under her ear. She snapped her fingers at me and mouthed, *Need you.*

"I have to go," I said to Rachel.

"Okay. Bye."

I hung up and gave Seema my attention so I didn't have to think about her card.

CHAPTER 41

RACHEL

I hung up.

That hadn't gone well.

What else did I have to do? How did I go about this? More roses? A card? A serenade?

His roses and chocolates came to the front desk. They were lost in the sea of flowers and balloons to writing and production. I carried the vase back to my desk in one arm as I tossed the heart-shaped box on the writer's table with the other. It landed next to three other heart-shaped boxes we were going to share, because who could eat an entire box of chocolate by themselves?

Maybe I needed to go bigger. Bigger balloons. More flowers. Just an extraordinary number of flowers. Wall-to-wall red roses.

"Get the permits." I heard Sandra from the hallway. "I don't care who you have to bribe. We don't have time to rewrite it. Go!"

Erin, one of our location specialists, trotted away.

"What happened?"

"'Love in a Click,'" she said with her hands on her hips, stating the title of the episode we were shooting. "The Hollywood sign's trademarked, apparently."

The final scene in this actor-falls-for-paparazza script had the hero taking his new love to the top of the Hollywood sign in the second act so that for his grand gesture, he could ask her to meet him there during his Oscar acceptance speech. If she still wanted him, of course. And of course she did.

"Do you want to start a rewrite just in case?"

"What's he going to do?" She paced to her office, and I followed. "Send her a dozen goddamn roses?" She stepped behind her desk and slapped her script down before quickly snapping two lengths of tape off the dispenser. "Happy Valentine's Day, by the way."

"Yeah," I said, suddenly realizing where I'd fallen short with Sebastian. "You too."

The day wasn't over yet.

Waiting outside his apartment building was kind of stalkerish. It was weird and rude. It pushed the boundaries of respect and common sense. Somewhere in the past few hours my sense of decency had taken a back seat to a frenzied need to get this right. His car turned the corner at 7:14 p.m. and stopped at the head of the driveway while the gate rattled open.

"You got this," I said to myself before I bolted out of the car as if it were on fire. He was already walking toward me, door open and beeping behind him.

"What are you doing?" he asked.

"I'm kidnapping you."

He tilted his head slightly, eyebrows knotted. I jerked my thumb behind me. "Get in my car." The gate clacked and stopped when it was all the way open. "Please."

"What's this about, Rachel?"

"It's about time."

"I don't want to ruin it," I said, turning into Griffith Park. The night was crystal clear with a slight bite to the air. "But you'll like it. I swear."

"I trust you."

"You do?"

"Mostly."

I parked the car in an empty space. "We have twenty-three minutes."

"The observatory," he said. "It's like you know me."

"Just like it." I popped the trunk. "Help me carry the stuff."

I laid out a serape Ruth had gotten me when she'd gone on a trip to Cabo. Sebastian laid the cardboard box on it. The lawn at the top of the hill behind the Griffith Park Observatory was dotted with blankets. Kids ran across the grass, chasing each other's glow sticks. The stargazing telescope in the dome was open to the public, and a line snaked out the little brass door inside.

The wineglasses clinked when Sebastian removed them. I spread out the cheese and bread while he uncorked.

"You didn't have to do this, Rachel. The roses were enough."

"But you don't even know what *this* is, do you?"

"A really nice picnic at the observatory." He poured.

"Better. There's a lunar eclipse tonight." A kid ran right at us and leaped over the blanket. "Partial. Really partial."

"Ah, I forgot!" For the first time since I'd picked him up, he seemed more than just generally pleased.

"They're shutting the floods right before to cut the light pollution." I tipped my glass to him, and we clinked. "Some lady on Twitter said it will be cool."

"Twitter knows all."

Silhouetted against the lights of the observatory, he tipped his wine into his mouth. A simple sip I watched with all the amazement of a woman seeing a great movie for the first time. I'd admitted to a feeling of romance. A gushy, pleasingly melancholy sensation that unhooked all the armor I'd built, and just looking at him made me want to rip that shield to pieces.

"I realized the roses were kind of . . ." I looked for the word. Trite? Cookie cutter? Obvious? Was I trying to be cool? Or was I trying to give him a gift? "Roses aren't really romantic."

"You tried. The question is . . . why?"

My first instinct was to deny, deny, deny. Cover it over with a clever turn of phrase. I had to resist that impulse.

I took a gulp of wine and laid the glass on the tray.

I wished I could see more of his expression. Or maybe the fact that I couldn't see his face in the dark was a blessing. I could imagine whatever I wanted.

Lying back, I looked at the sky above. He put down his glass and stretched out next to me. I could hear the chatter of adults and the laughter of children all around.

"I think," I started, pretending to talk to the sky. "I think I dated guys I knew would hurt me. I didn't have to look at myself then. I didn't have to think about where I was . . . I guess . . . failing to . . . why am I at a loss for words?"

Sebastian didn't answer. He took my hand and held it between us.

"I didn't have to get close to them or share anything," I said, "because I was always waiting for the other shoe to drop. And it always did. But you're different. There's no shoe. I didn't have to be afraid, so I didn't know how to feel."

The floodlights went out with a clap. Children giggled and screamed. Parents called them close. The moon was a glowing white disk above us.

"See how it's red at the edge?" Sebastian pointed with his free hand. "It's starting."

"That's cool."

"I didn't mean to scare you," he said.

"You're pretty overwhelming."

"When I shut you out, I wasn't trying to make it worse. I was trying to make it better."

The red section of the moon widened as if there were a dust storm on the surface.

"When we get married," I said, turning away from the sky to his dark profile, "I want to give it a try. I don't want to do it just to split up."

He faced me. The moon glinted off the white of his eye.

"Why?"

Not the question I'd expected.

The defensive answers piled up like too many clauses in a sentence with a single point. Why not / it might be fun / just because / no reason not to / might as well.

They all got crumpled up and tossed into the circular file because they were roses and candy.

"Because . . ." I bit my lip as if there was a part of me that wanted to hold it back. I only had so much strength. Even in the dark I couldn't look at him. I turned back to the moon, which was half-red, with a black bite out of the side. The eclipse was happening right before my eyes, and I hadn't said it yet.

"Because I love you."

He squeezed my hand.

"Are you sure?" he asked as the bite out of the moon got bigger. The edge was sharp and somehow spooky and unnatural.

"What do you mean?"

He laughed. "I mean . . ." He shifted to be closer and whispered in my ear. "Say it again. With feeling. Not like you wish you hadn't said it."

I turned to him. We were nose to nose.

"You want me to pitch it to you?"

"Yes."

"I love you. You make me feel safe. There were years, I know . . . when we were apart. I didn't feel right and didn't know why. I know now."

All the sounds and voices drifted far away, as if a bag had been put over them.

"I just can't be right without you. You remind me of who I'm supposed to be. Even if I'm not that. I can accept a life where I never become the person I wanted to be, and every plan I ever made goes bad . . . as long as I'm with you. You don't make me who I *want* to be. No. You make me who I'm *supposed* to be. Is that love?"

"I don't know," he said. "But I hope it is."

"I think it is. I know it is."

We kissed under the light of the moon as the earth moved out of the way of the sun, and it brightened to full again. I always thought love was exciting and thrilling. Maybe sometimes it was, but when I let him hold me, I felt nothing but relief, as if I'd come home after a long journey in the dark.

"I think it's done," he said, looking up at the sky.

"Was it good for you?"

"Amazing. Now. Pack up. You're coming to my house. You're going to forget any other man ever touched you."

I drove. The ride to his place was short but torturous.

Once we were going, he climbed into the seat behind me.

"What are you doing?"

"Pay attention to the road." He reached to the front and put his hands on my neck, whispering in my ear. "If it gets too hard to drive, say so."

"What—"

I couldn't finish. His hands were on my breasts, thumbs brushing against the bumps of my nipples. They twisted into pebbles.

"When we get back," he said, "I'm going to undress you slowly. I'm going to touch every inch of your body with my hands, then my mouth. If you squirm too much, I'm going to keep you on the edge until you stay still."

"That's . . ." I swallowed hard as he burrowed his hands under my shirt and bra. "That's cocky of you."

"Like I said. I'm a virgin. I'm not inexperienced."

"Left at the light?" I just wanted to be alone with him.

"You've been to my place before."

"I'm suddenly forgetting everything."

"Left. Then right into the driveway. I'll put the code in."

He plucked my breasts from behind until I stopped at the gate. He got out and opened it, drenched in my headlights. I parked behind his Porsche and cut the engine.

In the quiet dark before he opened my door, my breaths came out in gasps, and the whole of my body was tuned toward the ache between my legs. How was I not going to fuck him tonight?

—

We were barely in the door when we fell into each other, kissing two feet from the door as if we wanted to enter each other's bodies through our mouths. I went for his shirt buttons, but he pulled my hands away.

"What?" I said.

He reached down and scooped me up, carrying me to his bedroom.

"You forgot already," he said. "First, I undress you."

"And then you touch me all over."

He put me on my feet, facing his bed. It was high off the floor and neatly made. Glass doors leading to a deck let the moonlight in through sheer curtains.

From behind me, he pulled my shirt off with his palms running up my body, up my arms as they were raised. He unhooked my bra and let it drop to the floor. Keeping his promise, he touched every inch of exposed flesh. My nipples stood at attention when he drew four fingers over them.

"You're sexier than I ever imagined," he whispered in my ear before coming around me. He sat on the bed, pulling me between his spread knees. He looked up at me.

He laid his mouth on one, circling with his tongue before pressing his lips closed and sucking.

"Oh . . . ," I squeaked. I couldn't hold myself up. A channel between his mouth and my clit had opened up. He sucked one and kneaded the other, then switched sides, sending me into a twitching, blinding state of near orgasm.

"You like it."

"I love it."

He unbuttoned my jeans and gently pushed me back a step. He got on his knees in front of me and slowly pushed my pants down, getting my underwear at the same time. His fingertips brushed the space between my cheeks, inside my thighs, the backs of my knees, then my ankles. I stepped out of the jeans, then helped him get my socks off.

"I want you to get undressed," I said.

"I will." He kneeled before me, kissing my belly and hips, the triangle between my legs, running a hand between my thighs. "Open your legs, Rachel. I want to taste you."

When I spread my feet apart, he kissed inside my thighs and flicked his tongue over my swollen clit. I gasped.

He looked up at me, a sneaky hand drifting along the crack of my butt.

"I hope you don't need sleep tonight." His fingers slid between, finding where I was dripping wet but not entering me.

"No. I'm fine."

I had work in the morning, and I did not give a single shit.

Putting one of my legs over his shoulder, he said, "First one's just to make the rest last longer." He put his face between my legs and two fingers inside me. He licked and sucked, adding a finger inside until I came so hard I almost fell.

He held me up, and before I could even catch my breath, he guided me to sit on the edge of the bed. I watched him methodically undress until he was standing in front of me naked with a liquid-tipped erection. I wrapped my hand around the base of it and looked up at him.

I rolled my tongue over the salty liquid at his tip and kissed it, and after running my saliva all over it until every inch was glistening, I opened my mouth and took him down my throat.

"Jesus," he said through his teeth. I gave him three long thrusts, then popped off to breathe. "Fuck, Rachel."

"Have you never been deep throated before?"

"Not like that."

I went down on him again. He dug his fingers in my hair as I pressed my nose against his tight stomach. Again and again I took him until he jerked away with a gasp.

"Come down my throat," I said, holding him by the base. "I can take it."

"You're so sexy." He tightened his fist on my hair, and I took him until he bent over, grunting and then expelling a hiss as he came in a thick acidic stream.

I let it run down my throat, swallowing the last drops that landed on my tongue.

He pushed me back and landed on top of me.

"Let me kiss that mouth."

He kissed me, tongue trailing where his dick had just been. It was hard against my thigh in no time.

"Spread your legs," he said between kisses.

"Wait."

Instead of answering, he pressed my knees open. I was game. I was on birth control. I wanted nothing more than to feel him inside me. There was no real reason to wait for the wedding.

"Seb . . . we're not waiting."

"We are." He put the length of his erection along the length of my folds with the head at my clit and, leaning on his hands, pushed forward, moving the hood of my clit away to expose the most sensitive, tender parts.

"Okay," I gasped. He slid himself against me, both of us warm and lubricated. "Oh, God."

I got it now. I moved against him, stimulating myself against his shaft as he moved above me. I put my hands on his face, and he kissed the inside of my wrist.

Other things. This was part of other things.

It must have taken a massive amount of discipline not to shift slightly and enter me, but he kept using the surface of his dick to rub my throbbing clit.

"Faster," I said. "Do it faster."

"Look at you, though." He got down on his elbows. "You're so close."

"I am. Please go faster."

He rotated his hips, giving me a new sensation.

"In a minute."

"Please."

"Do you love me?"

"Yes. Yes, I love you."

"That's not going to make me let you come."

"Please," I begged, looking him in the eye. "I love you, but please."

He pushed hard against me, sliding against my pussy with skillful deliberation, then stroking again. And again. Moving faster. He bent his head, and when he straightened, his eyes were crunched closed.

The sight of him over me, tensed in pleasure as he shifted faster and faster, pushed me into orgasm. My muscles tensed, and my fingers dug into his back. I arched against him, hips jerking in an uncontrolled rhythm.

The base of his cock pulsed. He grunted again and spurted on my belly.

When he was done, he dropped his weight on me and kissed my neck, thanking me and telling me how much he loved me.

It was the best sex I'd ever had.

CHAPTER 42

SEBASTIAN

I was having a hard time focusing on work. The restraint it had taken to not enter her the night before had drained my reserves of discipline. My mind kept drifting back to the taste of her body and the sound of her voice when she said my name. She made every syllable sound filthy. It was better than the dirtiest dirty talk. I tried to leave her alone at work, but I didn't make it to lunch.

—I'm supposed to text you and thank you for last night—

She didn't text back until almost one.

—But you don't want to?—

—It seems inadequate—

I was tapping out a suitably wordy and corny addition when she texted back.

—You don't have an inadequate bone in your body—

I deleted my flowery response. She'd gotten it right. Directness was the heart and soul of romance.

—I want to see you tonight—

—Can't—

Three dots appeared before I could accept her denial with a petulant *okay* or *fine*.

—Wanna know why?—

—Nope

Joking—

—I'm going to get a dress with Mom later than I'd planned because—

The dots came and then disappeared without a message.

—Rachel?—

—They're doing a table read of the script about the video which isn't done and never will be . . . by me at least—

She'd stuck to her guns. Rock solid. A warrior. I slid my drawings of her from under a pile. The way she was when we were teens and the way she was now, with that laptop for armor. I dug around my drawer for an eraser and found one as her next text came.

—Now it's too late for anyone to write it so I'm blocking out time to get yelled at and fired—

What to say? I couldn't promise her it would all be worth it. But I could erase the fuck out of that laptop and roll her free hands into fists.

—I'm proud of you—

Seema came in and sat across from me. I hid the drawings like a teenager busted for looking at porn.

"Hey," I said, clearing my throat. "How was the meeting?"

"Good morning." She crossed her legs. "It was fine."

"Then why do you have a face like you're on a poster for an action movie?"

"You got into a fight at a club?"

A fight? I hadn't gotten into a fight since I was sixteen. Except that one time.

"It wasn't a fight."

"What was it?"

"I punched someone in the face. He had it coming. Why?"

"Because I heard this rumor, and I didn't believe it." She shook her foot in a rhythm. "But now I think I do."

"Can we just get on with it?"

"Bruce Geraldo from Overland? Is that the guy you punched?"

"He's an asshole."

"I know, but he's friends with Herve from Island Features, who went to Harvard with Kenny from Dominant Funds, and bottom line? Bruce is holding a grudge."

"What kind of grudge?"

"They want you off this deal."

"What about Rachel?"

"Bruce has been bad-mouthing her all over town."

My skin went cold. If Rachel got fired for doing what was in her heart, that was one thing. Losing her job because of my flying fists was something different.

"It's a big account," I said.

"We don't negotiate with terrorists."

I tapped my fingers and leaned back. Of course, as a company, we wouldn't make a personnel decision based on client demands.

A corner of my drawing stuck out from under the pile of paper. I wanted to finish it more than I wanted to do anything else.

"I've been thinking about leaving anyway."

Her head slowly moved from one side to the other as if she was drawing out a long no.

"You don't need me," I said.

A long silence followed, where Seema pushed her mouth to one side of her face as if she was holding back the wrong words.

"I left Bollywood because it was cruel and cutthroat. It ran on revenge and reputation. This is why I'm on the business side. I want to do better. And now you're going to leave because of this? This is the same thing!" She stood and pointed at me. "Do not let this happen. I'll never forgive you. If you bend to this pressure, I'll . . ." She pushed her full lips into a tight line. "I'll punch you in the face."

"Seema."

"Don't *Seema* me."

"Listen." I uncrossed my legs and leaned forward, but I didn't stand. I didn't want to add to the tension or let her think I was confrontational. "Let me figure out what to do about Rachel. I don't want her to lose her job because I popped her ex. Then we can talk."

"You better make it quick, and you better not leave because of this. I swear I'd rather sink this whole thing than be what I hate."

"Give me a few days, all right?"

"All right." She crossed her arms. "I'm sorry I said I'd punch you."

"You're not the first." I came around the desk. "Come on—let me buy you coffee."

Her shoulders relaxed as if a weight had melted off them.

Mine, however, were burdened with the need to make Rachel happy.

—

It took a few phone calls to verify that Bruce was indeed pulling strings to avenge his bloody nose. I'd been a fool to think he'd just let that go.

Calling in favors to counter his moves might work, or it might accelerate the entire thing. Rachel would flip out. She'd flip out if I didn't tell her. She'd flip out if I did. If I left, she'd punch Bruce in the face herself. So I did what any man would do.

I took a drive to Overland Studios.

"Mr. Geraldo is busy," the receptionist said. "May I take your name?"

The waiting room was a large sunken space below the offices above. It was ringed by a balcony with a plexiglass railing. I could hear voices up there and see ambitious people hustling from place to place. Bruce's voice cut through the echoing murmurs. I couldn't hear the words, but I'd recognize it anywhere.

"Tell him I'm on my way up."

Before she could pick up the security phone, I was bounding up the steps. I saw him right away, walking next to a woman in her fifties in a pencil skirt.

"We have to talk," I said.

"Whoa, there, buddy." He stepped back as if I was going to hit him again.

"I'll call security," someone said.

I didn't have a lot of time. When I took a step toward him, a young guy in a suit got between us. I shouted over his shoulder, holding up my hands in surrender.

"I'll quit," I said. "And publicly apologize or whatever you want."

Bruce waved security away and indicated an empty conference room.

"In here, buddy boy."

I straightened my cardigan and walked in. He closed the door behind me.

"You think I want an apology?" He leaned on the sideboard and crossed his arms, looking me up and down as if I was a curiosity. "Nah. You apologize on Twitter or whatever, and I gotta explain how a guy like you got the jump."

"So what do you want?"

"What do I want?"

"To make you leave Rachel alone."

He shook his head with a laugh.

"Dude, she got where she is because of me. She owes me. And what did I get for my trouble? For sticking my neck out for her? I got a shiner and a bunch of unanswered calls. You're gravy. Quit or don't quit. I don't give a fuck. But she used me, and she's not going further in this business. Not on my back." He stood away from the sideboard and uncrossed his arms. "She can start where she was when I met her."

He tapped my arm with his folder as he passed as if we were friends and he was delivering no more than uncomfortable honesty.

"She's too good for you," I said. "And you know it. That's why you have to keep her down. She reminds you of what a shit you are."

Halfway out the door, he faced me with a smug grin. He didn't care if she was a better person. He didn't measure people with the same ruler.

"I'll tell security to be gentle."

As he walked out, two guys in dark jackets and radios picked me up and kicked me out like a sack of potatoes.

That had gone exactly nowhere. I headed back to my car with my head down. You could stand up to a bully, but you couldn't play him at his own game. Bruce had too much practice being an asshole.

CHAPTER 43

RACHEL

Romancelandia ***Table Read***

"I'm going to say something to you, and you're going to stay still long enough to listen."

The actor's name was Ben Winthrop. He'd done some soaps and bit parts in movies. He sat at the long table reading from the script with the staff writers, the director of the episode, and the showrunner, Sandra, who hadn't read the script because the writer had handed them out at the last minute. That person would be me at the end of the table with shaking hands.

That person had put the "Viral Love" cover page on "Broken Promises."

Tamara East, the actress playing the heroine, read her line.

"Mention the stars one time, and I'm out of here." Then Tamara muttered, off script, "You go, girl."

"I'm giving it to you straight," Ben said. "No stars. No flowers. Because I'm not trying to convince you of anything but the truth. I love you. I loved you in high school, and I love you now. I love *us* together. And if you don't love me anymore, I don't blame you. But nothing you do . . . you can slap me in the face right now and walk away . . . nothing's going to make me stop loving you."

"What if I don't love you?"

"Ouch," Sharon whispered next to me with a nod. Ouch was *good*. We were three-quarters of the way in, there was no viral video, and she said *ouch*.

"But you do," Ben read. "You do, and it scares you."

Sharon read, "Amy turns on her heel and walks into . . . interior, kitchen, seconds later. Amy snaps open the dishwasher. Steam rises."

Tamara took over her line: "You don't scare me."

Sharon read the actions. "Amy grabs a handful of hot silverware and drops it."

Tamara: "Ow, damn it!"

Half the staff writers drew a line through the mild cuss. They were right, of course. We'd have to cut it. Across the table, CJ winked at me and gave me a sly thumbs-up.

Sharon: "Amy picks up the silverware. Jake tries to help, but she snaps the fork out of his hand."

Tamara: "Stop it! Stop trying to help. I was doing it on my own for years. You can't just come in here and act like I'm broken. I mean . . . I can't afford to be weak, and you make me feel weak—and raw. I could lose myself with you, Jake . . . if I let that happen, who would I be?"

Sharon: "Jake takes the silverware from her and puts it on the counter, then puts his arms around Amy."

Ben: "You'd be my North Star."

Sharon: "They kiss. End act three."

Pages flipped. Last act and an end credit teaser to go. I held my breath.

Sharon was about to start the first slug of act four when she prefaced it with two words to the table.

"Good stuff."

I covered my mouth so they wouldn't see me smile. I was dead meat at *Romancelandia*. Nothing would save my job. But I'd written good stuff, and no one could take that away from me.

"What do you think, gang?" Sandra said, flipping through the last few pages. "Can we shoot it?"

I gasped so loudly everyone turned to me.

"Hell, yes!" CJ cried.

"But there's no video," I said. "The guys upstairs wanted a video."

"I'll take care of them," Sandra said, flipping through the remainder of the script. "We'll use the locations we sourced for 'Viral.' Good is good. We're not leaving this on the table to chase a trend."

I covered my mouth so I wouldn't blubber all over the place, but my eyes sprang big, wet tears of joy. CJ clapped, and my fellow writers took up her cause, applauding my promotion into the life I'd always dreamed of.

I huddled behind the copy machine with my phone pressed to my ear.

"Hey," Sebastian said when he answered. "I've been trying to call y—"

"They're shooting it!" I sounded louder in my head than I sounded in the room.

"What?"

"They're shooting it!"

"No, I mean, what are they shooting?"

"'Broken Promises.' The one I've been working on when I should have been working on the 'Delete It' script? I just put the one I wanted in front of them, and it worked. I can't eeeveeee . . ." The last word morphed into a squeak of excitement.

"So this means, what? For you. You're not getting fired?"

"I'm promoted! I'm real! I'm rubber stamped! God, I want to drink champagne."

"Wow, that's . . ."

"You don't seem happy."

"Rachel, I'm not only happy—I'm bottle of champagne and balloons happy. I'm . . . jeez, after today, I'm indescribably happy."

"What happened today?"

He exhaled, paused.

"Nothing. I just had a tough day at work, and you made it better."

"Good! Next time I see you, I want that champagne."

"You deserve it."

We hung up, and I walked on air for the rest of the afternoon.

CHAPTER 44

RACHEL

The seamstress pulled straight pins from a stuffed tomato at her wrist and pinned the hem of the dress. We got one alteration with the cost of the dress, which would have to do since we didn't have enough time for a second go at it.

"I love it," I said from the little platform with the mirrors all around. The white dress was sleeveless with a scooped V-neck and a little lace trim at the straps. The bodice ended at a cute satin belt, and the skirt flared out just enough to be pretty but not overly dramatic. It was modern and flattering. Not too much. Not fake and overdone.

"It's *you*," Mom said as if reading my mind.

"It's a beautiful fit," the saleslady said. It was the second one I'd tried on after the first one had fit like a sausage casing and looked like a confection. "Let me go write it up."

"Don't forget the discount," my mother called as the saleslady was on the way out.

"Twenty percent!" she sang back.

Mom stood next to me, the uncontrollable hairs at her cowlick breast height as I stood on the platform. I had her eyes and face shape.

Her sloping shoulders and sense of humor. The seamstress excused herself to get more chalk.

Mom and I didn't move. She wore high-waisted jeans and a tight tank with a button-front shirt over it. Before the reconstruction she'd been relatively flat chested.

They'd taken part of her away and given her something fake, as if what was real about her could ever be replaced.

"You really do look beautiful," she said. "I'm so happy."

Her happiness was the point, wasn't it? That was why I was on that platform in a sample dress.

"I'm glad."

"There are so many things I wanted to do for your wedding, but Carol will take care of any plans while Dad and I are away."

She and Dad were going tomorrow. How had I not bothered to worry about that as well? But I'd been so happy about "Broken Promises" that I'd forgotten to worry. Like a bank collecting interest, the anxiety rushed back tenfold.

I fluffed out the skirt to hide an overwhelming sadness that filled me as if I were under a faucet.

"I want to give the toast at the reception," Mom said. "Do you think the best man would mind?"

"You going to be up to it?"

The sadness kept coming, turning into something hotter and more demanding, overfilling my heart with unbearable grief.

"We can do two. I—"

"You know what else I'd do?"

"Sweetheart?" Our eyes met in the mirror, hers surprised and mine filling with the hot liquid of overflowing grief.

"If I were you?"

"Maybe I shouldn't do the toast, then?"

"I'd tell my daughter if I needed more chemo." Gunk filled my throat, and my voice hitched. The tears of joy that had spilled out of me lubricated the way for a new flood. "I'd tell her even if it hurt her because she'd want to know. I wouldn't be a fucking martyr and hide it, Ma. I wouldn't lie about some vacation in Tahoe. I'd just tell her and let her deal with it."

She turned away from the mirror and to me, but I didn't look directly at her.

"I'm a grown woman," I continued. "And if the cancer's back, I don't need to be protected. So just say it."

"Say what?"

I looked at her from above.

"The cancer's back. Just say it."

Her brows knotted in confusion. "No."

"Is it bad?" I shouted through sobs. "Did it move to your lungs?"

"No. Wait a second."

"How bad is it?" My shoulders shook as I went from anger to a desperate plea. "Please just tell me. I'm not going to lie and say I can take it, because I can't. I won't take it well. I don't want to lose you, Mom. I've lost you a hundred times, and it hurt every time, but hurting is what we have to do, and it's okay to just feel it."

"Sweetie." She put her hand on my arm. "What makes you think . . . ?"

"You cut your hair!" I pulled the skirt up and got off the platform, but my eyes were fogged up, and I wasn't careful. I fell, landing in a heap of white satin.

"Ow!" I cried at a sharp pain in my foot.

"What?" She crouched by me. I'd taken a pin in the heel when my shoe came off. A tiny drop of blood appeared. Mom reached for her bag. "I have a tissue."

"Stop it! Stop trying to take care of me."

"You want a bloodstain on your white dress?" She shook out a tissue and pressed it to my foot. We paused there, and she shook out another tissue. I wiped my nose.

"I'm not sick. I cut my hair because I wanted to."

"What about the Zofran? I found an empty bottle in the trash."

"I had them from last year."

In the dark driveway, I hadn't looked at the date. Was she counting on that? Or was she telling the truth?

"You were tired that time I came over."

"So?"

"And Dr. Gelbart. The second opinions. The biopsies."

"Honey—"

"And Dad said you wouldn't tell me."

"Okay, wait a minute—"

"He said not to bother you because you didn't want to bother me."

"Is that why . . . well, that explains a lot." She shook her head. "The minute I got the results, your father wanted me to tell you. Wouldn't let up for a minute. 'Tell Rachel, tell Rachel,' like a broken record . . . as if you think about my health all day."

I waited, but she just stared at a spot on the floor with her lips pressed tight, as if remembering every time my father had pushed her the way she pushed him.

"Tell me," I said. "The results. Tell me. I can handle it."

She waved her hand. "Benign."

She thought one word would relieve the worry I'd spent so much time nurturing.

"Are you sure?"

"Do you want to see the test results?"

I blew my nose. "Yes, actually."

"You're calling my bluff?"

"Yes. I am. Because you care about my happiness more than common sense."

"I do, sweetheart." She cupped my face in her hands. "I do. But . . . the whole story. I did have some unusual cell growth in my cervix. Dr. Gelbart was very concerned because it was in a different place completely. So we got a biopsy that was inconclusive, so I had another, and it was benign. All right?"

"What about Dr. Friedman? He specializes in chemo."

"Right, well . . . first of all, my goodness, you must have been terrified."

"I was. Go on."

"Friedman's impossible to get. So Dr. Gelbart scheduled me for a workup while we waited for the biopsy so if it came back positive, we could start right away. He's very cautious."

I ran the calendar of events over in my head. Dad hadn't wanted to tell me anything as they were waiting for the second biopsy.

"I was trying not to worry you," she said, patting my hand. "I'm as healthy as I've ever been. I wanted to cut my hair and go on vacation and clean out the medicine cabinet. That's all."

"Do you swear?"

She gathered me in her arms, and I laid my cheek on her shoulder.

"I swear."

"And next time, you'll tell me everything right away?"

"I guess I'll have to."

I took a deep breath that hitched twice as the grief left my body.

Sebastian picked up the phone. He was breathing heavily.

"Are you all right?" I asked from the front seat of my car. Mom waved and pulled out of her spot. I should have waited to call. She could still change her mind and tell me the truth.

"I had the treadmill on a grade."

"I tried on the dress."

Mom pulled up to the gate and put her card in the slot.

"How did it look? No. Don't tell me."

"I can send you a picture."

When Mom's brake lights turned the corner and disappeared into the night, I believed her. She hadn't recanted. It was true. She was still in remission.

"Don't you know the rules? I'm not supposed to see it."

"Uh-huh." My sniffle was thick and wet.

"What's wrong? You're still not fired, right?"

"The job's fine. It's . . ." The sobs that racked my body were made of grief, but only because they'd been stuffed into the bottom of a bag for so long. They were released by relief.

"Seb . . ."

"What? Where are you?"

"David's Bridal on Ca-Ca-Camino."

"I'll be right there."

He was panicking. He cared. That felt so good and so unearned.

"Wait." I couldn't get more out before the tears of relief came out in a deluge. He heard it. I didn't want him to worry, but I couldn't get coherent words out. I got a stack of Starbucks napkins from my glove compartment and blew my nose. He waited, probably pacing his apartment or getting ready to jump in the car as soon as I gave him the go-ahead.

"Rachel?" he said when I was a little more controlled. "What happened?"

"God, Seb, it's a good thing."

"Okay. Good. Good . . . okay."

"Mom's not sick. She's still in remission."

"Oh, thank God."

"I misinterpreted everything. I was crazy. Out of my mind. And I feel so stupid but so relieved. I feel like . . ." My breath caught. "I feel like I'm the one who's been given a reprieve. You know?"

"I do."

"And I was holding this worry, and now it's gone."

"This is great news."

"It is." I wiped the fog out of my eyes and took a big swallow.

"We don't have to pretend we're getting married now."

Wait.

Was that great news to him? Did it matter?

Wait.

Hang on.

I was afraid this was all too fast but—

Wait.

We didn't.

"We don't," I said. "I guess we don't."

"That's a load off."

Wait. What?

"We knew we'd lose all the deposits," he said.

What was I defending?

Getting engaged to make Mom happy was stupid.

Not having to keep it up was a good thing.

But . . .

"We can still have a party," he added.

Right.

I liked parties.

But . . .

"I just paid for the dress. It was a sample, so . . ."

No deposit. Straight buy.

And, so?

You don't commit your life and body to someone because you bought a dress.

"Is it too weddingy to be just a dress?"

I realized I was spinning my diamond ring around my finger as if I was trying to unscrew it.

"Maybe? I guess it's not a big deal."

"I'm glad."

Glad.

He was glad.

He didn't have to be engaged to me, and he was . . .

"Glad?"

The lights for the bridal store went out, and the parking lot was nearly empty. I had a career, and I should be happy.

"That your mother is okay."

"Right." I had to put my head on straight. The engagement was fake. The wedding was a sham. I didn't have to do it, and I should be glad.

"Seb?"

"Yeah?"

"What does this mean for us?"

"Like, as a couple?"

"Yes."

"Since we're not getting married?"

Had we decided that? Had it been signed, sealed, stamped, and sent? I thought we were just talking, and now here he was stating a fact as if I was already supposed to know it. I thought we were just batting it around, but no.

It was off.

"Yes," I said. "Since apparently we're not getting married."

"This is what we planned. It's just happening sooner."

There were too many emotions swirling around. I didn't have an ounce of clarity. My mom was healthy. I was about to be a produced, credited writer. My fake wedding was off. I was in no condition to make a decision about anything. I tilted my ring in the parking lot lights to make it sparkle, then took it off and clamped my fist around it.

"We did all this in a kind of reckless heat," I said. "Let's stop and think for a minute, okay?"

"A minute? A literal minute?"

"A rhetorical minute."

Another heavy silence. I put the ring in the inside pocket of my bag and zipped it.

"You know what?" he said.

"What?"

"You're right."

"About what?"

"We didn't do this honestly. We were pushed. By us. We pushed. I mean, who even knows how we'd feel if we weren't sending invitations or getting measured for tuxes."

"You got a tux?"

"Yes."

"How does it look?"

"It's custom made, so I'm assuming it's going to look good."

Damn. Sebastian in a tuxedo. I wanted to see that.

"Custom's expensive. I thought you'd rent one."

"Look, I'll need tuxedos in life. It's not a big deal. I just . . . I think you're right. We need to take a step back."

"Yeah." I agreed because he was being sensible, but the fact was I didn't feel sensible. I felt defenseless and impractical. I felt as if my desired set of options was being shut down.

"It's for the best," Sebastian said, as if he were the adult in the room and I was an overfull bag of undefined emotions.

How had the conversation taken such a downhill slide? If I got in front of it, I'd get run over. Smashed to a grease spot on a steep incline.

I couldn't be part of this anymore. Not another literal or rhetorical second.

"I have to go," I said.

"Okay. Talk later."

"Later."

"I mean it," he said. "Talk later."

I hung up in a state of cold confusion, feeling as though I'd escaped falling off a cliff I'd wanted desperately to jump off. The shock lasted the drive home and was so overwhelming I dragged myself in the door and onto the couch, where I fell asleep in my clothes.

CHAPTER 45

SEBASTIAN

That went okay. Rachel's mother didn't have cancer. Couldn't spin that into a bad thing.

It hadn't gone okay. It had gone terribly. I hung up the phone knowing canceling the wedding had always been planned, and it was the smart, sensible thing to do. She had to know how I felt about her, and yet I'd hurt her.

To hell with that. I'd hurt myself. I wanted to marry her, but somehow I'd let the conversation devolve into what was reasonable instead of elevating it into what I wanted.

My tux was delivered to the office the next day. I took a picture of it on the hanger and sent it to Rachel.

—Should I wear it to the party?—

—Did you tell your mother yet?—

Right to the point, of course.

I hadn't told my mother because I didn't want to make it real.

—No. Did you?—

—I'm calling them at lunch—

The idea that you couldn't discern someone's mood from a text was false. I could see her sadness between the pixels.

—My feelings for you haven't changed—

—I'll return the ring as soon as I can—

Before I could reiterate my love, she texted again.

—I have to go into a meeting—

CHAPTER 46

RACHEL

I'd never seen Sandra with so many pieces of tape. They hung from four fingers like square-cut fake nails.

"Thank you for meeting with me," she said, ripping off another piece.

"Of course."

After yesterday's reading I'd been congratulated by staff writers so many times I thought a move up from the assistant's desk would only be hindered by the calendar. We were already renewed, and Harry was leaving the show to take care of his son. The space at the table was mine.

"We're waiting for Roger," she said.

"From HR?"

"Yes."

The promotion must involve signatures and agreements. I'd have the points to apply for the Writers Guild once the show aired. That status change probably meant a new contract.

There was a knock at the door.

"Come in," Sandra called, balling up all the tape by rolling it between her palms. She tossed it and went to the couches at the other side of the office, indicating I should follow.

Roger came in. With his ring of trimmed hair from ear to ear and around the back of his shiny head and dark suit that was two sizes too big, he looked the same as the day I'd met him at the beginning of the season. NDAs. Writers Guild. Employee handbook. W-something.

We all sat around the glass coffee table, me on the edge of my seat with my hands folded between my knees to keep the nerves at bay. Roger putting a folder on the table. Sandra in the chair across from me, looking . . . I couldn't read her.

"So," Roger said. "Ms. Rendell."

"That's me!" Was I too chipper? Definitely too chipper.

"It's come to our attention that there was a physical altercation in the early hours of January eighteenth between yourself and one of the executives at our parent company?"

My mouth fell open, and my arms suddenly drained of excited tension. My heart—I had to embrace the cliché—my heart fell in my chest as if a trapdoor had opened under it.

I glanced at Sandra, expecting some kind of encouragement. She wasn't looking at me. Her index finger tapped her thumb as if there were a piece of tape attached to it.

"Um, not me, exactly?"

He took a thick book with Post-its sticking from the side from the folder.

"Section one forty-two point four of the employee handbook"—he grabbed a Post-it from the handbook and opened to its page—"states that taking part in or encouraging acts of violence is a clear violation of the ethical behavior clause." He spun the book in my direction as if I wasn't too confused to read the fine print. "The gentleman you were with," he continued, "and who you left with struck Bruce Geraldo? Twice?"

"Yeah, it was . . . it was quite a night." A nervous laugh tacked itself onto the end of the sentence.

Sandra still wasn't making eye contact. She was gazing longingly at the tape dispenser on her desk.

My optimism had been pretty stubborn up to that point. Roger's opening salvo about the fight hadn't budged it. Optimism figured he was either making conversation or slapping my wrist over some garbage in the handbook. I was getting moved up, obviously. Right?

When Sandra wouldn't look at me, the reality sank in, and like bleach on a black shirt, it changed everything.

"So you don't deny it?" Roger asked.

What would be the point of lying? To save my job? Was that even possible? Or would I just be digging deeper?

"Would it matter if I did?"

Sandra finally looked at me.

"Just tell the truth," she said.

"Because you think I'll lie?" I turned to Roger. "Bruce and I used to date. He was a cheat and a liar, but whatever. When he saw me with someone else, he tried to start a fight with my date, but instead he got his clock punched. Twice."

I stood up and reached over Sandra's desk to grab the tape dispenser. I put it in front of her, and with profound relief, she snapped off four pieces of tape in quick succession.

"Ms. Rendell," Roger began in a monotone, "the network takes our responsibility to our viewers and our brand very seriously—"

"Are you firing me?"

"You can appeal," he said.

Fingers draped with tape, Sandra was looking at me with big kohl-lined eyes.

"You'll be paid to the end of your contract."

"That's like two months." And it wasn't the point either. I was supposed to be promoted, not booted.

Roger slid me a check. "One lump sum."

Great, and fuck him.

"Rachel," Sandra said. "Your show's still getting made. The residuals will still come for a full credit."

"No," I said. "No. This is bullshit."

"I suggest," Sandra said with a commanding tone that reminded me why she was the showrunner, and a pause after that loosened the valve on my sense of bullshittery. "I suggest that you take this in stride. You were never a great fit for this show. We can always get a fast typist, but your can-do attitude was what made us all want to help you. Staffing season is coming up. Don't forget that. If you maintain the attitude we all know and love, you'll have a dozen seasoned writers and myself in your corner."

Another snap of tape to make the point. They'd help me get another job as long as I didn't make trouble, and I couldn't get another job without them. Nothing would make a staff placement as easy as Sandra from *Romancelandia* picking up the phone on my behalf.

"This is going to follow me around," I said, pointing to the papers Roger was sliding out of the folder.

"It's sealed unless we arbitrate," he said. I glanced at Sandra for confirmation, and she nodded.

It would be fine.

It was terrible.

I thought Mom was hiding her cancer because she didn't want me to lose my job to take care of her, but she didn't have cancer, and I was losing my job anyway. All the promises of phone calls didn't change that.

Roger laid out the papers I had to sign, and I did what he asked without thinking.

No big deal. Hollywood giveth, and Hollywood taketh away. Right? For the best. All for the best.

I was escorted to my desk, where I packed up my stuff. I didn't make eye contact with anyone as I walked out. The writer's room was locked for lunch. CJ's desk was empty. When I drove out of the lot, I surrendered my parking pass and ID, then pulled over on a side street.

I slid the paper check out of the severance folder Roger had given me. There was no direct deposit when they booted you, as if that was more connection than they could bear. I'd been taxed at a higher rate, naturally, but it was still two months' pay in one place. I deposited the check with my phone.

For the best. All for the best.

I was back to being thirty and nowhere. Square one. Emotionally deflated. Empty. Above it all. My heartbeat echoed against the walls of my hollow chest.

No wedding. No Sebastian.

I hadn't even told my mother the wedding was off.

Sebastian texted as I was trying to find something to feel.

—I need to talk to you—

I couldn't deal with his love any more than I could deal with his distance. In a way, he'd broken up with me too.

He texted again.

—Call me when you can—

I shut the phone as an act of self-preservation. It was too much. He was too much. He'd tell me how wonderful I was, and that was the last thing I needed. I needed something to look forward to. It had all been there yesterday, and today?

Poof. Gone.

Maybe I did feel something. It was grief, and it scared me. I didn't want to be this sad. I wanted to be happy again. What did I have to do to get there?

I had time and extra money. There was something I could do for me.

CHAPTER 47

SEBASTIAN

When I got to her office in Culver City, CJ came out to reception and pulled me into the hallway without a word.

"Okay, so," she said. "She's not here."

"Did she go home sick?"

A sick day wouldn't require a conversation in front of the elevators. I knew it in the middle of asking the question.

"They let her go."

I groaned and looked up at the ceiling to curse the heavens.

"I know," CJ said. "It was stupid. There was some fight at a club."

My fault. I'd decided to stand up to the bullies at the expense of the one person who had always protected me from them. Nice fucking work, dweeb.

"Did she say where she was going?"

"I didn't even know about it until now. I'm going to stop by her place later."

"I'll go now."

—

She wasn't there. I knocked until my hand hurt and the neighbors would have had cause to call the police. I dialed my mother to see if Rachel's car was in the driveway across the street.

"Not that I can see," she said. "Rob's not back from work, and Mona's out shopping. Do you need something?"

"Just call me if she shows up."

"Is everything all right, dear?"

"No, everything's fucked."

"Do you want me to throw cards for you?"

"No. Please, God, no. Just . . . give me Mrs. Rendell's number, would you?"

She rattled it off, and I wrote it on a scrap of paper I held up against the stucco wall.

"I'll throw a spread anyway," she said.

"Just keep your eyes out, okay?"

I hung up. Tried Rachel again. Nothing. Called Mrs. Rendell.

"Hello?"

"Hi, Mrs. Rendell, this is Sebastian."

"Well, hello!"

"Have you seen Rachel?"

"Why?"

Why? Because I was her fiancé, and I wanted to know. Except I wasn't her fiancé, and Rachel was calling her mother at lunch, which had long passed. She probably knew the wedding was off, and Lord only knew how Rachel had painted it if she was upset.

"Because," I said, "she's not home."

"I was wondering why she wasn't at work," she said.

"So you talked to her."

"She's coming by the house to pick up her passport."

"Her passport? Where's she going?"

"Oh, I didn't think she was going anywhere. I thought she needed it for ID maybe."

My phone beeped. Carol. I hung up with Mrs. Rendell.

"Is she there?"

"Just walked in the house. Seb. The cards say there's a separation. I have the Tower crossing the Hanged Man."

"Stop her."

"How?"

"Just do it."

"You don't have to be so bossy."

"Please."

Rachel had obviously been on the way out because I heard the screen door creak before she called out across outdoor background noises.

"Yoo-hoo! Rachel."

"Oh, hi." Rachel's voice. "Can you—"

"Carol!" I shouted. "Put her on!"

My mother's voice: "Of course."

Rachel: "Thank you. And I'm sorry. Tell—"

"Ma!" I shouted, abandoning her first name.

My mother: "I will, but—"

"Put her on!"

Fabric rustled against her phone as if the phone was being transferred, but when the noise cleared up, it was Carol's voice I heard.

"Sebastian? Are you there?"

"Where is she?"

"She had to catch a flight."

"Where?"

"The six forty out of San Diego."

"I mean, where was she going?"

"France."

I cradled my face in my palm. Her flight would be gone in two hours, and there was no way I'd get to the San Diego airport at rush hour on a Friday in under three hours.

"I'm so sorry, Seb, honey. And she says she's sorry too."

"Paris," I muttered.

"What happened?" she asked.

"I ruined her life."

"I'm sure you didn't."

"I did."

"She didn't seem mad. She left you an envelope. Do you want me to open it?"

The last thing I wanted was my mother reading a note from the love of my life over the phone.

"No."

"If I hold it up to the light, I can see it's handwritten."

"Stop."

"There's a key in it."

"Put it down. I'll come down there and get it."

Dear Sebastian,

I've stared at that comma after your name for twenty minutes already.

I don't know what I want. That makes me really uncomfortable.

I want to write you something so romantic the earth shakes, but I'm just not built that way. I can make the words, but they don't fit right even if they're true.

So instead of trying to be romantic, I'm going to bite the bullet and be brutally honest.

Romancelandia canned me today. It doesn't matter why, except that it was Bruce. I don't know how I ever thought I loved such a jerk. Bad judgment. Maybe I confused him getting me a job with kindness. I hate that I fell for that. I thought I'd never trust a man again. Then, boom. You show up, and you're perfect.

Then Mom being sick-not-sick and the wedding-not-wedding, then with the career-not-career?

I'm falling apart. Everything is just crashing. I'm a mess. I don't want you to see me like this, and I especially don't want you to tell me it's all going to be okay. It's not going to be okay. When we called off the wedding, I was crushed. I felt like my heart was being stabbed repeatedly, and I couldn't make it stop.

But why? Really, why? We're not ready to get married. And we're not getting married for the best reason ever . . . because I get to keep my mother. We're not even breaking up. But here I am, feeling broken because I lost you.

You know what? I have a secret behind door number two.

I knew you had a thing for me. I knew it hurt you when I dated, but I enjoyed our friendship, so I didn't say anything. And after high school when we were on opposite sides of the country? I didn't think about you much. Even when I was getting my heart broken by some dumb actor. And then, as soon as I saw you again, I tried to use you to make my mother happy.

I know that makes me awful.

The fact that I love you now doesn't change the fact that I'm not worth it. I'm nowhere. You're loyal and smart. Successful and confident. You're complete in a way I'm not. I miss you already. When you're around, I have someone to look at and say, "This is who I want to be like." And to see you look at me with affection and love? It makes me feel complete too.

See? I just said you complete me. That's . . . true. But so icky. There must be some truth in the ick.

I want to marry you now. Today. But that's not sensible. You're sensible, and that's what I love you for. The irony isn't lost on me.

So I'm going away through hiatus. Paris. The most romantic city in the world, supposedly. Can I even tell if it's romantic without you there? I'll let you know when I'm back.

I love you.

Rachel

PS: I didn't want to leave the ring in an envelope or someplace not safe. Here's the key to my apartment. It's in the spinach box in the freezer.

PPS: If you still want me when I'm back, I want to be your first.

The last postscript gave me a half a boner and made me laugh at the same time. I was sure that was what she was going for.

"Well?" Carol asked. We were still in the street. Rachel's mother had just pulled into her driveway with a pink bag. "Mona!" She called her over.

"Sebastian!" she said, hugging me. "I'm so sorry. I tried to talk her out of it, but she insisted. She said we could just have a party without her."

"There's no point in losing the deposits," Carol said as I read the letter again and again, looking for inspiration. She blamed herself for everything, and what had I done? Had I ever told her how I felt? Or had I just assumed she could never love me and guarded myself against the possibility?

"What does she say?" Mona looked over my shoulder. I pressed the paper to my chest so she wouldn't see the postscript.

"She needs time," I said.

"That's what she told me, and I said, 'In a bad hotel in Paris? Can't you take time here?' but no—"

"The charts didn't say anything about travel," my mother said, brows knotted.

"The charts are bullshit," I said.

She slapped my arm.

"They predicted you'd be practical and straightforward like your father was." Behind her, Roy pulled up in his truck.

"Oh, Carol," said Mona, grabbing for the letter I wouldn't give her. "It's all bullshit."

"What? After Rachel's chart was so accurate?"

"The chart said she was getting married next week. Bullshit."

"How dare you!"

Roy got out of his truck.

"What's going on here?" he said as if he was going to have to be the man around here and break up the catfight I was too chickenshit to get involved in.

"Rachel's up and gone to Paris for her wedding!" Carol cried.

"What's he doing here, then?"

A cacophony of voices chimed in, but I didn't hear them anymore. None of them were more important than hearing Rachel's voice behind her letter.

She'd been hurt by the world.

She felt small and inadequate.

She thought she didn't deserve happiness.

All that was wrong, and I wouldn't let her stew alone for a minute longer than I had to, but I wouldn't rush any more than I had to either.

I got out my phone. "What's Joy Tabona's number?"

CHAPTER 48

RACHEL

The rental was tiny, with a kitchenette and a little balcony with two chairs and a round table and a cast-iron railing that overlooked a narrow cobblestone street. The street was on a slope and curved in both directions, making it feel cut off from the wider world.

My balcony was one of many. I was surrounded by them on either side and across the street. I had coffee there in the morning, and so did a couple across the way and down a floor. They were in their twenties, and I recognized a few words of Italian from a show we did about Tuscany. Three mornings in a row, he put a fresh rose in the vase and pulled her chair out. When they spoke, he always touched her chin and held her hands.

"They are so in love." A man's voice came from behind me. I turned to see him on the balcony next door. Tall. Sandy-brown hair cut into precise disarray. Green eyes under eyebrows that arched suggestively. His shirt was open so I could see he was built like an actor determined to land leading roles.

"Yeah," I said. "It's kind of nice."

"I think he's just trying to get her into bed." I couldn't place his accent. "Or keep her in bed."

"Why do you say that?"

"He pours her coffee before himself. Picks up the plates. He's like a servant. Men don't act like this unless they're thinking about the bed."

I watched them below. She laughed and flipped her hair over her shoulder. He ran a lemon peel along the edge of his cup. I leaned over the railing to speak to Green Eyes more softly.

"They listen to each other," I said. "They never interrupt. Look at how she's making eye contact when he's talking and how he's taking the time to explain whatever it is they're discussing, right."

"Right, right." He put his elbows on the railing between us.

"Look," I said. "She doesn't answer until he picks up his cup. He's signaling he's finished, and now she answers. And you can tell she disagrees, but he's listening and nodding."

"She is." Green Eyes wasn't looking down at them, though. He was looking at me.

"They're real," I declared.

"Maybe so. What are you working on?" He indicated the laptop on my table.

"Oh." I slapped the computer closed. "Nothing."

"You're a writer?"

"Sometimes."

"Is it a book?"

"No." I looked over at him for a second. He seemed harmless. I'd built up a resistance to all the beautiful men in the world but one. "I'm writing a screenplay."

"About what?"

"Love."

"Wow."

His *wow* was as fake as a candy-store diamond and was accompanied by a glance down my shirt.

I went inside and handwrote Sebastian another letter I wouldn't send. This one would be about the distance between the couple downstairs and the insincerity of chatty men on balconies.

My first two nights, I walked to the Eiffel Tower. If I passed a doorway with music or people, I stepped in and had a glass of wine. On the third night, I flipped open my spiral notebook to write Sebastian a letter.

> *Dear Sebastian,*
> *I might send you this one, just so you don't think I'm ditching you. I'm not.*
>
> *Actually, I keep passing places and seeing things I have to make a note of so if we ever come here together, I can show them to you.*
>
> *Today, I was in the plaza in front of Notre Dame. It was super early, so there weren't many people around. There were so many pigeons the ground looked like a moving gray ocean. This kid who was about four ran into the middle of them, and they all took off like a wave, revealing a chalk drawing under them. One of those colorful ones artists do while you watch. It was of a woman with a dozen roses, and you'd have no idea it was there under the pigeons. It was like the kid had pulled a curtain open, and when he ran back to his mother, they all came back like they'd never left.*
>
> *I wanted to nudge you and say it was like the pigeons were door number two. They had a secret they'd only show when they were so scared they had to run away, but they'd always hide it when they were too comfortable.*

The difference between me being too scared to show myself and showing myself even when I was comfortable is you. When I come back, I don't think I'll need to hide again.

Love,

Rachel

The minute I'd arrived, I'd bought a stamp and an envelope in the airport but had been afraid to use them for fear of sending something mawkish or sentimental. In the café, with my wine half-finished, I put the letter in it and mailed it on the way back to the apartment.

CHAPTER 49

RACHEL

I was having a dream where Sandra was behind her desk, surrounded by tape dispensers. She was saying something about how the scene needed to open up. She said my name over and over, and every time she said *Rachel*, she rapped her knuckles on the desk. The building was burning. The sound of licking flames nearly drowned her out as she cried, "Come out, Rachel, come out!"

I shot upright in bed, twisted in sheets. It was pouring rain.

"Rachel!"

The voice came from outside. I opened the balcony doors. The rain smacked against the little table and chairs in silvery explosions.

"Rachel!"

I stepped outside in my bare feet and looked down to the source of my name.

Sebastian stood on the cobblestone street, wearing a trench coat and holding an umbrella that only partially protected his legs.

"Good morning!" he shouted over the crackle of the rain.

"What are you doing here?"

"Getting wet."

I ran downstairs. Through the beveled glass in the front door of the *pension*, he was out of focus and broken into pieces, but I'd know him anywhere.

My fingers slipped on the dead bolt before I could get a good twist. When I threw the door open, he closed the umbrella.

It took a second for me to believe he was there, smiling at me as if he was as glad to see me as I was to see him. It seemed impossible that his breath was taken away. Or that all his worries were swept away by seeing me. When he saw me, he couldn't have felt the loose ends of his life being tied together the way I did when I saw him.

"Seb," I whispered.

"Can I come in?"

"Oh." I realized where I was, as if waking up from a dream, and stepped aside. He shook out the umbrella and came in. I closed the door and leaned against it. I had things to say. Big things. Meaningful things I'd written in a letter he couldn't have gotten yet, but the sight of him shook the words into a jumble.

"I'm sorry to come unannounced," he said.

"It's okay."

"I can't stop looking at you."

"Yeah. It's . . ."

. . . what we mean when we say *romance*.

. . . the stolen breaths.

. . . the full heart.

. . . the feeling that your feet aren't touching the ground.

"Upstairs," I said and ran up as if I couldn't be alone with him quickly enough. He pounded up behind me. By the time we made it to my room, we were laughing, gathered in each other's arms, all lips and tongues and relief like a dam breaking.

When I reached under his coat, he pulled my hands away.

"Wait."

"You came all this way to wait?"

"No." He laughed to himself. "The opposite."

"I love you." The words burst out of me, and they still seemed inadequate.

"I thought I loved you," he said. Past tense. Yet I wasn't worried. "All those years, I thought what I felt was love. But it wasn't. I worshipped you, but I didn't love you. Not until you showed me who you were. When I saw the fragile Rachel and the sad and the sentimental parts of you . . . then . . . then I loved you."

I thought he was leaning forward to kiss me. I was ready for a kiss to end all kisses. A kiss that would make the background music swell into a crescendo.

But he wasn't leaning in for a kiss.

He got on one knee. My face got hot, and my fingertips shook as he got a little robin's-egg-blue velvet box out of his pocket and opened it.

A new ring, with an emerald that caught every bit of light in Paris.

"Rachel, my North Star. Will you marry me? For the right reasons this time?"

The rain went silent.

He held out the box, sapphire eyes lit from within. Even on his knees, he wasn't the boy who couldn't defend himself—but he was. He was that vulnerable boy and this strong man. Both together, and something wiser, stronger, more complete than the sum of the parts of his life.

"Today?" I asked. "Now?"

"Or we can wait. As long as you know I'm yours."

"God, Sebastian. I'm going to cry again."

He took the ring out of the box, gently raised my left hand, and placed the ring at the end of my fourth finger.

"Will you have me?"

Have him? How could I want any less for myself? Of everything in the world that was right, giving myself to him was the rightest. Success or failure, I could be anything with him at my side.

"Yes," I said. "A million times, yes."

His smile was mine and mine alone. I had to bite back a sob when he slid the ring on my finger. It was given not as part of a deal but as a symbol of our promise.

When it was on, he kissed my hand and stood. We couldn't take our eyes off each other.

"It's too much to ask that we get married in Paris, isn't it?" I asked.

"You're dreaming too small."

"Our parents would kill us if they weren't at the wedding."

There was a knock at the door. He cleared his throat.

"I didn't want you to feel pressured. I wanted you to be able to say no or next year or whatever."

"No." I shook my head with confusion. "Now. I want you now, but—"

"Rachel?" Was that my mother's voice on the other side of the door? Was it her pounding on the wood as if she had ten hands?

"They were supposed to wait for my signal," Sebastian said.

"Honey!" A man's voice . . . was that . . . Dad?

I unlatched the flap covering the little window in the door.

On the other side . . . faces.

"Holy crap." I opened the door. The hallway was crowded with people. Mom. Dad. Carol.

"Tiffany?"

She burst past me. "There is, like, zero reception here."

"What—" I was pushed aside by a flood of people, too stunned to object or make a fuss. "Roy?"

"You have bathrooms?" he asked.

"Down the hall. What are you doing here?"

Mom was already standing by the french doors, shaking the rain out of her hair. A man brushed by me, and I spun around to find Father Jamie.

"Hello," he boomed.

"Hello, wh—"

"Right or left?" Roy's voice came from the hall. "I can't find sh—"

When I saw Joy Tabona with her little rolling suitcase, I cut off my own sentence.

"Left," I called to Roy, except I wasn't calling. My voice had gone missing.

"My God, the French know how to put on a rainstorm," my mother said as Dad helped her with her soaked coat.

I looked back at Sebastian, who was taking his trench coat off to reveal a tuxedo, but for one difference.

"Don't worry," Wade said, holding up a garment bag. I remembered him from the strip club. "I brought the jacket."

"No," I said. "I like the grandpa cardigan." I ran my fingers down the collar of Sebastian's black sweater. "Even the toggles."

"It's on, then?" Mom asked from somewhere a million miles away, outside the tunnel of attention between my love and me. Sebastian's smile was all the assurance I needed. He was the calm center in the chaos and babble.

"I said yes."

A small ovation went up from the crowd that had gathered in my room.

"Is it today?" Carol said. "This was the date the stars aligned, and we have two hours before the date changes at home, so get on with it."

"Mom?" I said, still looking at my real, true fiancé.

"Yes?" she said from somewhere to my right.

"Did you bring my dress?"

"It's in the car."

"Good. I don't want to get married in my nightgown."

Turned out you needed a permit to get married under the Eiffel Tower, so we did it guerrilla-style. With the help of Mom, Tiffany, and Carol, I wrestled myself into the dress in the back of the car. Sebastian was in a separate car with the guys and Father Jamie.

The rain had stopped. The sun split a crack in the clouds for the time being.

When I was dressed, Mom handed me a plastic-wrapped supermarket bouquet.

"That was all they had at the Paris airport."

"They're beautiful."

"Shit," Tiffany said after Instagramming the proceedings. "Something old, something new."

"The dress is new," I said.

"Here." She snapped her phone case closed and handed it to me. "Blue and borrowed."

"Thank you," I said, holding the Tiffany & Co.–cased phone like the treasure it was. "Am I supposed to hold a phone during my wedding?"

"Everyone does," Tiff said.

"I brought something old." My mother dug in her bag.

I tucked the phone under the belt, and Mom found what she was fishing for. A piece of three-hole-punch lined paper.

"Our contract," I said.

"I thought you'd want to have it."

"Mom," I said. "Thank you. For everything."

"I'm the one who owes you." She folded my hands in hers. "I love you so much, little girl. And I'm so proud of the person you are. Be as good to him as you are to me."

"I will." I squeezed her hands. "I will."

The driver stopped the car on the east side of the plaza and called back to us.

"I'll be on rue du Général Lambert."

I folded the contract up and put it in my garter.

We ran out, ready to break French law so fast we wouldn't get caught. I slipped on the wet stones, laughing into Sebastian's arms as Father Jamie stopped between us and our families folded around. Wade put a ring in the groom's hand.

"Do you," Jamie started, "Sebastian Barton, take this woman to have and to hold—"

"To love and to cherish." Sebastian gleefully cut him off. "All the rest of my days forever and ever. I was born loving this woman!" He shouted it to the sky, and I laughed with delight.

He put the ring on my finger, on top of my emerald.

"And do you, Rachel Rendell—"

"I take him," I said as Wade pressed a ring in my palm. "For my husband. My lover. My best friend. To protect and treasure." I slid the ring on. "To let him protect and love me. To show him all the scary, icky parts of myself because he's the only man I trust with them."

"I now pronounce you—"

We kissed before Jamie finished, and applause broke out just as a policeman asked for our permits in French.

"They didn't even need me," Father Jamie said somewhere far away, in Paris. Voices seemed closer now that the circle of family was breaking up.

But we didn't let go. Even when I felt Tiffany slide her phone out of my belt, our arms stayed wrapped around each other so tightly I felt my husband's heart beat against mine.

CHAPTER 50

SEBASTIAN

What had just happened didn't hit me until we got to the party.

I'd paid Joy Tabona whatever she wanted to get the job done, and she had. She'd found a hall in a seventeenth-century parsonage and laid it out in white and silver.

We stood at the entrance, hand in hand, the whirlwind calmed to a breeze, and I had a second to think.

Holy shit.

She married me.

Not for her mother's sake, but because she loved me.

I looked down at her.

My wife. Rachel.

When her eyes met mine, I looked for an ounce of doubt and found none.

"Are you happy?" I asked.

"So happy."

I leaned down to speak into her ear.

"The things I'm going to do to your body later? You're never going to forget it."

"I'm ready for you," she said. "So ready."

Only a few guests could fly to Paris on a moment's notice, even if I was covering the expense. Her roommate. Seema and the kids, but not Teddy. Wade, of course. Ace was at the podium wearing a white-on-white tuxedo. The rest of the band wore black on black. Tiff had her phone up, ready to blast social media with her boyfriend's screams.

"That's going to sound really loud in a room this small," I said.

"I'm going to love telling our kids about our first dance."

Our kids. This woman was giving me everything I ever wanted.

"Hello," Ace said into the mic. The acoustics were pretty bad, so it wasn't too loud. His croon was buttercream smooth. "Ladies and gentlemen. Boys and girls. I'd like to introduce you to Sebastian and Rachel, husband and wife, as they have their first dance."

We stepped in. Our family applauded, and the guitarist hit the first note. I cringed. But the second note complemented the first, and when Ace started singing "All of Me," he sounded like Frank Sinatra.

"I didn't know he could actually sing," Rachel said as we danced.

"Tiffany told me he was trained in opera. I didn't know if we were getting Sid Vicious or Luciano Pavarotti."

Her parents joined us on the floor. Roy danced with my mother.

"Did you pick the song?" my wife asked.

"I didn't have time for that. I just told him to do romantic music. I had no idea what he'd come up with."

"So far, so good, because you have all of me."

"I wouldn't take any less."

Somehow, I made it past the food (deeply French), the toasts (my wife wept openly), and the garter (I removed our contract before tossing it over my shoulder—Ace caught it) to get to our suite at Hotel Montaigne. I guess when you'd waited for something as long as I had, another few hours didn't make much of a difference.

Getting up the elevator, however? Pure torture.

"Penthouse suite," the elevator guy said as he rattled the gate open to two doors in a small hallway.

"Thank you."

"I can open the door for you," he said. "Show you the amenities."

"Nope," I said, helping Rachel out of the elevator. Her shoes had not been kind to her. "We're good."

"Monsieur."

I pulled a folded twenty-euro note out of my pocket. "We have it."

"Of course. *Bon.*" He took the note, stepped back, and slid the door closed.

Rachel had her hand on the wall to take a bit of pressure off her feet. I swept her up and carried her to our door.

"Better?" I asked.

"Better." She got the key card out of my chest pocket and waved it over the scanner. It beeped and went green. She laid her hand on the handle but didn't push down.

"You said something about what you were going to do to me?"

"I did." I reached under her and opened the door. "I spent all day thinking about the fastest way to rip that dress off you. I'll throw you on the bed and eat your pussy until you beg me to stop."

"Will you stop?"

I put her down and kicked the door closed.

"Only to fuck you."

CHAPTER 51

RACHEL

We had a view of Paris I had no time to appreciate. As soon as the door closed, I felt him behind me, yanking my zipper down, getting the straps over my arms, pulling the dress to the floor, unhooking my bra, sliding my underwear off. It took five seconds to get me in no more than my shoes. From behind, he put one hand on my breast, another between my legs, and his mouth on my shoulder.

"You're wet," he said.

"I've been wet all day." I bent my knees so his fingers could probe deeper.

He came around and picked me up for the second time. I wrapped my knees around his waist and kissed him as he carried me to the bedroom and threw me on the mattress, as promised.

Fully clothed with an erection stretching his perfectly tailored tuxedo pants, he stood at my feet.

"See something you like?" I said.

He pushed my knees open, looking right between my legs, where I was softest and most sensitive. A shot of arousal went through me.

"Yes."

Carefully, he took my shoes off, kissing my feet around the blisters, running his hand inside my thigh. With my free foot, I pushed against his erection, and he groaned.

"When I fuck you," he said, working his way down my leg to my knee, "I'm going to go slow. I'm going to savor every minute of our first time." The inside of my thigh quivered when he kissed and licked it. "Slow and deep."

He opened me with his fingers, pulling back the hood of my clit, exposing the most tender flesh before he put his tongue on it.

"God, Seb." I clutched his hair. Slowly, he ran it along my seam, into my entrance and out, back up again over my clit. "Do that one more time, and I'm going to come."

"If you insist."

"Wait—" But it was too late. His tongue teased my orgasm out with a few flicks, releasing a day's worth of pent-up desire.

He stood up and quickly got undressed. I watched as the perfect suit was removed piece by piece to reveal the perfect body. He crawled on top of me.

"How do you want it?" I asked.

"Start simple," he said, kissing my collarbone. "We can work through the Kama Sutra by morning."

"Are you nervous?"

"A little."

"I'd say we can wait." I reached down and took his dick in my hand. "But it's time."

He took my hand away, then grabbed my other hand and put them over my head, pressing down so I couldn't move.

"It's time."

He slid himself along my seam until I gasped with pleasure, then rested at my entrance.

"Yes," I whispered, shifting my hips against him. "I want you inside me. I love you, and I want you inside me."

He let go of my arms and shifted forward.

"Ah, wow."

Forward again, and he closed his eyes as he entered me.

"It's good?" I asked.

"You're amazing." With one last push, he was buried to the root. "Worth it. All worth it."

He kept his promise to go deep and slow. Years of discipline had left him totally in control. I dropped my legs and pushed against him when he was deep, and I felt every inch when he pulled out. His rhythm was reverential, as if he was feeling and appreciating every moment.

I took his face in my hands.

"I love you."

"I love you." His lips moved against my cheek, and a heat grew between us like a slowly boiling pot.

"I'm—"

"Me too."

He didn't speed up. Not one bit. We rolled onto our sides, holding each other so close we were one body, one heart. He let it boil over slowly, until I was clutching the skin and muscle of his back in one long, drawn-out orgasm, and with a shuddering exhale, we came together.

"Rachel?" he breathed into my neck.

"Yes?"

He got up on his hands.

"I don't think I got that right."

"What? You were amazing."

He wrapped his arms around me and rolled over onto his back with me on top of him.

"Again. I want you again."

"Oh no." I bent my knees, bridging him so there was space between us.

"What?"

I rolled off him and sat up.

"You're going to be completely insatiable, aren't you?"

Laughing, I leaped off the bed. He caught me halfway to the bathroom. We wrestled to the floor, and we twisted together again and again until the sun set and the sounds and lights of the most romantic city in the world joined us in love.

EPILOGUE

EXT: ROOFTOP—NIGHT

White tablecloth. Silver flatware. Two candles. The lights of the city twinkle over the edge of the roof. REX picks up a crystal goblet and holds it out to SERENA. She CLINKS hers to his with a subtle smile.

REX

Happy anniversary, darling.

SERENA

It's been quite a—

She stops when one of the candle flames goes horizontal and dies.

SLOW MOTION as Rex pulls his gun out of his waistband with one hand and reaches for Serena with the other.

When a bullet knocks over the candlestick, we realize the candle was snuffed by the first shot. Coming fast now, pop-pop-pop, the dishes *shatter* as

"Rachel!"

Goddamn it and a woman couldn't get a lick of work done around here. Not without voices coming through the door or dinner smells coming from downstairs.

"I'm working!"

I turned back to my laptop, grumbling about getting up at five in the morning to write, only to get called at six thirty. My show, *Deadpan*, was wrapping up a season of intrigue, twists, turns, and gunfights. Once I was done with these last two pages, I'd relax, and I could do them if I had a solid hour.

The door to my office swung open. Sebastian had a hand on the knob and the other on the jamb like a bridge over the opening. His pajama bottoms hung low on his waist, and his T-shirt hugged his biceps better than a grandpa sweater.

"It's Christmas," he said.

"Honey. Two pages."

"Nope." He came in the room. "Everyone's up."

"Page and a half."

Wedging his arms between me and the chair, he picked me up under the knees and shoulders.

"No. Even the showrunner needs Christmas off."

I put my arms around his neck, pages nearly forgotten.

"You're going to get laid tonight if I don't have this hanging over me."

"I'm getting laid tonight no matter how much you type."

He took me out of the room. We were on the upper floor with a hall so wide he didn't have to turn to carry me along it.

"Really? You think so?" I ran my fingers through his hair.

"I know so. Venus is going direct."

"Mom!" Andrew stood at the base of the stairs. At six, he already had glasses and his father's childhood whip-shaped frame. "Come on!" He waved us down the hardwood steps, jumping in his footed baseball pajamas.

I would have sworn Sebastian slowed down the more his son tried to rush him.

"No!" Kellie screamed from the kitchen with the full-throated depth of a girl much bigger than two years old.

"You have to wait!" Mom said from the living room.

"Come on, Daddy!" Andrew said, waving his hand to hurry us up. "Put her down! She can walk."

I rested my head on my husband's shoulder and let him take as long as he wanted.

"For the love of Pete." Roy met us at the bottom of the stairs. "Can you two get moving already? Put her down, for crying out loud."

Sebastian dropped me to my feet and kissed me, stalling for Roy's sake.

"Merry Christmas," he said.

"Santa came! Come on, come on!" Andrew pulled me into the living room. I grabbed Sebastian's hand and let our oldest guide us to the tree, where our family waited.

"I wonder how he fit a bicycle down the chimney?" my mother asked with a rhetorical lift in her voice. Her hair was still short, and she was still with us, rolling the blue-and-silver two-wheeler away from the tree so Andrew could get his hands on it. Kellie was jumping up and down like a pogo stick while Dad read the name tags. Roy sat back on the couch with a cup of coffee next to his new wife, Carol, who sat on the edge of the cushions. Tiffany was in a chair, phone put away, while Ace sat on the arm.

"We're all here," Sebastian said. "Youngest does the honors. That's you, Kellie."

Dad handed her a package. "This is for Grandma Barton."

"Carol, please," she said, taking the box from Kellie.

"Gamma Carol!"

"That will do."

Every time Kellie handed out a gift, she got to open one of her own, and the floor bloomed bright paper in no time. Sebastian opened my gift. A plaque of his children's book, *Whose Star Is That?* on the *New York Times* bestseller list, along with cutouts of his best reviews.

"Thank you," he said, kissing me.

"I'm so proud of you."

"Let me see." Tiffany reached for the plaque and read it with Ace. "So cool."

Her brother had stopped being a dweeb and had become admirable. Cool, even.

Roy got Carol an out-of-print astrological concordance. Tiffany got Ace hard-to-get tickets for the Grunts.

Kellie ran up to me with a package and ran back to open one of her own.

"That's from me," my husband said.

I opened it. It was a tourist's scale model of the Eiffel Tower. I read the card.

> *My Only,*
> *The last time we were in Paris, we rushed.*
> *Let's go again, but slowly this time.*
> *I love you,*
> *Sebastian*

"This is . . ."

"Our parents can watch the kids for two weeks."

"Two weeks?"

"During hiatus."

Shows didn't run in July. Technically, I had off. But that was when pilots were developed and pitches bought. I didn't have two weeks, but that was only part of the reason. I looked up at him to tell him a week might be better, but the tunnel between us closed out the chaos of ripping paper and squealing children.

"That sounds perfect," I said. "Two weeks. Just us."

"In the most romantic city in the world."

"July." I remembered something I hadn't told him yet. "That could be tough."

"Don't say no."

I took a second wrapped box out of my pocket. "I'm not."

He took it, looking at me suspiciously. We'd agreed on one meaningful gift.

Kellie ran into his legs, jolting his gaze away. She held up a horse toy strapped to the box so securely only a daddy could liberate it.

"Open."

He crouched by her, putting my package on the floor while he wrestled the thing out. Roy joined in with his pocketknife. Andrew sat on his bike, kickstand deployed, and pretended he was ripping down the street as Mom collected paper and Dad grumbled about breakfast.

That was when I noticed the way Ace was standing in front of Tiffany with a little box in his hand.

Slipping my phone quietly from my pocket, I poked Sebastian with my foot and hissed at him.

"Psst!" When he and Roy looked up at me, I jerked my chin toward his sister. I started videoing them. The room went quiet just as Ace got down on one knee.

"My girl," he said with the blue box closed between them. "You're the ground under my feet when I reach for the stars. The chord string every song is based on. The driving theory behind my life. You're the foundation the house of Ace rests upon. I can't live without you."

He opened the box, revealing a single stone in the six-pointed Tiffany setting.

"Ace, baby, you are such a jerk," Tiff muttered.

"Be this jerk's wife."

Even the kids stopped breathing. I looked around the screen to see her answer in three dimensions.

"Okay."

"Okay?" he asked.

"Yes. Yes, you big lug. Yes, I want to be Mrs. Ace. I've always wanted to be Mrs. Ace."

We exhaled and cheered as the couple hugged and kissed. I stopped the video after he put the ring on her. Carol suffocated her daughter in a hug. Kellie's plastic horse was freed. Andrew abandoned the bike for a box of trains.

"Oh, that was so romantic," Tiffany said. "I wish I had video."

I'd tell her later. For now, Sebastian was unwrapping the second package to reveal a Rolex box. I kneeled next to him.

"I know we agreed on one gift," I said. "But this turned up, and I really had no choice."

"I don't need a watch."

"You need this one."

He took the top off. There wasn't a watch inside.

"Oh my God," he said.

"So I know we said we didn't want to be outnumbered . . ."

"What is it, Sebbie?" Carol looked over at us. Everyone gathered around. He handed her the box so she could see the pregnancy test, but his eyes were on me.

"Will you still take me to Paris all knocked up?"

"Rachel Rendell." He cupped my face in his hands. "I'll take you to Paris as many times as you want to go."

He kissed me, and I curled my body around his. Our families laughed and applauded in the most sentimental, clichéd, icky, perfect, joyful scene I could have written.

And we lived happily ever after.

ABOUT THE AUTHOR

Photo © 2017 Liz Lippman

CD Reiss is a *New York Times* bestselling author. She still has to chop wood and carry water, which was buried in the fine print. Her lawyer is working it out with God, but in the meantime, if you call and she doesn't pick up, she's at the well hauling buckets. Born in New York City, Reiss moved to Hollywood, California, to get her master's degree in screenwriting from USC. In case you want to know, that went nowhere—but it did give her a big enough ego to write novels.

Reiss is frequently referred to as the Shakespeare of Smut, which is flattering but hasn't ever gotten her out of chopping that cord of wood. If you meet her in person, you should call her Christine. Text *cdreiss* to 77948 to get a notification whenever she has a new release.

ABOUT THE AUTHOR